I0667782

WINDOWS OF THE SOULLESS

A Novel

Kathryn Horsley

Vendera Publishing

To Patrick,
who helped me stop procrastinating.

Chapter 1

There's a darkness we all keep, tucked away deep inside our souls. But for creatures like me, soulless, there's nowhere to hide it. It consumes us. We give in to it. And it defines us. I suppose that's what brought me here to this field with blood smeared across the blades of grass. Old and dry, it flakes away. Bodies are scattered on the ground. Once full of life, now just hollow shells. What I wouldn't give to have been in this field when they were still fresh, blood pouring from their wounds, sweet and luscious smells, death all around me. It's enough to make my mouth water and my throat burn with thirst.

I stoop down close to a nameless face and inhale deeply. It smells pleasant enough, though it lacks the temptation it should possess. Reflexively, my fingers wipe across his face, tracing lines in the wet crimson. I press them to my tongue, hoping for the delicious warmth to ease the hunger inside me, but the taste is insufficient. The blood is cold and stale, and I feel the grit of gunpowder on my lips. It's revolting, making my stomach twist and churn into knots. I cannot deny myself for many more nights the simple pleasure in taking a life.

I rise to my feet and walk through the field, stepping around the bodies and weapons. They're all soldiers, and aside from their uniforms, they all look the same. Young and weak before, now their eyes are glazed over, the color gone from their cheeks.

I stretch my arms out and close my eyes, feeling the stillness around me, and let the aroma of death encase me, filling my lungs with its delicacy. Standing still, I inhale deeply. Subtle variations in their blood make the air intoxicating.

The wind blows across my face, bringing with it the scent of fresh blood and the sound of a beating heart. Instinctively, my eyes open, my senses heighten. My eyes, intimidating and frightening, turn entirely black, no whites, no iris, no pupil. I see a child a hundred yards away as clear as though he was close enough to touch. My fangs press against my tongue as they grow behind my lips.

My stomach hungers for him, my throat is set ablaze. Every atom of my being aches for him. Four centuries ago, I would have enjoyed drinking his blood, making him last for hours, dragging out his pain. But killing children only brings regrets. Hearing their faint whimpering, feeling their tiny necks between your teeth, holding a pale and limp little body in your hands is hard to forget.

I close my eyes, letting the desire leave my lips and feeling my fangs recede. My nostrils still draw the smell of the boy in like a magnet, baiting me like a fish. But I ignore the way my muscles twitch toward him, the way my mouth waters for him. I listen to my breathing, the steady rhythm of air entering and leaving my mouth. My eyes open, and they are a soft green again, like when I was human, making them seem trustworthy and kind.

More composed, I venture closer, running as quickly and silently as I can until I am only twenty feet from him, but it is far too dark for his human eyes to notice me.

At this distance, I am close enough to perceive the desperation behind his hazel eyes. He stares at the body for only a moment before he moves to the next soldier. Leaning over another dead German, he hovers barely inches from his face. His shaggy blond hair, oily and streaked with dirt, hangs heavily as he searches for someone.

I inhale once more, smelling the pleasantness of the warm blood pulsating in his neck. My throat is set on fire as it beckons me to surrender to my thirst, but I draw from what's left of the compassion I had as a human and regard the boy as a child and less as prey.

I clear my throat, making myself known but doing nothing for the pain.

Startled, the boy turns quickly, holding a lighter between us.

"Who's there?" he blurts out bravely. But his heart pounds against his chest hard and quick. His pupils dilate, trying to make me out in the shadows.

I walk closer to him, loudly snapping a twig under my feet, much the way a human would. In the light of the small flame, I don't appear very frightening. I am not a large man, only five feet ten, with a medium build. Although my muscles are sculpted, my clothing conceals them well. My dark hair is trimmed and neat, in keeping with the modern style. My strong jaw and straight nose, which may have made me appealing as a human, look merely average in the eyes of a vampire.

"I didn't mean to alarm you," I say with a roughness in my voice that makes me sound more human than my usual enchantingly smooth tone.

"I wasn't afraid."

Even as a human, I would have caught how poorly he lied. It was something in his body language, standing stiff and rigid. Defensive.

"It's a little late for you to be out here, isn't it?"

I can hear his heart rate slowing down. He is making the mistake of believing that I am not a danger.

His answer is full of defiance and confidence. "You're out here, too. And I'm pretty sure you're not a grave digger."

I genuinely smile, pulling the right corner of my mouth up further than the left, making it lopsided, which I've been told is an incredibly endearing feature.

I smell the flesh begin to burn seconds before he drops the lighter. "Ow," he groans as he puts his finger in his mouth to cool the skin.

"Who are you looking for?" I ask.

"My father." He stands up, facing me though he cannot actually see me. "This is his infantry. He would've fought here today. And I have to know if he's out here."

The clouds move enough to let a glimmer of pale moonlight shine down on us. In the cold light, my skin appears whiter than usual. It doesn't help that I haven't had any fresh blood in me for nearly a week. A fresh kill would have given me an appropriate human coloring in my cheeks.

Looking at him in the pale light, my heart softens. "I'll help you," I whisper.

Concealed by the darkness, I breathe in deeply, separating the intricacies in the scent of his blood. Then, turning my back to the boy, I inhale, smelling the mixture of blood and gunpowder still hanging in the air. I stand very still, letting the perfume of death titillate my nostrils, pulling apart the beautiful aroma as I search for similarities to the boy's blood.

The clouds part enough for the moon to cast its glow on us. The light makes the bodies on the ground more visible, even to the boy, making it feel more like a necropolis than a pasture. Sensing it too, the boy shudders and wraps his arms around himself.

"He's not here," I state honestly.

I hear the rustle of his clothing as he drops his arms, no longer concerned by our location.

"How do you know?" he asks suspiciously.

Though his stern approach to me was amusing at first, it annoys me now. I look up at the clouds. Timing this is imperative.

"I can smell it," I reply in my smoothest, most unnatural voice.

With my eyes still solid black, I turn around to face him. His eyes widen when he looks into mine, just before he screams. He steps back and trips over a soldier's corpse. Landing on his back, he kicks himself away from the body quickly.

As I predicted, clouds cover the moon once more, plunging the boy into full darkness. With quick and jagged breaths, he looks around wildly. His heart pounds against his chest. I suppose it was cruel of me to frighten a child, but then what kind of child tries to intimidate a man who spends his nights in a field of death?

The air vibrates between us, resonating with his fear. "What are you? A demon? Or a devil of some sort?" he stammers out.

His hand rolls over a stick and he grips it tightly. His knuckles white, he raises the stick and makes an attempt to appear threatening.

"Don't be stupid, boy," I say. The smell of his cold sweat captivates me. Humans will never comprehend how alluring their terror is.

"Do you mean to kill me?" he asks.

"If I wanted you dead, you wouldn't have even seen my face."

I watch as his mind processes what I said and he lays the stick down beside himself. He keeps his hand on top of it, though, not really trusting me, which is the only clever thing he has done tonight.

"What do you want then?" His breathing is beginning to regulate itself despite the way his chest thumps intensely.

I bend down and take the lighter in my hand. The cold metal feels smooth as I rub my finger across it, outlining the ridges of an eagle.

I stand up again, looking down at him. "I want you to forget what you saw here. I want you to go home before I change my mind about killing you." I toss the lighter at him and look up at the clouds. They will part soon, and when they do, I don't want to be standing here in front of a scared little boy.

With only seconds left to make my escape, I run as swiftly and quietly as possible and disappear into the trees.

Although I am faster, stronger, and more keenly aware of my surroundings than any human, there are things that daunt me, things that belong in these trees, whereas I don't.

The canopy of leaves prevents even the smallest fragment of moonlight from reaching the ground, making it impossible for a human to see anything. But a human isn't what I worry might find me here.

Putting aside my concerns for a moment, I slow my pace to a walk to admire the woodland ambiance. I rub my fingers along a tree and feel a vine that twists upward, reaching desperately for the light. Although the undergrowth is thick, I make out the flowers that have shut themselves for the night.

I listen to an owl screeching, searching for its next meal as I sit down on a fallen log. The smell of the rot beneath me wafts up, encircling me.

My peace is broken by the thumping of small paws rushing toward me. I rise to my feet quickly, listening intently. It's a hopping sound, like rabbits. Not just one, but several. They're running from something. Something silent.

My heart sinks as I consider it. "Werewolves," I whisper to myself. I draw in a deep breath and find what I was searching for. It's an unmistakable smell. Musky and strong, it carries a rich wooded scent mixed with the blood of a wild human.

I don't stick around to consider how the contradicting scents could confuse a younger vampire or how it could even trick them into believing it was a simple human waiting in the trees. I run as fast as my legs can move, crushing the ground beneath my feet loudly. I could slow my pace and be silent, but I am after speed. I rip through the leaves in front of me. When I reach a narrow stream, I leap over it, landing with a thud far on the other side. Pushing myself even faster, I clear the trees quickly.

Perhaps I shouldn't have run quite so fast, because I don't see the gravel road until it is too late. As soon as my feet hit the loose rocks, they slide out from under me. I land on my back hard enough to throw the tiny stones into the air around me. I am not sure where humans get the idea that we are graceful, but if they could see me sprawled out on the ground now, they would reconsider.

Before the rocks can fall back to the ground, I am on my feet. I closely watch the trees for any signs of movement. I sniff the air, but the wind is blowing away from me, taking the forest scents with it. I listen for the sounds of panting or growls, but there are none. There is only me, standing alone on the rocks that shift under my shoes.

It is possible the wolves never knew I was there or that I outran them. More likely, they had never met a vampire before and weren't sure what they were smelling. That means they are young. Too young to have taken part in hunting us centuries ago.

Taking no chances, I decide to make my way home by slipping through the farm bordering the forest until I reach the highway. From there, I could run the twenty miles to my home unnoticed.

I walk to the fencing along the road and bound over it easily.

As I walk through the night, dreading the impending daylight, I am slightly jealous of the wolves. They have all the best parts of being a vampire, the strength, speed, the heightened senses. They live forever yet they still get to be human when they choose. Walking through the sun, having children, meeting people that you don't want to kill, I'll never have that. And it simply isn't fair.

Chapter 2

The night air is unseasonably warm as I walk slowly, the dirt road crunching beneath my feet. I appear quite human walking along the road in the dark. But I'm not doing this for show, I quite enjoy emulating a human. The way people naïvely approach me, so welcoming, so friendly. They try to make me belong to a world that has long since disowned me.

I see my home just ahead. A large Colonial, it was never quite compatible with the European countryside. It sits peculiarly on a two-hundred-acre farm, which, without livestock or crops, isn't utilized properly. I walk alongside the crumbling rock wall that outlines the farm, running my fingers along the coarse stones. The wrought iron gate moans loudly as I push it open.

I walk up the stairs at one end of the large porch, which has grand columns that reach up to the second floor. I see the intricate detailing on the top and bottom of the columns despite the darkness. The white paint on the wood siding is beginning to fade and flake away, leaving chips of paint lying on the porch.

Impressive in its day, the house was built more than two hundred years ago under my close supervision. I made sure the workers didn't want to disappointment me. I think they knew there was something different about me, since I met them only at night, and I refused to have windows anywhere on the first floor.

Although the house is worn and old, it still feels new to me. That's probably because we stayed in the house only three years after its construction due to some local murders casting suspicion on us. We had other homes to choose from, so we took up residence elsewhere.

Leaning back against the house, I watch the tire swing rock side to side as the breeze rolls over my skin. The moment is broken by a most enchanting voice. "Nicolas," she says from inside the house. "Come to me, my dear."

Obediently, I push myself away from the house, but reluctant to go inside, I linger, watching the fireflies. Their tiny lights twinkle against the immense darkness that the moonless night creates.

"Nicolas, don't keep me waiting," she says in a honey-laced voice.

I hesitate at the door, knowing my words will soon dishearten her. She is expecting me to have completed an imperative task, but alas, I haven't. Instead, I spent my time reveling in my own personal reverie, surrounding myself with death most of the night. A most selfish habit of mine. But then vampires do tend to be self-centered.

I turn the doorknob slowly, listening to the way the metal of the deadbolt scraps against the strike plate. I push the door open and step inside. The room is dark, far too dark for human eyes, but with my eyes I can see the way the vaulted ceiling extends into the second floor, opening up so that you can see the landing of the grand staircase that spirals down into the foyer.

Elegant and refined, it's the type of staircase that a Southern belle would descend toward the man of her dreams. But the woman on the staircase is no Southern belle. Her blond hair hangs straight, cut into a bob at her chin. Full of body, it bounces as she walks down the steps. The bright red of her lipstick contrasts starkly with her pale skin. Her sharp features complement her blue eyes, which even now look cold and vicious. A true killing machine, she walks with a confidence approaching arrogance.

Beautiful and intimidating as she is, I have never been afraid of her. Not even when she rescued me from my own personal hell. Though she's not my creator, she is still my mother. The only vampire I owe my life to.

Her hand glides along the banister, leaving little traces of her fingers on the polished wood. The silky blue dress she wears drags along the steps behind her and hides much of the movement of her legs underneath.

I reach over and push the light switch up. It shines down on us, casting shadows on the dark hardwood floors. The crisp white of the walls amplifies the brightness of the incandescent bulb.

"Living in the Dark Ages again, are we?" I ask.

The corner of her mouth turns up as she steps off the last stair. "You don't need electricity when you can see in the dark."

"True, but look at how it makes your skin glow," I reply, appealing to her vanity.

A wide smile appears on her face, exposing her teeth. She walks over to me with great poise and takes my hand. The coolness of her hand against mine reminds me of my failure, and I begin to despair as she leads me away from the door.

"Don't let the bugs in. Those thirsty little bloodsuckers are always taking what belongs to me," she says as she closes the door.

I smile at the word bloodsuckers. After all, that's what we are.

She puts her chilled hands on either side of my face, wrapping her fingers along the base of my skull. "Nicolas, my dear, you know you're my favorite. Now tell me you were a good boy," she says softly.

It would be easy for a human to get lost in the captivating sound of her voice, which sounds temptingly gentle and alluring while lacking the unnaturalness mine contains.

"About that..." I start.

I feel the sting of her hand on my cheek before I realize she has moved it. A simple slap, I had expected worse.

She puts her fingers to her temples and rubs them in circles. I can hear the force of her breath as she exhales while I watch her eyes flutter with anger.

"I want my sheep," she replies through gritted teeth.

A sheep, as she so lovingly refers to them, is a human kept alive for feeding purposes. While it sounds like a terribly cruel thing to do to a person, it's not. The sheep are incapacitated. Although they resemble their usual selves, they lose the ability to make their own decisions. Acting only on our commands, they are here to please us, and it satisfies them to do so. They have no memories of their former lives and therefore do not miss them. Perhaps it is slightly cruel to relieve them of their free will, but in the grand scheme of things, there are much worse things we could do to them.

"I'll get you one tomorrow," I offer.

She looks up at me quickly with narrowed eyes. "You said that yesterday."

The harshness in her face leaves me feeling more shameful of my actions tonight than I ought to. My eyes drift down toward the floor and away from her.

"I'm sorry, Marcella," I say in a voice barely above a whisper.

She grabs my chin, pulling my face to hers. "Sorry? Save your pathetic apologies for Claire. Explain to her why she isn't feeding tonight," she snaps at me and jerks my face away.

Claire, the youngest of Marcella's children, is still a baby among vampires. Having been a vampire for only three years, she requires more of everything—more blood, more sleep, more attention.

Marcella moans exasperatingly. "Why, Nicolas? Why must you do this to me?" she whines. She wraps her arms around me, laying her head on my chest. "If you do not help me, I will find one for myself."

"No," I say quickly. I take her hands and push her away from me. "I will do it."

Though Marcella is superb at enthralling her sheep, she isn't selective enough for my standards. Without caring about the consequences, she takes whomever she wants, be that young or old. I, on the other hand, select only those nobody will miss. With no one searching, there are no eyes looking in our direction, no suspicions cast on us, no angry mobs with pitchforks and torches, no need to flee the country quickly. Just us and our sheep. Just the way I prefer it.

Marcella places her cool hand against my cheek, making me look her in the eyes. It has been said that the eyes are the windows to the soul. That seems more fitting for vampires than for any other creature. Effortless as it is for us to hide our emotions, the eyes never seem to lie. Piercing blue, Marcella's eyes are soft and forgiving.

"Don't disappoint me again," she says gently.

As she drops her hand, I catch her fingers and pull her hand toward my mouth. "I shall not ever again." I press my lips to her knuckles, making her smile softly.

Then from across the room, I hear, "Making promises you can't keep again? Seems like your forte, if you ask me."

I don't need to look to know where the voice came from. If I had to guess, which I don't, I would venture that a large vampire is leaning against the doorframe with his arms crossed over his chest. Arrogant and obstinate, he wears a smirk on his wide face. His bald head is shining in the light. The bulge of his muscles and the darkness of his skin are visible through his thin white shirt and his dark eyes are set on me.

I glance at him to verify my assumptions. "Hello, Luther," I say evenly. It is no secret in the house that Luther and I aren't the best of friends. In fact, we're not friends at all. His pompous attitude has annoyed me from day one, precluding any possibility of camaraderie, and I know my disdain infuriates him. "And what, pray tell, are you talking about this time?"

"Time to update your vocabulary, nobody says pray tell anymore, pops."

Ignoring the way his snide comment makes my jaw clench, I lean toward Marcella, placing my cheek against hers. "Rest well, Mother," I whisper to her.

The wood creaks as Luther pushes himself away from the doorframe with his foot. I hear him forcefully exhale his disgust. I know what he is thinking. He believes I am trying to ingratiate myself with her, to keep my place as her favorite. But I don't need to employ false flattery. I will not fall from her good graces, no matter what I do. But to annoy him, I kiss her on the cheek softly and press her hand with mine.

I let go of her and walk toward the door where Luther stands lurking, brushing his arm with my shoulder as I pass him. Much to my disappointment, he turns to follow me.

"What do you want, Luther?" I mutter as I enter the library. With masses of books stacked high along three of the walls, the room smells of old paper and leather, and remnants of smoke and dust remind me of a time not so long ago. A time when reading and writing weren't just pastimes but necessities of sorts. A luxury of those who could afford an education. On the wall opposite me is a large fireplace with a stone surround that reaches up to the ceiling. Staring at the elaborate façade, I doubt if Luther has ever really noticed its beauty.

I take a book down from the shelf and flip through the pages, the smells of its past wafting in my face.

"I want to know how long you plan on letting Claire suffer. You're letting her starve, you know," he accuses.

Even the sound of his voice, though it is charming to most, grates on my nerves. Aggravated, I come across as more defensive than I mean to. "Don't exaggerate the situation. A week without feeding will not kill her. It may even teach her a lesson about not slaughtering the sheep."

He snorts at my response. "I am so sick of your self-righteous attitude, Nicolas. You're not better than any of the rest of us."

I refuse to look at him or reply to his comment. The truth is I don't think I am better, just more experienced, and that counts for something for a vampire. I place the book back on the shelf next to the other leather-bound ones and start toward the kitchen.

"I guess if Claire gets desperate, she could always feed on my sheep. I'd take care of her," he adds.

Something about the idea of him taking care of her makes my pulse quicken and my face heat up. I spin around to face him. "Claire is not to touch Harvey. And make no mistake, he is Kate's sheep, not yours. She is gracious enough to let you use him because you lack the control it takes to capture one for yourself, the control it takes to be a real vampire. You're just a parasite. Like a tick, you try to drain us. But one day, you will be plucked away and tossed aside. And I hope it's me who does it," I snap.

I turn back around and try to focus on my breathing. I actually don't have a problem with Claire drinking from someone else's sheep. What I have a problem with is the idea of her drinking after an animal like Luther. Perhaps I am being a bit territorial, and I know I shouldn't be, but the thought of her soft lips against the flesh of a human that Luther calls his own sickens me. And her lips really are soft. Plump and luscious, they beckon to be caressed. The way she bites them at times, her teeth pressing against them gently, it's enticing.

I put away my thoughts of Claire and enter the large kitchen. Rows of tall, off-white cabinets give it a comfortable country feel. The walk-in pantry is more than necessary in a house built for vampires, but I've heard no complaints about it yet.

As I walk through the room toward the landing of the stairs that lead to the basement, I hear Luther huff.

"You know what, Nicolas," he begins.

I turn toward him and put my hand up to stop him. "Stay here, Luther. I haven't the time for your petty conversation," I say before I start toward the stairs again. To my surprise, he stays where he stands.

"Seems to me, time's all you got," he says with a smirk.

I am not sure why his improper English bothers me as much as it does, but I correct him anyway, "Have. Time is all you have. Get it right," I say irritably.

But he's made a valid point. Time for me does seem abundant. The world changes around me while I continue to live in a ghost of a life, not truly living but not longing for death, either.

I stop on the landing at the top of the stairs. In front of me is overwhelming darkness, but that isn't why I linger there. Part of me—albeit, a small part—considers apologizing to Luther. Regardless of how impudent he is, I should not be so harsh.

I look back, but he is gone and I am not much disappointed by it. I don't feel guilt for being so severe with him, but I know it was wrong. If I am honest with myself, I know it won't be the last time.

I start down the stairs, letting the darkness swallow me. My eyes don't need time to adjust to the lack of light. I can see every step in front of me, though it's dark enough that with my green eyes I can only slightly make out the wood grain on the treads.

At the bottom of the stairs, I turn left, walking toward the bedrooms. When I reach the first two-bedroom doors, one opposite the other, I notice my door is slightly open, and I hear water from the shower. I push the door open further and listen closely to the sound of the water beating the shower floor as someone wrings out their hair. The scents of expensive soaps fill the room.

"Wrap it up, Kate," I say just loud enough for her to hear.

When she doesn't answer, I add, "You have three minutes."

I start to walk away when I hear, "Ten," from my bathroom.

I smile to myself. "I'll be back in five. Not a minute longer."

I start down the hallway again before she can contest it. As I make my way toward Claire's and Luther's bedrooms, I think about what I will say to Claire about not finding a sheep and try to anticipate her likely reactions. But mostly I think about the way I've let her down yet again.

I hear soft music emerging from her room as I walk toward it. The mellow tones, rhythmic and peaceful, overshadow the crackling of the record. Stopping in front of her door, I hesitate. With my failure and her certain disappointment weighing heavy on my heart, I hold my breath, listening to her light steps as she dances across the floor just on the other side of the door.

I let myself imagine what she must look like swaying to the music, her blue eyes closed, letting the melody consume her, her red hair swinging gently from side to side, her arms wrapped around herself, pretending someone is holding her. I place my hand and lay my forehead against the door, longing to be the one she is thinking of. Yearning for her, I exhale slowly.

The needle scratches the record as the music stops, startling me. The door swings open, and the light from her room floods the hallway, highlighting her silhouette in the doorway.

She smiles a most irresistible smile. "Hello, Nicolas."

But before I answer, her face turns serious. She steps close to me, placing her hand on the back of my neck. With her fingers entwined in my hair, she lays her head against my cheek, smelling my neck. I try to keep in mind that the scent of death still lingers on me, but it doesn't change the way my body craves her. I flex my fingers to keep me from placing my hand on the small of her back and pulling her closer, closing the space between us. I do, however, let myself inhale the aroma of her hair, smelling the roses in her shampoo.

She steps away too soon. "Sorry," she whispers. She bites her lip, embarrassed, and she has me hooked. "You just smell so inviting. What is it?"

Lost in her eyes, it takes me a moment to comprehend that she has asked me a question. "A, um, battlefield," I stammer.

She walks into the bedroom where the light makes it easy to see the soft features of her round face. The way her freckles bridge across her nose and cheekbones. The way her hair, curled and pinned, frames her face perfectly. The way her lips are parted slightly, beckoning me.

"I could hear them fighting most of the day," she says. "I wasn't aware that there would be anyone still alive."

I know where she is going with this, but I have to tell her anyway. I walk into the room and close the door. "There wasn't."

She sits down on the edge of her bed. "Then how did you get a sheep?"

And just like that, I am back to reality. "I didn't."

She shifts uncomfortably on the bed and looks away from me, sighing. She tries to hide the distress and anguish in her eyes, but I can read people well.

I want nothing more than to take her in my arms and console her, but I know I shouldn't. Instead, I walk to her and bend toward her. I take her hand in mine, making her look at me. "I'm sorry," I say quietly.

She smiles softly at me. "It's all right."

The way she forgives me only makes me feel worse. I lay my forehead against our hands. I begin to tell her not to absolve me, but she starts again.

"I don't blame you. If I had the chance to go to a battlefield that smelled so wonderful, I wouldn't think of me either."

My head jerks up. "I think about you all the time," I admit before I have a chance to consider what I am saying. I stand up, dropping her hand. "I mean, I think about everybody that relies on me," I blurt out, trying to camouflage what I really meant.

Smiling slyly, she says, "If you say so." Her voice is soft and sultry, making it difficult for me not to tell her more.

Refocusing, I start again. "Claire, I will bring you a sheep tomorrow, I promise."

"I'm not rushing you."

She leans back on her hands and crosses her legs. A tempting position that makes her dress cling to her body all too well. I'm not sure if she knows that sitting that way enhances her breasts and narrow waist. Or that leaning back pulls her dress up high enough to make me think about the ease of sliding my hand along her thigh all the way to her bottom, where with a firm grip I could... Stop, stop right there, I tell myself.

I take a deep breath, looking at the wall behind her. "Goodnight Claire." I turn around and walk away.

When I open the door, I hear her say, "Goodnight."

Compelled, I look at her one more time. "I'll see you tomorrow," I tell her softly.

She smiles at me and says, "I'll count the minutes."

I cannot help but smile back at her, my lopsided smile. "I should go."

She rolls onto her stomach, letting her dress hug the shape of her butt. "Then go," she says.

Deep down, I almost believe that she knows exactly what she does to me. I look at the door, trying to get the image of her lying on the bed, ripe for the taking, out of my head. When so many of my fantasies involve her lying on that very bed, it is difficult. I keep my eyes on the door. Although it lasts only seconds, I wonder if she notices my hesitation to leave her. Then, with a great deal of willpower, I walk out before I can change my mind.

Once I'm in the hallway, it's easier to think clearly. I start back toward my bedroom, putting my hands on my face for a moment. Then, sliding them up through my hair, I exhale forcefully. Relieved that I hadn't said or done anything inappropriate, I enter my bedroom.

The water from the shower has been turned off, but I still hear it dripping from the faucet. I lean back against the wall near the bathroom door and let my head fall back, making a light thump.

"Why must you shower in my bathroom?" I ask. "You do have one of your own."

From inside the bathroom, I hear, "Yours is bigger."

I smile, considering the comments I could respond with. But I won't be impolite, and I keep my mouth closed.

"Besides, you don't have to share yours," Kate says, her voice muffled by the door.

"Apparently I do," I reply.

"Luther and I are going out tomorrow, if you want to come with us," she offers.

"I would rather spend the night in a chapel," I mutter to myself.

"What was that?" she asks.

I smile, knowing she would have heard me clearly enough. "I said I'm busy."

She laughs to herself, a soft, gentle laugh. I hear something hit the bathroom floor faintly, like a towel dropping. "What do you have against Luther?"

I consider the way I want to answer her, but decide the truth would be most fitting. "He's conceited."

"So you see yourself in him?" she jokes.

I laugh lightly. "No." My smile fades as I turn serious. "Honestly, though, he's going to get himself killed. My only hope is that he doesn't bring us down with him." I look toward the door as I hear the smacking of her bare feet on the stone floor coming closer. "I don't want you to get hurt because of him."

She opens the door and steps toward me, her flowing white gown making her reddish-brown skin appear even darker. Her hair, heavy with water, hangs to the top of her hips. Chestnut-brown and perfectly straight, it's draped over one shoulder. Her high cheekbones and straight nose give evidence of her Native American origins, but she gave up her heritage long ago, saying she was part of that world for only twenty years, a fraction of her time alive.

"Don't waste your concern on me. I can handle myself," she tells me with conviction.

I push myself off the wall and step toward her. "I'm obligated to be concerned. You're my only friend."

She nods. "It's hard to believe I'm your only friend when you smell so strongly of Claire."

I knew this was coming. It is the same lecture she has given me every night for the past month. I groan and walk to my bed, waiting for the verbal attack.

"I was just in her room talking. Much the same way you are in my room talking to me," I say as I sit on the edge of the bed. The lie does me no good. She knows it's not the same. I have never felt for her the way I feel for Claire, have never yearned so intensely for a being in all of my vampire life.

Kate walks over to me and bends down in front of me. "You can't be with her. If you two are together and you bite her, it will create a bloodlust that she doesn't have enough restraint for."

"I know. It'll be at least another couple of years before she has that kind of control. I can wait. I can." I try to reassure her. "Really, when you've lived as long as me, what's another few years?"

"I hope you're right. Because if you're not …"

Closing my eyes, I interrupt. "I know." I don't want to hear her finish. I don't want to think about how a bloodlust in Claire could be so dangerous. I don't want to hear about the victims she would consume or how their blood would be on my hands. But I especially don't want to know how a loss of control so early in life could be the end of her.

I open my eyes slowly and see the look of distress on Kate's face. "I know," I tell her again. This time, however, my voice cracks, and I am sure she can see the pain in my eyes.

She stands up in front of me, but I keep my head lowered. She rubs her hand through my hair, then leans down and kisses me on top of the head. Silently, she walks to the door.

"You know, you shouldn't be so hard on Luther," she says softly.

I look up at her, confused but relieved at the change in conversation. "Why's that?"

She shrugs. "He's been a vampire for eighty years and hasn't gotten himself killed yet."

While her argument sounds reasonable, she has forgotten a very important point, one that I don't hesitate to remind her of. "He's never been up against anything as deadly as him either. No werewolves, no nomadic vampires, no angry mobs ready to burn us out of our home. He's been lucky. But his luck will run out, and when it does, either someone will rescue him or he'll die."

She can tell by the tone of my voice that I believe what I am saying, and the sadness in her eyes shows me that she believes it too. "I hope you're wrong," she says quietly.

I don't respond. I am not sure I trust myself to say something respectful. She does not wait for my response and tells me, "Goodnight."

After she goes, I walk over to the record player. The record crackles as I place the needle on it, but when the music starts, I pay no attention to that. I listen and find it hard to believe that such a voice could come from a human.

I take my time in the shower, letting the water wash away my day and taking with it all remnants of the smell of the battlefield and of Claire. It's disheartening to lose such wonderful scents, but not being constantly reminded of Claire will help me sleep. Although a lack of sleep will not make me tired, I will be stronger tomorrow if I rest well.

As I finish my shower, the singer on the record belts out a note that would be difficult for most humans to match, but I have no trouble keeping up. I sing out the words loud enough for most of the house to hear.

Someone pounds on my bedroom door. I hear Luther yell through the thick wood, "Knock it off."

Continuing to sing as I dry myself and brush my hair, I ignore the way Luther beats on my door, and by the time the record stops, I feel better.

I move the tone arm back to its resting position. Turning toward the door, I casually say, "Goodnight, Luther."

"I hope you die a terrible, painful death tomorrow," Luther spits out.

I listen to him stomp back to his room and slam the door shut. Knowing I have infuriated him makes me smile ever so slightly as I get into bed.

I lie still for a long time, long enough to have drifted into sleep when I hear my door open. Always defensive, I open my solid black eyes, ready to kill. But who I see in the door makes me think I am dreaming. I sit up and look at her. Flawlessly stunning, she stands in my doorway in her nightgown.

I blink, letting the black of my eyes fade into my usual green. I can see the way she bites her lip nervously. That's when I realize this isn't a dream, because if it were, she would already be in my bed.

"Claire, is everything all right?" I whisper low enough so that nobody else hears me.

She leans against the doorframe. "I can't sleep alone."

I knew that, though she had never actually told me. Conflicted between what I want and what I should say, I ask her, "What about Marcella or Kate? Can't you sleep with one of them?"

She looks away from me. "They don't want me to. They say I'm difficult to sleep with."

Since I cannot see her eyes, it's hard for me to tell whether or not she's lying. Though it does make sense, because vampires are vulnerable in their sleep, and we don't happen to be trusting creatures.

"Can't I sleep in here?" she asks innocently.

Although I would very much like for her to be in my bed with me, pressing her body against mine, resting her head on my chest, it wouldn't be the wisest thing for me to agree to.

"I don't think that's such a good idea," I tell her, and I watch as disappointment clouds her face.

"All right, I understand," she whispers. Her shoulders slump forward, and she looks so discouraged and depressed that I nearly yield to her. But I am in control of my desire and determined not to tempt myself beyond my limits.

I am not prepared, however, for what she says next. "I'll just see if Luther will let me stay in his room." Then she turns to leave.

And just like that, my jealousy gets the best of me. "Wait," I tell her. I pull back the blanket and pat the bed beside me.

Her smile lights up her face. With light steps, she walks to my bed. Just as I had imagined her doing on countless occasions, she slips into my bed gently. Her body so close to mine, her hand as she pushes a lock of hair behind her ear, the way her chest rises with each breath make it hard to focus on sleeping.

"Thank you," she says, bringing me back to reality.

She reaches her hand toward me but I grab her wrist. "Just try to stay on your side of the bed, all right?" I tell her as I let her go.

"Of course," she replies. She lies on her side away from me and pulls the blanket up around herself.

I lie perfectly still, worrying about my ability to control my response if she were to tempt me. Would I be able to keep my hands off her? Would I say something I should keep to myself? But more importantly, could I stop myself if she were willing?

It isn't long, though, before I hear her breathing change to a slow and steady rhythm, indicating that she is asleep. Relieved that my questions will not need answers tonight, I roll over with my back to her, and, listening to the cadence of her breathing, somehow I fall asleep.

Chapter 3

I can sense the day has not yet ended even as my body pulls itself from sleep. Vampires do not dream often, and this time was no exception. I haven't slept well since Luther came to live with us, but somehow I managed to do so this day.

Even before my eyes are open, I smell the scent of roses, strong and close. A pleasing scent, it reminds me of Claire. And there is someone soft and cool under my arm.

My eyes shoot open. Without moving, I analyze my position. My head is lying on a woman's shoulder. My arm is draped across her abdomen. Thankfully, I haven't pressed myself against her, and there is a narrow space between us.

Before I can take pleasure in how wonderful this feels, I jerk away from her, sitting up and sliding across the bed quickly. Shocked by my indiscretion, I keep my eyes on the wall in front of me, not daring to look at her.

I feel the bed shift as Claire sits up. "It's all right. I didn't mind."

I move to the edge of the bed and place my feet on the rug that covers most of the stone floor. "I'm sorry," I murmur. Truly though, I am only sorry that she took notice of me holding her.

She rises to her knees on the bed and scoots over behind me. Her hand slides across my shoulder and down along my chest as she pushes her body against my back. "I think it just means that you trust me," she whispers in my ear.

She may not be aware of it, but there is seduction in her voice, and her hot breath on my neck has the hairs on my arms standing on end as my whole body tingles. I close my eyes, losing myself to the sensations.

"Really?" I ask, simply to hear her speak again.

She pulls me closer to her, which I didn't think was even possible. "Maybe even more than you trust Kate."

I open my eyes, thinking. Kate. I give a small sigh. Leave it to Kate and her lectures to spoil my fun. With my head cleared, I pull away from Claire and stand up. For the first time tonight, I look at her. She's beautiful as ever, and it's hard to believe that someone can sleep an entire day and still look so appealing.

With her standing on her knees and her gown pulled taut between her legs, it's difficult to focus, but I manage to say, "You should probably go back to your room so that nobody knows you were here."

"What are you going to do? It's not dark out yet," she says, making no effort to remove herself from my bed.

I walk to my dresser and open the drawer. "I'm going to get ready. I have to get you a sheep, don't I?" I pull out some clothes and set them on top of the dresser.

"Are you going to get me a soldier?"

I look at her sitting on the edge of the bed, a devilish grin on her face. She's intrigued by the idea of having a soldier in the house.

I close the dresser drawer without taking my eyes from her. "No." I grab my clothes, walk into the bathroom, and close the door.

As I change my pants, I hear her start again, this time right next to the door. "You're going to get a woman again, aren't you?"

I most definitely would be hunting for a woman. A woman without family or friends to look for her.

I slide my shirt on. "I like women. Their skin is delicate. Easy to bite." I pull open the door.

Beside the bathroom door, Claire leans against the wall, her hands behind her. She looks at me, soft concern lighting her eyes. "They're calling it World War Two out there."

"I know," I say quietly.

She steps close to me, looking up at me from the tops of her eyes, drawing me in. "You be careful tonight," she whispers with a silkiness in her voice.

"I'm always careful," I tell her. I look away from her, trying to keep from losing what little willpower I have with her.

She places her hand on my cheek and turns my face back toward hers. "You come back to me, you hear?"

I nod slowly, keeping her face just inches from mine. Absorbed by her touch, her gaze, her honeyed voice, I long to taste her lips on mine.

She glides her hand along my neck, down to my chest, making it hard for me to breathe. My hands tremble as I fight to keep them by my side.

"I'll see you soon," she says softly. She pulls her hand back as she turns around. I feel my body sway forward slightly toward her as she starts walking away. I watch her until she is gone and the door is closed, and then I exhale, utterly regretful that waiting to kiss her is a necessity.

I finish getting ready, taking more time than I need, and eventually find myself waiting on the staircase in the foyer. Sitting quietly on the steps, I can hear Harvey upstairs noisily fumbling through his armoire. A middle-aged man, he has been with us nearly six years, which, surprisingly, is not a long time to retain a sheep.

"Harvey," I yell up to him.

After a few moments, he appears at the top of the stairs. Speckles of white streak through his black hair, making him look older than he is. The joy in his hazel eyes matches the smile on his round face. I like to see him so happy. It makes me feel better about what we've done to him.

"Are you hungry? Do you want me to make you something before I leave?" I ask. The scent of his blood fills my nostrils. Heavy and overpowering, it's probably the reason Kate picked him from the crowd, but the fresh punctures on his neck make him less tempting than he should be.

He shrugs his shoulders. "I'm all right."

I am slightly disappointed, as I do quite enjoy cooking. "All right. Well, we're going to have a new friend joining us soon. So if you could please get a bedroom ready."

He nods, and it reminds me of a child about to start school, half excited, half anxious.

"Use the white linens and the quilt that's pink and white," I instruct him, though I try not to sound too imperious. "You do know which one I mean, right?"

"The one you got from Paris?" he asks.

It always surprises me that for someone who cannot remember his past, he can retain so much of what we say.

I smile to myself and nod. "That's the one."

I can feel that the others in the house are beginning to wake. I sense them much the same way that I feel the night approaching. I close my eyes, listening intently. I don't hear anything, but I know they are close.

I look up at Harvey, still standing at the top of the stairs, and smile mischievously. "Tell Marcella I said thanks for the car."

I hurry to the door and grab the car keys hanging on the wall. Knowing it is dark enough, I rush outside, running to the side of the house where a car is covered with a tarp. I stare at the silhouette of the vehicle, contemplating whether to take it out or not. The automobile was a gift from Kate, and Marcella has always been selfish with it, not allowing any of us drive it without her permission.

I pull back the tarp, exposing the 1936 Horch 853. In the dim light of the moon, the light gray paint appears darker than it is. It's difficult not to stop and admire everything about it, from the high rolling fenders and round headlights to the step boards and split windshield.

I glide my hand over the slick hood, feeling the cold metal. I pull the door open and slide inside. The smell of leather saturates the stale air. I could have simply asked for the car, and Marcella would have said yes. But where's the fun in that?

I turn the key inside the ignition, and the straight-eight engine comes to life. Knowing everyone in the house heard me start the car, I don't waste any time. I drive down the overgrown driveway quickly, trying to make my escape a clean one. The driveway is rough enough to bounce me around at this speed, but, brutal though it is, it has me smiling.

I don't need to stop to open the gate since I hadn't closed it the night before. I press the gas pedal down farther as I approach it. Speeding through the entrance, I turn sharply, making the tail end of the car slide across the dirt road wildly. Laughing loudly, I regain control of the car.

With an impenetrable cloud of dust behind me, I race down the dirt road until the house is invisible in the mirror. I turn on the lights just before I hit the highway, not to help me see the road but so that the humans can see me. I roll down the window and let the cool night air push against my face.

As I get closer to the city, I see more homes that have been hit by the bombers. Half of a brick two-story stands along the road, rubble in the yard, the grass charred. I watch the house as I drive by, wondering what kind of people had lived there. Did they escape the house, or the city, or even the country? Germany isn't the safest place to be right now, even for us.

To my right are the remnants of another home. Scorched splinters of wood sprinkle the lawn. Only the porch is recognizable, though it's half sunken into the crater the bomb left. A small bicycle lies on its side in the front yard. At least one child lived there, probably a happy child before warfare scarred its life.

I turn my attention back to the road and drive slowly as I enter the city limits. The destruction does not end here. Rubble from the lime mortar and brickwork of several buildings is heaped on the sidewalk, yet across the street the buildings remain standing. An eerie sight to drive past, the ruins reflect the shadow of a once prosperous city. Lights are shining in the windows of adjacent buildings, a futile attempt at prewar normality.

Numerous citizens have taken shelter in neighboring towns, trying to escape the attacks. The city, however, is anything but dead. Troops still reside here along with families with nowhere else to go. Pubs and taverns litter the streets, providing the only solace in this cold time.

I stop in front of what once was the road, now just a loose pile of stone. I back the car into the alley and park it where it will be concealed by darkness. With the headlights off, I put the keys in the visor.

Not the most secret hiding place, but it will keep a thief from ripping out the panel to hotwire it.

I get out of the car quietly and stand in the darkness for a moment, making sure nobody has taken notice of the car. Feeling positive that no one is around, I start walking. The air is cooler than it was last night. Since I didn't wear a coat, I wrap my arms around myself in an attempt to appear as cold as a human would be.

I hold myself and shudder slightly as the wind whips between the buildings, keeping up the charade. I walk only a few blocks before I reach the pub. Cold and gray, it blends in with the other nondescript buildings surrounding it. I hear laughter and music pouring from within, loud and obnoxious. It isn't my preferred place to spend my nights, but nonetheless I am here.

A sign, painted in red and posted near the door, states, NO WEAPONS ALLOWED. I smile to myself as I enter the tavern, revealing the most unsuspected of weapons, my teeth. So many humans have fallen prey to them. Too many to count. If I had such a desire I could annihilate the entire pub. No witnesses, no one escaping, with plenty of time to spare. But those days have long since passed for me. I have lost enough of myself to mindless carnage.

"That's an awfully big smile for a man without a coat," jests the rough voice of a woman.

I look over and see a small woman, short and thin, standing behind the bar. Her black hair is pulled back into a ponytail loose enough that some strands dangle in front of her face. Her round face looks worn and weathered, but I assume that most of her aging has taken place just in the past few years.

I walk to the bar and sit down on the stool beside an inebriated man. "My wife just had our first son," I lie in my best German.

"Congratulations," the barmaid says. "First round's on me." She leans over the bar, accentuating her cleavage, and there is plenty to flaunt. But that isn't what catches my attention. The pendant she wears, a cross, I cannot take my eyes from it. If it were larger, it would have bothered me more, but it's small and only makes my pulse quicken and my skin crawl. Elusive and untouchable, it dares me to feel the way it would burn against my flesh. Captivated, I watch it rise and fall with her breaths. I am sure, however, that she mistakes what I have set my eyes on, because when I finally look up, she is smiling assertively. "What's your poison?"

"Rum." As a human I had a strong preference for rum, though I had a very low tolerance for it.

"Nice choice." She rubs her finger along her collarbone and down her chest. "Do you want to buy me a drink?"

I am still human enough to enjoy when a pretty lady shows interest in me, so I smile and say, "I'm married, remember?"

She raises her eyebrow seductively. "That's my favorite kind of man."

"I'm going to say no, for now." It does not please me to pretend to be a sleazy man, but let's face it, humans are corrupt. I rub my finger over the back of her hand. "But if you ask me again after I've had a few shots, the answer might be different."

She grabs the bottle of rum and a shot glass from under the bar. "What's your name?" I ask her.

She pours the rum to the brim of the glass and smiles at me. "Gretchen. But you can call me Gret." She sets the bottle of rum back under the bar. "And just what name will I be calling out tonight?"

She's direct, I'll give her that. Her frankness keeps me smiling, "I'm afraid I don't entirely know. But my name is Nicolas."

She smiles broadly. "You let me know when you're dry, Nicolas."

I slide the shot glass toward myself as she walks to the other side of the bar and starts serving an older man with two days' worth of stubbly, white beard on his face. I look at the man beside me. His head is lying on the bar, his hand still clutching his half-drunk pint. I couldn't have asked for a more perfect opportunity to discard my drink.

I glance around the room. The pub isn't crowded, perhaps twenty-five people are here. They're mostly young men, making me seem to fit in, but in reality, I am nothing like them.

When no one is watching, I pour my rum into the older man's pint. As I set the shot glass down, I notice a photograph partially hidden under his other hand. I reach over his head and slide the picture gently away from him. Staring back at me from the black-and-white photo is a man, no, a boy, of around eighteen years. A private in a Wehrmacht uniform, he stands holding his weapon to the side. His light hair is peeking out from under his cap, and his eyes, young and innocent, suggest the photograph was taken before he fought in any battles.

I can hear Gretchen approach long before she stops in front of me and fills my glass with rum. "That was fast," she jokes with a smile in her voice.

I look up from the picture and notice that the top button of her dress is undone, where it previously had not been. A desperate action by a desperate woman, I suppose.

"I was thirsty," I reply. It is not a lie, only misleading.

She smiles at me and I admit it makes her look more attractive. I flip the photograph around so she can see it. "Do you know this man?"

She barely looks at the picture before her smile fades. "That's Samuel's son." She nods her head in the direction of the older man beside me. "Samuel just got word that he was killed earlier this week."

I look at Samuel sleeping on the bar and feel a sort of pity for him. "Did he die here in Germany?"

"Poland. Poor sap's been in here every night since." She takes the photo out of my hand and lays it on the bar beside Samuel. "But we don't need to talk of such sad things, do we?"

I slide the shot glass toward me, taking care not to spill any rum. "Most of the men in here, they're soldiers, aren't they?"

"They are." She rubs her hand over mine. "But I'm not looking for a soldier. I'm looking for a man like you."

Just because I am curious, I ask, "And how do you know I am not a soldier?"

She laces her fingers through mine, and it feels nice to have someone drown you with affection even when it is unwarranted. "Because you've never killed anyone. I can see it in your eyes."

Before I have time to react properly, I burst into laughter. The idea of my having so much innocence packed into my eyes is ludicrous. "You're really good at reading people." I have to fight to keep my voice from sounding sarcastic.

She rests her forearms on the bar. "Thank you. I should be. I see enough men come through that door. It's nice to see a real gentleman, like you, for a change."

Perhaps I like being called a gentleman, or perhaps I just want to prove her wrong, but something makes me hunger for her. I lean across the bar until I am close to her, and I place my hand on her neck softly. I entwine my fingers in her hair and pull her toward me forcefully. "Truth is, sometimes I'm not so gentle."

I can feel her breath, ragged on my face, and hear her heart pounding against her chest. She is not afraid, merely excited. The way her skin heats up under my hand as the blood rushes through her body makes it difficult to think clearly.

I keep my face close to hers, staring at her widened eyes. "Now, if you will excuse me, there is something I have to do," I say smoothly.

I settle back on my barstool, letting my hand glide across her cheek. I am not misleading her entirely. The animal inside me realizes how effortless it would be to take what I want from Gretchen. Her blood would soothe my burning throat, but I have to keep in mind that I have a goal for the night. Others are depending on me.

Vampires are not the cold, calculated killers humans portray us as. We are more impulsive predators, acting on desire and instinct. It can be difficult for some of us to focus on more than one thing at a time, but right now my attention is on a man playing billiards. I noticed him as soon as I entered the pub, marked him as a pawn in my plan. Unknown to him, my plan begins to unfold.

I glance back at Gretchen. As I do, I walk directly into the man playing billiards, making him miss his shot.

"Sorry," I mutter. But in that second it took to bump him, I have his wallet and a booklet in my pocket without anyone noticing.

The man tosses his pool cue on the table and turns toward me with a cigarette in his mouth. He inhales strongly, making the end of the cigarette burn red.

"I don't want any trouble," I tell him, though it's not entirely true.

He blows smoke in my face in one long breath. Choking and coughing, I fan the air in front of my face, trying to clear it.

"Well, you got trouble," he says in a raspy voice. He pushes my shoulder back powerfully with his hand.

From across the room, Gretchen calls out, "Come on Pete, leave him alone."

He pushes my shoulder again, knocking me back a step. "What's he going to do?" he asks her.

I ignore Gretchen's pleas to Pete about not fighting indoors and concentrate all my attention on appearing human, despite feeling my teeth tingling. "You're making a mistake," I say to him quietly.

He smiles at what he perceives is a challenge, though I hadn't meant to imply one. "Really? Make your move." He pushes my shoulder back again. "Do something." He slaps my cheek hard enough to turn my head, but it doesn't hurt me. "I dare you."

He pulls his hand back to slap me again but I grab him by the hair and slam his head against the pool table. I hear his cheekbone snap and see blood stream out of a laceration just above his eye. I grab the pool cue and break it against the table, making a sharp point. Before his friends can move to help him, I press the tip to his neck.

I lean close to his ear and let the darkness show in my voice. "Do something. I dare you."

Breathing hard, he puts his hands up in surrender, but I keep the pool cue close to his throat, aching to press it into the artery just beneath his skin. "Please, you don't... you don't want to hurt me," he stammers out. "I'm an officer. You'll go to prison."

It is true that I don't want the attention the death of an officer would bring down on my family. Although I am certain no prison could hold me, I toss him to the floor like a rag doll. "Then be respectable, like an officer should be," I warn him.

I hold up the broken pool cue. "I'll be keeping this. If you follow me, I'll pierce your liver with it."

He nods. As I walk toward the door, I steal one more look at Gretchen, expecting to see disappointment or sadness. But she stands at the bar, twirling the end of her hair, half biting her lip, and her eyes fix on me, revealing the lust behind them. It is strange how violence affects humans, frightening some and arousing others.

KATHRYN HORSLEY | 33

I step outside into the cool night air and toss the pool cue to the ground. I take out the wallet I stole and open it. Inside is more money than I anticipated. I shove it into my pocket even though I didn't take it for money. I look at the booklet. It is what I expected, a military identification book. I open it. Stamped across it in bold black letters is the name LT. P. MUELLER. I slide that in my pocket, too, and go back to searching through the wallet until I find what I'm looking for. A hotel key with the number 403 etched into it.

I have already done enough reconnaissance to know which hotel the troops have established a base in. Now I have a room number to go with it. After I put the key in my pocket, I pitch the wallet across the street and start for the hotel. It isn't far, only a few blocks away, and I get there quickly.

When the hotel was evacuated, the guests left most of their belongings behind. Clothing in the closets, suitcases on the floor, coats on the racks, everything was forgotten. The soldiers take advantage, pretending there isn't a war and dressing as civilians when they get the chance which is convenient since it means nobody has to die for me to get my hands on his uniform.

I enter the hotel lobby knowing the obstacles awaiting me. First, although hotels have public accessibility, the rooms themselves are private enough that I require permission to gain entry. There is a loophole, however—anyone's permission will do. I just need the right kind of chump to give it to me.

And there, sitting behind the counter, is such a chump. Dusty blond hair and thick plastic glasses make him look younger and more naïve then he probably is. His uniform, while pressed reasonably well, screams private. He's leaning back in a chair, his feet propped up on the desk. His relaxed body language suggests that the letter he's reading is most likely from his mother.

I walk to the counter and wait for him to look up at me.

When his blue eyes meet mine, he asks, "Can I help you?" I can tell by the way he asks that he is hoping I'll say no.

"I left my key in the room. I'd like to use your spare to go in and get it," I tell him in fairly convincing German, though it is not my native tongue.

He sits up straight, dropping his feet to the floor. He looks at me suspiciously. "You're a soldier stationed here?"

I nod. This is where it gets tricky. If he knows Lieutenant Mueller, then perhaps I was wrong about nobody having to die for this uniform.

"What room are you staying in?" he asks with his eyebrows drawn together.

"403."

He flips through pages attached to a clipboard, and from where I stand, I can see that they contain a list of room numbers, a soldier's name beside each. On the fourth page, he stops. He trails his finger over the list until he reaches close the middle of the paper.

He looks up at me with his eyes only. "Name?"

"Lieutenant Peter Mueller," I say with the authority I assume a lieutenant should possess.

He lets go of the papers so that they fall back down onto the clipboard. "Do you have identification, sir?"

"Of course." I pull out the ID book and hold it up toward him, keeping my fingers over the picture of the real Lieutenant Mueller. The private leans close, squinting to read the scratchy handwriting. I pull the booklet back away from him and tuck it inside my pocket.

"I didn't really get to see-" he starts.

I interrupt him. "Are you going to let me in my room or not?" I huff, crossing my arms. "I've told you my name. I've shown you my ID book. I even know exactly where my key is. I left it on the nightstand."

"Lieutenant, sir, you do realize that I must follow protocol. And protocol states that I must inform the major of all soldiers attempting to gain access to a room without the proper identification"—I start to say something but he continues—"and a key. Sir."

I had known that but was hoping he had not. "I am well aware of the protocol," I tell him. I lean against the counter. "And are you aware of what time it is? The major is sleeping. He will not want to be awakened, forced to come down here, only to hear of you hassling an officer over a petty issue that can easily be resolved." I say it forcefully enough that it sounds almost like a threat.

The private shifts in his seat uncomfortably. "Sir, again, protocol states…"

I cut him off again. "It states that you must notify the major to obtain his approval in order to give me the key. However, I don't need your key. If you would walk with me and let me in the room, I could get my key and show it to you. That way you would know I was telling the truth, and since I will not be touching your key, there will be no need to wake anyone."

I watch as his mouth twitches slightly as he considers. I add, "You can tell the major I ordered you, if you like."

He looks me in the eye, and I can see him yielding. "You're sure you know where the key is, sir?"

"Yes."

He opens the drawer and takes out a large set of keys, the type of keys you would picture a janitor carrying. "And what if you can't find it, sir?"

I half-smile to myself, knowing I've won. "Then I'll wake the major myself."

He closes the drawer as he stands up. Then he calls over his shoulder, "Keller. Come watch the desk for a minute."

"Sure thing, Krause," a man says from an adjacent room.

Private Krause walks around the counter and motions for me to follow him as he heads toward the elevator. "Let's get your key, sir."

I follow him to the elevator, taking care not to walk faster than him and so seem too eager. He presses the button to call the elevator car and watches the needle above the doors as it begins to move.

I hear papers shuffling at the counter, so I turn and look, as any curious human might. A private stands at the counter, staring at me, confused. I assume he is Private Keller, but I have been wrong before.

The elevator stops and the door opens, redirecting my attention back to the task at hand. Private Krause gestures for me to get on the elevator first. I suppose if I were a dangerous human, I would want the private to stay in front of me so that I could monitor his actions. But I am a vampire, so his position is of little consequence to me.

I smile at him and step onto the elevator. Looking around at the rich fabrics and lush carpeting, I can tell this must have been a luxury hotel at one time. Now just a shadow of its once glorious existence, it has become subdued by the tribulations of war. Private Krause seems unmoved by the sadness the atmosphere evokes as he gets into the elevator and presses the button for the fourth floor.

As the elevator moves upward, I say, "Private Krause?"

"Yes, sir?" I can hear in his voice that he is still uncertain about me. "How old are you?" I ask him.

"Almost nineteen, sir."

Merely a child. I am glad I didn't have to kill him. "Do you have a wife back home?" I ask.

He laughs slightly. "I'm a bit young for that, don't you think?" Then he adds, "Sir."

The truth is, I don't think eighteen is too young to be married. I was born in a time when most people were married and had children by the time they were eighteen.

"Do you, sir?" he asks.

And for reasons I don't quite understand, I tell him the truth. "I had a fiancée once. But that was as close as I ever came. Her name was Ann." Maybe I just wanted to hear the sound of her name, or maybe all I wanted was to let someone get close to me for a moment. To understand me. To think of me as a human.

"Is she waiting for you, sir?"

He must notice that I keep my eyes averted from his and pause a moment before I speak again. "She died," I say quietly.

"I'm sorry, sir."

I shrug. "It was a long time ago."

The elevator stops on the fourth floor. "Begging your pardon, but it couldn't have been that long ago, sir. You're not that old."

I laugh a little to myself as we walk off of the elevator. "Right." We start down the hallway. "I'll tell you, though, I do feel older."

I watch the numbers on the room doors get lower and lower as we pass them.

"War will do that to you, sir," he says as he flips through the keys.

"Yes, killing the innocent does have a way of aging you. It dims your soul." I grab his shoulder, stopping him. "Try to keep your head down until the war is over. Try not to lose yourself in it."

He draws his eyebrows toward each other, gauging the gravity of my comment. "Yes, sir."

I nod my head toward the room door. "We're here."

Private Krause looks at the door beside me and sees the number 403 just above the brass knocker. He smiles and steps past me toward the door.

He slides one of the keys into the lock, and as he turns it, I ask him, "Private Krause, would you mind if I entered first?"

He pushes the door open and motions with his hand. "After you, sir."

And there it is. Permission to enter. The only thing I really needed from the private. There are easier, quicker ways to get it. There is the threat of death, followed by death itself. But I don't want to kill anyone if I can help it.

I walk into the pitch-black room. It is small but adequate, especially for a soldier during war. At least it is shelter, which is better than some of them have. Along the wall to the right is the bed and nightstand.

Before Private Krause can flip the light switch, I rush to the nightstand and set down the key from my pocket. When the light comes on, I am standing at the foot of the bed.

I look at the nightstand as though I hadn't seen it in the dark. "See, there it is," I say as I walk over and pick up the key, holding it up so that Private Krause can see it.

He smiles, satisfied. "Goodnight then, Lieutenant." He closes the door as he leaves.

Once I am alone, I know I must hurry. The real Lieutenant Mueller could be here at any moment, and I do not want to have to explain that.

I go to the closet and pull open the door. There, hanging alone, is the uniform I want, earthy gray and freshly pressed. I smile to myself as I rub my hand along the sleeve. I take it down and lay the uniform on the bed. I take the ID book out of my pocket and set it on the bed. I am sure Lieutenant Mueller will need it more than me.

I kick my shoes off and I undress quickly. I slide the pants on, the coarse material feeling rough against my skin. As I anticipated, they fit me well. I chose the lieutenant because his build is similar to mine. I do admit I am glad I will be portraying an officer, someone who gives orders instead of merely obeying them.

After I dress, I look in the bottom of the closet and am pleased to see the lieutenant's shoes, polished and shining, lying on the floor. I put them on and though they are about a half size too big, they will work well enough.

I take my clothes and go to the window. I pull it open and look down at the four-story drop below. I know it will sting a bit when I hit the ground, but I have jumped from higher.

I sit on the ledge and let my legs hang from the window. Behind the hotel is a small yard surrounded by a fence with razor wire along the top. A row of bushes runs alongside the base of the hotel walls. A lone guard walks near the fence, looking everywhere but up. He doesn't notice me, and once he walks around the corner of the building, I push myself off the ledge and drop to the ground.

I land in a squat, hidden by the bushes. I know I could easily make the distance of the small yard, but another guard appears from around the corner of the hotel. I remain crouched between the bushes until he walks past. Seeing no other guards, I rush up behind him. Very quickly, I reach around him and grab his gun. With a jerk, I pull it from his hands and hit him in the face with the butt. He drops to the ground, unconscious. I grab him by the shirt and toss him and the gun into the bushes.

I run at the fence and jump over it with little effort. Once on the other side, I take the long way back to my car, hoping to avoid Lieutenant Mueller.

The car is still in the alley. I place my clothes inside, but my night is not over. On the contrary, my real mission for the night has just begun.

I start toward the other side of town, the seedier side. It isn't long before I find myself walking amidst the shabby, rundown apartment buildings where the filth of Germany still crawls. I see them hiding in the shadows like cockroaches, waiting for an easy target, someone weak and helpless. Someone not like me.

I ignore them and keep walking until I reach a five-story apartment building with no name or address on the door. A perfectly disreputable place, I had chosen it well. Nobody will miss a girl from this part of the city.

I knock on the door robustly, and I do not have to wait long before it opens. A slender woman with blond hair and intense blue eyes stands in the doorway staring at me.

"Are you lost, officer?" she asks.

I take off my lieutenant hat and start, "Good evening, Madame-"

She interrupts. "Evening? Don't you mean night?" She leans against the door frame. "It's an awfully late hour for a man to be calling on a woman."

"Yes. And what will the neighbors say if you keep me outside for all to see?"

She smiles at me. "What would they say, indeed?" She pushes the door open the rest of the way. "Come in, Lieutenant."

I suppose I shouldn't be surprised that she can recognize a lieutenant's uniform. She probably has had loads of soldiers here. I assume she has had loads of every type of man here.

I walk into the warm room. Though it was once the lobby of an apartment building, it looks more like a large living room with couches and pictures and some wilting flowers in a vase.

She closes the door behind me and says, "What can I do for you, sir?"

I turn around toward her. "It's not what you can do that I am concerned with. I am afraid I couldn't afford you." I smile at her gently. "I'm looking for a woman. I believe she works here."

The Madame sits down on one of the couches and crosses her legs, letting them hang out of the slit in her dress and exposing them up to her thigh. "You'll have to be more specific."

"She's about this tall." I hold my hand up to show that I mean about five feet, six inches. "Medium-length black hair, enchantingly pale skin, small hazel eyes, straight nose leading to a pert little mouth," I say describing the woman I have followed most of the week.

She rubs a fingertip over her knee in a circle. "I know who you are talking of. Her name is-"

I put my hand up to stop her. "No. I don't want to know her name." It's better if I can think of her more as prey and less as a person.

The Madame uncrosses her legs and sits up straighter. "I'd very much like to have yours, though."

"Of course, how rude of me. I am Lieutenant Emmerich Hager." I often use the surname Hager because of its meaning: stranger. Which is exactly how I wish to remain when I use it.

She stands up and walks over to me. "You have money, Emmerich? My girls are not cheap."

I smile slightly at her. "Nor did I assume they would be." I lean in closer to her and say, "Don't fret, pretty lady, I have done this before." Which is true but deceptive, as I am sure we are talking about two very different things.

"Good. Follow me," she says and then turns and heads toward a hallway. It is apparent that someone has attempted to keep up the building to some degree, although the hardwood is worn, and the white paint on the walls has yellowed. I follow her silently to a staircase with poor lighting.

She starts up the creaky stairs. "You'll have to forgive us. This building was built in 1863 and no elevator was ever installed."

"I don't mind the exercise so much as long as she is not on the fifth floor," I joke.

The Madame laughs slightly to herself. "No sir, only on the second."

The light flickers above my head. "I'm sure I shall find the stairs invigorating then."

She looks at me with an odd smile on her face. "You speak as though you are very old."

I smile. "And wise. Don't forget wise."

She laughs. "Yes, how could I?" At the top, the stairs open to another hallway. This one is much better preserved. The hardwood shines under the bright lights, and the wallpaper is no more than a few years old.

We stop in front of the second door on the left. The Madame knocks lightly, and a moment later the door opens and there she is. Beautiful and desirable, she wears only a peach silk slip.

She looks at the Madame and then at me and smiles flirtatiously. "Hello."

The Madame says, "Be a dear and show the lieutenant a good time, won't you?"

"Of course," the young woman says. "It would be my pleasure." Then she takes my hand and says, "Come in." She pulls me inside and closes the door.

The room feels as though it used to be a living room and now is masquerading as a bedroom with too little furniture. Aside from the bed along the wall, one nightstand, and a vanity desk, there isn't much to look at. The underwhelming bedding is tossed about, signifying to me that she has already had another customer in her bed tonight. In which case, I will not be lying on that bed.

"Madame did not tell me your name," she says.

I walk to the chair in front of the vanity and sit down. "It's Nicolas Rider. And I'm going to call you Lilah, if that's all right."

She smiles slightly. "You can call me anything you like so long as you pay."

I take more money than necessary out of my pocket and drop it on the vanity. "Lilah," I say softly. "Come here."

As she walks toward me, she starts to pull her slip off. "Leave it on," I tell her.

With the slip pulled up around her waist, she slides onto my lap, her legs straddled across me. "What are you wanting from me?" she asks, unbuttoning my shirt.

"You'll see," I whisper.

I pull her face to mine and crush my lips against hers. As she pulls my shirt out of my pants, I can hear her heartbeat quicken. My own heart pounds in response, making it difficult to stay focused. I slide my hands down her body, feeling her warm skin through the thin slip. She rubs her hand up across my chest as she kisses along my jaw line toward my ear. My body shivers with desire. I grab her butt and pull her closer until there is no space between us. She entwines her fingers in my hair and pulls my head back. Her tongue traces its way up my throat toward my chin, and my fingers press into her hips as I fight to keep my eyes a soft green. I let out a heavy breath and glide my hands up to her back. Keeping her pressed against me, I kiss down her neck, feeling her arch her body into mine.

With my eyes still green and my fingernails short, I let my fangs grow out. I bite into the base of her neck. Her body tenses and tightens against me. I can hear her raspy muted attempts at a scream. I feel the way she tries to push away from me, afraid and alone, thinking death is coming for her.

I drink, allowing her blood to quench my burning throat, marking her as my own. Her life, her will, her soul belongs to me now. I can feel her resistance fading. Her attempts to scream cease, leaving behind only jagged breaths. She grows calm in my arms. I drink just a little longer until my belly is satisfied, and she begins to slump against me.

I don't intend to kill her, so I stop myself there. I carry her limp body to the bed and set her down gently. Unconscious, she appears much more fragile than she had before. Her eyes begin to flutter, as if she is dreaming.

I kiss her forehead and whisper, "You are mine now. Rest well, for I will be calling you soon."

I walk back to the vanity and sit down again. All that is left to do is wait. Leaving too soon would only raise suspicions. Then I will go home, where Claire will be waiting. I smile at the thought of seeing her.

Chapter 4

One could believe that vampires would care very little for the stars, as they see them all the time. But I find the stars very interesting. They are part of nature, yet are similar to me. The same unchanging constellations have been in the skies for centuries. Beautiful and distant, they are surrounded by a sea of others yet stand alone.

As I lie on the cool grass gazing at them, I cannot help but question my place in the heavens, too. But after killing so many of such a beloved species, which god could look upon me with forgiveness and compassion? In all my time, the only answer I have come up with is: none.

I hear the grass bending and know that the light footsteps belong to Kate. I lie very still and let my eyes phase to black, pretending not to hear her. A slow smile spreads across my face when she stops and crouches down. She pushes herself off of the grass, scraping the ground with her shoes as she lunges at me. I jump to my feet and grab her arms, pulling her over. We tumble over one another twice before I pin her to the ground, my teeth close to her throat. Lying on top of her, I let my fangs extend slowly until they press against her skin.

"Do it. Take what you want," she tells me quietly.

I raise my head to look into her black eyes and smile. "If I ravish your body, it'll be with something much bigger than my fangs," I joke.

Laughing, she playfully hits my shoulder. "Get off me, you dirty old man."

I roll off her and lie on my back in the grass, smiling. "You know it would be like sleeping with my sister," I tell her as I let my fangs recede and my eyes change back to green.

She shifts onto her side, leaning on her forearm. "Well, you never know about you fourteenth-century men, you might enjoy it," she teases, raising her eyebrow.

I laugh lightly. "Oh, I forgot, we were so uncivilized then, it was so long ago."

"You smell like sex, you know?" she says bluntly.

I frown at her. "Kate, you shouldn't say things like that, it's not proper."

"You can say it and I can't?" she snaps.

"I didn't make the rules," I tell her, smiling. I look back up at the stars. "It's from a brothel. The whole building smelled this way."

She rolls onto her belly, laying her head on her hands in the grass. "I don't know why you bother yourself with that trash."

I look at her. "Those women are not trash. They work in the oldest profession in history. They perform a great service for men everywhere. Worldwide. It's a huge industry."

She smiles softly. "Mm hm. And did these women service you?"

The truth was, they had, but not tonight. "I'm not going to indulge you with this."

She leans up onto her elbows. "Why do you always speak with an American accent? You're English. Speak like an Englishman."

I look away from her. "I like America. I watched it grow up."

She smiles mischievously at me. "You know I will win this. All I have to do is make you angry. You always speak English when you're pissy."

I continue to stare at the stars. She is right, of course, I do speak English when I'm upset. But she won't have to make me mad, I'll do it for her anyway.

She rubs my collar. "You have lipstick on your shirt. It's a trashy color, too." She rubs her finger down my chest. "I wonder if there's lipstick somewhere lower." Her fingers trail down my abdomen.

I grab her hand at my navel. "Blimey, Kate," I say with a heavy English accent. "Don't go all sixes and sevens on me."

She laughs. "There it is."

Keeping my English accent, I continue, "Honestly, you know I didn't shag that girl. I never mix business with pleasure." Then I add, "Often."

"You should talk like that all the time. It suits you."

I let go of her hand and drop my accent. "I'm not English anymore." I haven't been in England for centuries, nor do I wish to go back. Nothing is there for me but bad memories.

"Really? Where were you born?" she asks.

I smile slightly, knowing where she is going with this. "England." She shifts herself closer to me. "And where did you grow up?"

Even after all these years, I remember my father. I see him every time I look in the mirror, though I'm not sure he would be proud of what I've become. He raised me alone after my mother died during childbirth, which was common at the time. I look up at the sky and exhale loudly. "England, again."

"And your parents, where were they from?" she asks with a smirk.

"They were English."

"And where did you have your first love?" she asks sweetly, batting her eyes.

Ann was my first love. She was my only love. Pain crosses my face as a flood of memories begins to pour in. "You made your point," I say quietly, knowing that if she hadn't taken me by surprise, I could have hidden my emotions better.

Kate's expression turns serious. "I'm sorry," she says. "I shouldn't have brought her up."

I can hear the remorse in her voice, but it only makes the memories that much clearer.

I close my eyes and see Ann in the town square dancing with her younger sister under the night sky. The lights surrounding the square give off a soft glow, not that she needs any help to look beautiful.

"Nicky, say something," Kate pleads with a guilty voice.

But I don't want to stop remembering yet. "Just give me a minute," I tell her.

With my eyes still closed, I can feel the heat of Ann's hand when I cut in and the softness of her green back-laced gown.

I open my eyes, knowing that the memories will take me to a place I don't want to think of. I stare at the stars and try to remember something else, anything else.

"Can you still navigate by the stars?" Kate asks me.

I assume she is only asking to distract me since she knows the answer. It isn't something I am about to let myself forget how to do. As a human I was a sailor, and in those days, you needed to be able to tell direction from the night sky as well as a compass. It's a skill that is slowly disappearing, which is a shame. "Yes."

I look at her as she gazes up at the stars, her eyes lost in wonder. I smile at the thought that she enjoys the stars as much as I do.

She reaches over and takes my hand. "Do you want to know a secret?" she asks without looking away from the sky.

"Is it that I look spectacular in this uniform?" I joke, referring to the uniform I still wear.

She laughs lightly and then looks at me. "You know it is." She rolls onto her side and faces me, smiling as though she is about to burst.

"All right, what's your secret?" I ask her.

She leans close to my ear. "Luther sleeps in the nude."

Before I have time to think about my reaction, I grimace. "Ugh. Why would I want to know that?"

She gives me a discouraging look, but I continue, "How do you know that?"

She smiles broadly, raising her eyebrows and biting her lip, "Well..."

"No, Kate. That's disgusting." The idea of Luther and Kate together has my stomach churning. "He's repugnant."

She giggles in a way that makes me believe that she probably agreed with me once. "He's not that bad."

"He is. This is so repulsive, I think I may literally be ill," I tell her.

She pushes my shoulder. "Don't be so dramatic."

I can hear the uncertainty in her voice. I know that as her best friend I should be more supportive, but honestly, did it have to be Luther? I sit up, draping my hands over my knees. "Do you really like him?" I ask quietly.

She sits up beside me. "A lot."

I admit, I had noticed her flirting with him on several occasions, but I never thought it would become more serious than that. I sigh and run my hand through my hair. "Then I suppose that as long as you're happy, I'm happy for you."

She smiles softly and says, "Thank you." She loops her arm around mine. "Come on, let's go inside."

We stand up together and start toward the house. "Don't think I'm going to be nice to him from now on," I tell her.

"Oh, I don't expect miracles," she jokes. "I sincerely doubt that the two of you know how to be civil to one another."

I smile. She knows us too well. "I can be courteous if he can. So long as you are in the room and I'm obligated."

She laughs, thinking I meant it as a joke. I suppose I will have to try harder to be nice to him. I know Kate would choose my friendship over her relationship with Luther if it came down to that, at least I hope she would. But I will do my best to make sure she doesn't have to make that choice. However, I cannot say that Luther will make it easy for me.

We go inside and I am pleased that Luther is nowhere in sight.

She slips her arm away from mine. "I'm going to go take a shower." She playfully hits my shoulder. "Do you want to tussle in the gym first?"

I know how much she enjoys a good fight, but she tends to be a sore loser, and I am not really in the mood to be called a cheater. "Not tonight."

She shrugs. "All right." She leans over and kisses my cheek. She starts to walk away but then turns toward me, smiling. "Oh yeah, Marcella wants to see you."

I groan slightly, making her laugh.

"I hope you live through the night," she adds as she walks out.

I smile at the way she sashays out of the room, full of enjoyment and humor. Surely, she believes that I will be punished severely for stealing the car, but I know better. Marcella always forgives me, especially when I have good news.

I walk into the sitting room, which is relatively small considering the size of the house. The furniture is scaled down appropriately, though, so it doesn't feel claustrophobic. A sofa with an atrocious floral print sits across from two uncomfortable chairs with a small table between them. It's my least favorite room in the house.

However, I did make a bet with Luther that by 1950 it will contain a television, which I feel will be a very successful invention. Luther, on the other hand, believes it will fade away in a few decades. But Luther is an idiot.

I am sure Marcella is wondering what's taking me so long, so I make my way through the adjoining dining room toward the gym, as that is surely where Marcella will be. She's probably training Luther, though it seems pointless to me to waste so much time on him. In the nearly eighty years that he has been with us, he has learned very little. It's not that he can't be taught; it's that he won't be. He hasn't the discipline to accept other people's suggestions, which is one of his many flaws.

I walk into the large gym. Flails, crossbows, daggers, spears, swords, nunchucks, double-headed axes, we have it all, hanging along the walls, ready to be used. We don't need any of them to win a fight, but being able to wield a weapon is a good skill to have.

Marcella and Luther are in the middle of the room, fighting with a set of martial arts sticks. She sweeps the stick around, knocking his legs out from under him. He hits the floor hard enough that I hear him let out a forceful breath.

"Get up," Marcella barks at him.

He rolls backward, pushing off the ground with his hands so that he lands on his feet. Before he can block it, Marcella jabs him in the stomach hard enough to make even me flinch.

To his credit though, he doesn't stop attacking. He swings his stick around at her head. Being Marcella, she blocks it easily and the sticks collide, making a loud cracking noise, but I can tell she's holding back.

"Find your attacker's soft spot, their weakness, and exploit it," Marcella instructs him. She pushes him back with the sticks.

I chime in from across the room, "If you want something soft and weak on Luther"—I tap the side of my skull—"it's in his head."

I hadn't intended to interrupt them, but sure enough, Luther looks over at me. Mercilessly, Marcella mashes the stick into his groin, lifts him over her head, and slams him into the floor. I almost feel bad as he lies on the ground rolling around holding himself. Almost.

Unaffected, Marcella yells at him, "Don't be so pathetic. Distraction is for the weak."

I smile. I remember her saying that to me once, but only once. "Yeah, Luther, I know I'm a handsome devil but you don't have to stare," I taunt.

He sits up and narrows his eyes at me. "I haven't missed your tedious and pointless remarks. I was really hoping the city would be bombed with you still in it."

I simply smirk at him. "Tedious. That's a big word for you, isn't it?"

"That's enough," Marcella snaps at us both. "If I wanted children, I would have changed one."

I know she would never change a child. It's too dangerous. Children are even more impulsive and selfish than the typical vampire, and they usually wind up getting everyone killed, human and vampire.

"Luther, excuse us," Marcella tells him.

*　　*　　*

He gets up, leaving his stick on the ground. As he walks past me, he hisses as though I should find him intimidating. It only makes me smile at how absurd the idea is.

I walk over and pick up his stick. "You should put a muzzle on him," I joke.

But it is apparent that she is not in a joking mood. "Where is my car? I didn't hear it pull into the driveway," she says firmly.

That's because I left it in the alley. I walk over to the wall and hang up the stick. "It's safe," I reply, which is possibly true.

I hear the air chopping behind me and turn around in time to catch Marcella's stick, which was flying toward my head.

I smile at her while I spin the stick around my hand. "You're getting slow."

She smiles back, taking it as a challenge. "I wasn't trying to hit you. Hang it up for me."

I turn toward the wall to hang up her stick, knowing she will try to attack me from behind. I would never fight her out of anger, but this is just for fun. Besides, I know she can handle it.

I place the stick on the wall and step to the side as her foot drives into the wall where I was just standing. I elbow her in the nose. She responds with a slew of punches, most of which I block. When I see my opening, I strike her chest with my hands, knocking her back across the room into another wall.

I grab one of the flails as she grabs both swords. I swing the chain and spiked ball in a circle beside me and in front of my chest until she charges at me. She jumps in the air, flying with her swords aimed at me. I roll away just in time. She lands, driving her swords into the floor. I sweep the flail around, knocking her feet out from under her. Then I bring it up in the air and back down at her, but she is gone before the flail hits.

She swings the swords around. As I move away, they slice my shirt across the abdomen. Without delay, she swings one around toward me. I wrap the flail around it and jerk it from her hand, but with only enough time to stop the other sword by blocking it with my forearm. The sword goes deep into the bone. I pull my arm away and kick her back, making her lose her grip on it. She starts for the wall as I run up along the opposite wall, grabbing a whip. I jump away from the wall, flipping in the air and landing on my feet. Just before she reaches the other wall, I wrap the whip around her neck and jerk her back toward me.

With her back pressed against me, I pull the sword from my forearm and hold it close to her neck, though my fangs are just as close and would be more effective. "You just lost," I tell her.

She laughs and turns around to face me, wrapping her arms around my waist. I drop the sword and embrace her. Looking up, I see Luther standing in the doorway. I point to him and boast, "That's how it's done."

He huffs as he walks away. "Where is my car?" she asks me.

I lean away from her so that she can see my face. "You don't expect me to make a human walk from the city, do you?"

Her face lightens with her smile. "You got me a sheep?"

"Us a sheep," I correct her. "We're sharing, remember."

She starts toward the door. "Not for much longer. Claire is quickly gaining control; she'll be ready for her own soon."

"How soon do you think?" I ask, not because I care about whether she gets her own sheep, but because I want to know when she will have that much control.

She raises one eyebrow, knowing what I am really asking. "Close to one more year. So don't fuck her yet," she says coldly.

Though it pains me to hear a woman be so crude, I do not reprimand her. "Such sound advice, and you put it so eloquently," I tell her.

"Your sarcasm is wasted on me, Nicolas," she says.

I walk over to her. "I'm sorry, Mother. I will behave myself," I say softly. I cup her face in my hands and kiss her forehead. "Goodnight."

I leave her standing in the gym and walk out through the dining room. Hearing heavy footsteps, I stop. I know exactly who it is, and just when I expect him, Harvey hurries around the corner and nearly walks into me.

"Oh, I'm sorry, Nicolas. I didn't see you there," he tells me.

I give him a shrug. "It's all right." I decide to change the subject, "Did you get that room ready, as I asked?"

He nods. "Mm hm." Then he notices the slashes in my shirt. "What happened to your shirt?"

I glide my finger along the bottom of the slit across my abdomen. "Just a bit of fun." I look up at him. "But what happened to yours?" I put my finger on his chest.

He looks down and I raise my finger, bumping his nose up in the air.

His light chuckle makes me smile.

"Goodnight, Harvey." I walk past him and step into the kitchen. All the lights are on, so as I head for the basement, I flip most of the switches off.

I start down the stairs into the dark, as it is rare that the lights are ever on downstairs. The air always seems to be stale and thick in the basement. I walk to my room quietly, trying not to attract attention.

The last thing I want is to talk to Luther again. All I really need is to try to get a few hours of sleep before I call Lilah to me.

I push the door open and step into my room. It isn't the way I left it. The bed is made, and my dirty clothes are in the hamper. This isn't so unusual though; being the favorite has its perks.

I can hear the water from the shower beating down on the floor as someone rings out their hair.

"Kate," I call as I unbutton my ripped shirt.

I hear Kate say, "Yeah?" but the voice is not coming from my shower. In disbelief, I drop my hands, letting my shirt hang open, and stare across the hall at the door to her bedroom. Kate is somewhere behind it. My pulse quickens as only one thought crosses my mind: Claire.

After a moment, I say, "Goodnight," which is not what I had intended to say. I close my bedroom door even before she has time to respond.

I fix my eyes on my bathroom door, knowing who is inside. I walk to the bathroom and put my head against the door, longing to be able to see through the two inches of wood dividing us. I imagine what she must look like standing in the steam-filled shower, water coursing over her body. It's enough to make a lump form in my throat. As I try to swallow, my hand unconsciously goes to the doorknob.

My hand twists the knob, and I tell myself I'm just checking to be sure it's locked, but the knob turns freely. Before I have time to analyze the situation, I push the door open.

The steam rolls out around me, warming my skin. Everything in my mind is screaming for me to stop, but my body doesn't listen. I walk into the bathroom and wet humidity engulfs me. My eyes skim the fogged-up mirror and see the thick towel lying on the sink, but they quickly find their way to the shower where what I see there stops my breath.

The shower curtain has not been closed completely, leaving a gap of a few inches. Although I cannot see her, I know I very easily could. I take a deep breath as I try to convince myself to leave now while I still can. But my feet do not move; instead I cock my head to the left and lean ever so slightly until I see what I came in here for.

Her hands are tangled in her hair, and lather from the shampoo covers most of her red locks. My heart quickens as I watch suds slide down her spine over her milky skin, which is flushed from the heat of the shower. The foam trails down her back, tracing the curve of her body. My hand aches to follow the same line with my fingertips, to feel her soft skin under my hand. The suds run over her bottom, and though they continue down her leg, my eyes stay where they are.

Imagining all the things that I could do to her makes it hard for me to breathe as I fight to keep my eyes green. I let out a small sigh, which is louder than I intended it to be.

She stops washing her hair and stands completely still, more still than a human could. Knowing that she heard me, I stop moving, stop breathing, but I cannot stop thinking. I should be nervous that she may be angry with me. I should be ashamed, but I'm not. My thoughts circle around desire and passion—no not passion, lust.

She starts to glance over her shoulder and I drop my head as I lean away out of view. "Sorry, I-" I start, but that's a lie. I'm not sorry at all. I raise my head up and stare at the curtain. If she wants me gone, she'll have to tell me to leave. I step to my left so that I have a clear view again.

Facing me now, she keeps her head tilted back, rinsing the shampoo from her hair. The water rushes down her chest, dripping from her breasts, her flawless perky breasts, with soft pink nipples and … I know vampires are supposed to be perfect, but could anything be this perfect?

She lowers her head, opening her eyes and looking into mine. She lets a sly smile slowly spread across her face. I don't know how long she knew I was watching her, but I know she liked it. Her hand trails along her hair and down her neck. I inhale slowly trying to regulate my breathing as her hand rubs over her breast and down her abdomen. It flows all the way to the top of her hip where I see a birthmark, not really in the shape of anything, just a dark, little patch of skin, making her seem more human and so much more desirable.

My body yearns to touch her, to feel her wet flesh against mine. She raises her hand and curls her finger, motioning for me to come to her. My eyes phase to black as my willpower begins to slip. I close my eyes, trying to hide the hunger in them, and pinch the bridge of my nose, focusing on regaining control. I can hear her turn off the water and walk toward me.

Smelling roses, I open my eyes, which thankfully are green again. She is closer than I expect, still dripping wet and making a small puddle at our feet. She slides her hand up along my bare chest as she leans in closer to kiss me.

I turn my face away slightly and place my hand on her shoulder. "Don't," I nearly whisper.

She doesn't lean away, instead she stays close to me. "Why? You want something, and I don't think it's my blood." Her voice is intense and sultry, making me work to keep my composure.

Her hand slides slowly down my chest and abdomen. Without taking her eyes from mine, she begins to unbuckle my belt.

I grab her wrists, "Stop," I manage to spit out, though even I can hear the weakness in it.

She pushes herself against me until she is a mere inch from my face. "Make me," she challenges.

It's enough to have me back her into the wall, pinning her arms beside her. Keeping my cheek against hers, I glide my hand along her arm toward her body, inhaling her sweet scent. I can feel her chest press into mine and feel her hot breath on my neck.

My hand slides down to her waist and pulls her into me. I place my other hand on the side of her neck, and using all the control I have left, I whisper, "Have you ever been with a man, Claire?"

"Once," she says a little breathlessly.

I pull my face to hers so that our noses are almost touching. "Hold on to that, because we'll not be making new memories tonight." I lean away enough to grab her towel from the sink.

Her eyes narrow as she snatches the towel from my hand. Pushing my shoulder, she knocks me back a step and then stomps out of the bathroom, slamming the door behind her.

I exhale forcefully, finally able to breathe again, and run my hand through my hair. Looking in the mirror, I see a man who is weaker than he should be. Not physically, of course. Physically, I'm the strongest in the house, and though Luther would contest that, it is the truth. No, this man is losing control. I am losing control. But only the control I need to have with Claire.

I haven't wanted anyone since Ann, and I'm not prepared for this. I feel my resistance to Claire beginning to falter. It's as if I'm standing on ice that's starting to melt. There are thin spots all around me, and if she presses on one of those spots, I'll fall through. Sadly though, the more I think about this, the more I think it wouldn't be such a bad thing.

I walk into my bedroom and though it is pitch black, I can see the lump under the blanket that is Claire. She lies with her back to me, so I go to my dresser. I'm slipping on my shirt when I hear a sniffle come from the bed and realize she's crying.

Guilt washes over me, and my heart drops into my gut. Quietly, I go to the bed and crawl in beside her. "Claire," I start softly. "I'm sorry." I say it with enough vulnerability that she should know I mean it.

She wipes her face with her sleeve. After a moment, she says, "Don't you want me?"

"Of course, I do." I pull back the blankets from her shoulder so that I can see some of her face and realize the shirt she's wearing is mine. "We can't get too close, and you know why. When vampires are... together, they like to bite. And biting a vampire causes a bloodlust that you're not strong enough to handle. Yet."

She rolls onto her back and looks at me with sadness in her eyes. "Couldn't we just not bite?"

I smile to myself. "I could. But it takes a lot of focus and control, more than you have right now."

She sits up beside me and lets a tear hang heavy in her eye. "Could you at least kiss me?"

"I shouldn't," I say simply.

"That's not what I asked you."

She blinks the tear from her eye. As it rolls down her face, I place my hand on her cheek and wipe it away with my thumb. My hand slides back until my fingers are at the base of her skull, pulling her face toward mine. I close my eyes, brushing my lips across hers, and for once nothing is telling me to stop. I press my lips to hers. Soft and plump, they're better than I imagined, and the fire that's growing inside me makes me gasp slightly. As heat courses through my body, I part her mouth with mine and let my tongue slide over her lip. Her fingers wrap themselves in my hair as she pulls herself closer to me.

Slowly, I pull away from her, before I succumb, but I keep my face close to hers, not wanting this to end. I slide my hand back to her cheek and rub my thumb over her lips, feeling their softness. She inhales deeply, parting her lips slightly, and it sends a shiver through my body.

"You can't tell anybody about this," I say quietly. "And if they ask, you have to lie."

She places her hand on mine. "I lied to you once, when I asked to sleep in your bed."

Unable to read her eyes, I ask, "Is that the truth?" She smiles broadly.

"I don't know. Is it?"

I have no idea if she is lying or not, and I'm usually good at picking out lies. If I can't tell, nobody else in this house will be able to tell, either. I smile and lean in for one more kiss. This one is soft and simple, just enough to let me feel her lips again, just enough to forget why I ever hesitated.

When we part, my hand moves to the side of her neck. Looking into her eyes I find something other than blood and battlefields to look forward to. "Goodnight, Claire," I whisper.

I pull her toward me and kiss her forehead gently. I lie down in the bed. She smiles at me and lies down beside me, tugging up the blankets. She takes my hand and rolls over, pulling me onto my side and into her back. I bury my face into her still wet hair and let the smell of roses surround me. As soon as I close my eyes, I hear her sigh happily and think, *I could get used to this.*

Chapter 5

When a vampire sleeps, his senses are muted, and some consider this the best time to hunt a vampire. But there is a better time, a time when our senses are not merely dulled but null and void. A time when we disconnect from reality. A time when we call our sheep.

It goes against my instincts to call to Lilah with another vampire sleeping so close to me, but I like Claire here. I like her smell hanging in the air around me. I like the rhythmic sound of her breathing. I like the way her body feels under my arm.

Trying not to wake her, I sit cross-legged beside her on the bed, as though I'm preparing to meditate. I place my hands on my abdomen and feel the rising and falling of each breath. I close my eyes, letting go of my inhibitions and concerns, blocking out everything my senses are telling me, and search for the delicate thread of energy that links me to Lilah, feeling for the thin web I have spun between us, the web that will convey my wishes to her, bringing her to me.

Like a single hair blowing against my skin, I can feel her, though only slightly. I focus my senses on connecting to her presence until I can feel the beat of her heart thumping quietly inside my chest. The smell of old sweat that saturates her room fills my nostrils.

At my will, her eyes open and I can see her room, foggy and blurred through her human eyes. Like a puppet on a string, she sits up, and I see her in the mirror, her black hair as straight as when I lay her down on the bed. Her peach slip is straight and smooth, as if she hasn't moved since I left.

She/I look around the room. There, hanging near the door, is a long woman's coat, the type one would wear on an evening out, not suitable for the early morning hours. I compel her to put it on anyway. Even though they don't match the coat, I have her put on the first pair of shoes I see, rain boots.

I stay connected to her, leading her down the creaky stairs and through the dull hallway into the lobby, past the Madame and a few of the other women who work there. Some of them look at us strangely while others pay little attention despite the vacant expression on Lilah's face. Nobody tries to stop us as I guide her out the door and into the morning sun.

I pause here a moment, letting the sun warm her skin, enjoying the way the light makes her flesh glow in a way no man-made bulb can. This is the closest I can get to experiencing the sun for myself.

The streets are not the same as they were last night. Different types of people are on the sidewalks, men on their way to the few jobs still remaining in this city, children smiling and running in the streets. High above the alleys, women are leaning out of windows, hanging their laundry.

I flood Lilah's mind with images of the streets she will use to find the car, where the keys are, the roads she must follow to get to our farm. I show her the door to my house and me waiting for her. As I show her these dreamlike images, I whisper, "Come to me."

I sever our connection, leaving her on the steps of the brothel, and return to my body, letting my senses begin to process the information surrounding me in my bedroom again. I smell roses again, lightly at first but growing stronger.

I open my eyes slowly and am pleased to see Claire sitting on her knees in front of me, her face only inches from mine. Without hesitation, she presses her lips to mine quickly before I can truly react to her kiss.

She smiles brightly. "Good morning."

I rub the back of my fingers along her cheek and jaw line. "I didn't mean to wake you."

Her finger trails down my chest. "Well, when you say 'Come to me,' I listen."

Grabbing her hand, I correct her. "You know I wasn't talking to you. I didn't even mean to say that out loud."

She leans in close to my face again. "I think you meant it for me, you just don't know it yet."

I grab her around the waist and drag her down onto the bed, leaning over her. "I know exactly what I want."

Claire runs her hands up around my shoulders and pulls her face toward mine, but I lean back slightly. "I want to make Lilah some lunch because she will be hungry when she gets here," I tell her.

She sighs and collapses back onto the bed, letting her arms flop down above her head. She has no idea how beautiful she is when she's not trying, the way her blue eyes draw me in, alluring and inescapable.

I slide my hands up along her arms, pinning her wrists, and position myself to where I am almost completely on top of her. When I kiss her, I put enough force and urgency behind my lips to make it clear that I'm not thinking about Lilah anymore. I can hear her heart beat harder as she matches my need with her lips.

Her arms push against my hands as she tries to caress me. But I know my limits, and it's easier for me to control this if she is not touching me, although keeping her pinned has my body nearly trembling with desire.

By the time I move my lips to her jaw line, we're both breathing heavily. She lays her head to the side, exposing her throat. I kiss along her neck, my hot breath giving her body goose bumps. She closes her eyes, and I hear the beginning of a moan that she's trying to conceal. The muffled sound sends an unexpected rush of heat throughout my body.

Thankfully, one of us is thinking clearly. "I thought you said you wanted lunch," she says breathlessly.

I lean up so she can see my eyes. "I'm working my way down there. Just be patient."

She smiles at me and laughs quietly. She is right, I should stop myself now. Although I'd rather not, I tell her, "Come on, let's go upstairs." I let go of her wrists and sit up. "The moment's gone, anyway."

She sits up, leaning back on her elbows. "I hope it takes you longer than a moment," she jokes, smiling mischievously.

I grab her knee and slide her toward me, leaning close to her face. "I'll take longer than what you're going to need," I say with enough intensity to make her inhale sharply.

"You want to prove it?" she challenges.

"Yes, I do. In"—I look at my wrist as though I'm wearing a watch, which I am not—"three hundred and sixty-four days."

She laughs, but I can tell she's disappointed.

"You need to get dressed, and in something other than my clothes," I tell her. "It might make people suspicious."

She sits up, making me lean back. "Really? I would love it if you tried to take this off of me."

I smile. I'd like that too. "You can keep it."

She slides off the bed. Her hand trails along my cheek as she starts to walk away, turning my face toward her.

She walks slow, trying deliberately to drive my senses wild. Opening the door, she looks back at me. "This shirt doesn't smell like you now. I don't think I want it anymore."

She pulls the shirt off and drops it on the floor near her feet. And just like that, she's standing in my doorway wearing nothing but a pair of lacey panties. She blows me a kiss and exits.

Damn. I'm in trouble.

After I begin breathing again, I get dressed and head upstairs. I take out the cutting board as I contemplate what to make for Lilah's lunch. I don't worry about being quiet, knowing I won't wake up Marcella. She can sleep through anything.

I hear the sound of light feet on the stairs and smile, knowing Claire is not trying to conceal herself from me. I take the large skillet from my, not as impressive as I would like, selection of pans and set it on top of the stove.

"So, what are we making?" Claire asks as she sways her way over to me. She walks behind me, letting her hand glide across my shoulders. There is an ease to her simple touch that makes my smile spread into a little lopsided grin. It's as though there is nothing more natural than her affection toward me.

She leans back against the counter and props her elbows on top of it.

My eyes fix on her and notice everything. The way her pale blue dress plays off the freckles that parade across her flawless skin. The way the casual ponytail she's arranged her red hair into makes her appear so innocent.

"Chicken cordon bleu," I tell her.

She shifts slightly. "Why did you choose that?" she asks, though I can tell she's not really interested in the answer, as she lets her eyes gaze across the room.

"Because most women like chicken. And I, sort of, have a thing about pleasing women."

She looks at me quickly, probably to gauge my seriousness.

I let her stare at me, frozen for a moment, analyzing the way I keep my eyes locked with hers, before I smile softly. "Will you hand me the bread?" I ask as though I hadn't insinuated anything just a moment ago.

She half-smiles and pushes herself off the counter as I head toward the refrigerator.

Thankfully, Harvey had previously laid out the chicken and left it on a plate, which I'm sure he won't mind me using. As I balance the plate of chicken and the Swiss cheese on my forearm and take the eggs and milk in my hand, Claire approaches me quickly.

"Do you want me to take anything?" she offers.

I grab the plate with a very small ham on it with my other hand. "Just get the door, will you?" I say, nodding toward the refrigerator.

I go to the counter where she had set the bread down as she closes the refrigerator. I lay everything out on the counter and grab three large bowls from the cabinet. Claire walks over to me and kisses me on the cheek softly, making my lopsided smile spread across my face again. "What was that for?" I ask her.

She shrugs. "Do I need a reason?"

I shake my head. "Not as long as you're prepared for the consequences."

She smiles. "Consequences? What did I do?"

I step closer to her, narrowing the space between us. "Left me wanting more."

She places her hand on my chest and rubs her fingers along the buttons of my shirt. "Maybe that's what I intended." She looks up at me from the tops of her eyes and they draw me in. "Just how much did you want?"

I whisper, "Everything." I lean in close until my lips almost touch hers. "But I'll settle for this." I kiss her softly, letting my tongue slide along her lips.

As she arches her body into mine, she runs her hands up my back, pulling me toward her. I place my hands on both sides of her neck, allowing my thumbs to graze her cheeks, and continue to kiss her, letting her feel the desire behind my lips.

I pull away from her slowly, feeling the energy between us still electrifying the air. With my eyes closed and my face near hers, I listen to her heartbeat as it slows to its normal rhythm.

Opening my eyes, I move my hand up to her cheek and rub my fingers across her skin. She takes my hand and guides it to her lips and kisses my palm gently.

I half-smile at her as she brings our hands down between us. I glance at the ingredients on the counter and nod my head toward them. "Do you know how to separate everything into the bowls?"

She nods. "I've made this before."

"Good." I let go of her hand and grab one of the eggs. I roll it over my hand and down my forearm. I straighten my arm suddenly, sending the egg into the air and into Claire's hands, making her laugh.

"Do you cook often?" she asks as she cracks the egg and drops it into one of the bowls.

"Considering that I never eat, yes, I do." I take out a knife and slide the plate with the ham on it toward me.

She glances at the ham and smiles. "Did you make that?"

I look down at the ham, slightly charred and extremely dry, and I realize she's never seen anything I've cooked. "No. Harvey made this mess, which is a shame, because it's a prosciutto."

"Where did you get an Italian ham?" she asks while she tears the bread into tiny pieces and places them into another bowl.

"Times being what they are, I cured it myself," I tell her as I cut the ham into thin slices.

She looks at me curiously. "I thought it took several months to cure a ham that way."

Ten months to be exact, and I was rushing it. "It does. So you can imagine that when I found the disaster that used to be my ham, I was, um, I was a little... irritated."

A warm smile spreads across her face. "I bet." She slides the third bowl to herself and grabs the flour out of the cabinet, standing on her tiptoes to reach it.

I watch her pour the flour into the bowl, and a white mist of powder rises around her hands. But I'm not focused on that. I'm staring at her face, amazed at how stunning someone's profile can be.

Dusting her hands off on her dress, she starts again, distracting me. "You must really like to cook."

Her eyes are soft when she looks at me, making it easy to talk to her. "Yes, it makes me feel more human."

She leans against the counter as her eyes scan my face and body. She bites her lip gently and looks away, slightly embarrassed, and I have never wished so badly to know what someone else was thinking as I do this moment.

"Do you miss being human?" she asks with tenderness in her voice.

I do, in fact, though I'm not sure I truly miss being human as much as I miss what I had as a human. I had Ann. "Sometimes," I tell her, keeping my eyes on the cheese so that she can't see the secrets hiding in them.

She takes my hand. "Do you want to know what I miss?" I nod and she continues. "I miss the outdoors. I miss the wind on my face. I miss the way the air smelled in the winter. Do you know what I mean?"

The winter air is crisp, clean, and cold. I enjoy it as well, so I nod.

"I know I can't be around a lot of humans yet, but sometimes I just wish..." she looks away and lets go of my hand.

Shaking her head lightly, she shrugs. "Anyway," she starts again, but this time there is sadness in her eyes. "Do you have a meat mallet I can use to flatten the chicken?"

I can attest from experience that a vampire's early years are difficult to get through. I remember coming to grips with what I had become, fighting for control, feeling stronger and yet weaker than I ever had before. Many vampires don't make it through their first year.

I turn her face toward mine slowly. "Hey," I say softly. "I spent the first five years locked in a basement with a dirt floor, and most of that time I was alone. So trust me when I say you can do this."

A gentle smile lights up her face. "Thank you."

Letting go of her face, I begin again. "That being said, I know we're the only two in the kitchen, but we're not the only ones in the house, so we will not be using a meat mallet."

"How do vampires do this, then? I don't suppose you want me to use my fangs to suck the juices out," she says. "I don't think it would make it thin enough anyway."

I don't even try to hold back my smile. "Funny," I tell her. "Actually, we're going to use a rolling pin."

I take the rolling pin out of the drawer near the stove and hand it to her. As soon as I do, she raises it in the air. I stop her. "Don't hit the chicken. What did it ever do to you?" I joke.

She smiles despite herself as I walk behind her and take her hands. "Let me help." I lay the rolling pin down at the base of the chicken with her hands under mine. "Put a little weight into it. One fluid motion. Roll it thin." Together we flatten the chicken until it's approximately a quarter of an inch thick.

I know I could have easily told her how to do it, but I wanted to have my arms around her, close enough that the scent of roses becomes intoxicating.

Without thinking about my actions, I move my hand to her lower abdomen, pressing her into myself. My other hand brushes the end of her ponytail to the side. Starting at the base of her neck, I kiss her skin tenderly. I let my lips inch their way up along her neck as she leans her head to the side. The chills covering her body and the way her breath catches make it difficult for me to think clearly.

I imagine her eyes are closed and her mouth slightly parted. She rubs her hand over my arm and laces her fingers in mine.

When my lips reach her ear, I drag my teeth, pulling at her lobe, and her grip on my hand gets tighter.

I know I cannot go too far with her, so instead of proceeding the way I want to, I lay my head next to hers and hold her against me since I'm not ready to let go yet.

Standing in the silence, surrounded by the floral fragrance that is Claire, I linger in the moment, but it ends much too quickly.

"Nicolas," she begins. "Did you tell Marcella to turn me?"

I loosen my grasp on her and step back slightly, taken aback by the question. "Where did you hear that?"

She turns around to face me with an expression that I cannot read. "Kate told me. Is it true?"

Damn Kate and her big mouth. I know the look on my face is more of worry than shock, and Claire would easily know if I was lying. Besides, I do not want to lie to her so I don't. "Yes and no. I asked her to give the option, and I hoped you would choose this."

"Why?" she asks. I'm pleasantly surprised that there is no anger in her voice.

"I don't know. I saw you and there was something about you that captivated me, so I followed you. I kept thinking you would do something that would turn me away, but you didn't. The more I watched, the more I wanted you. Not just physically. I wanted to know you, I wanted to keep you, make you mine."

Slowly, she smiles. "And you still feel the same as you did three years ago?"

No longer worried, it feels appropriate to be open with her. "It has changed some. In the beginning, it was easier to keep my distance."

Stepping close to me, she places her hand on my chest. "You're not the only one who has been waiting, you know? I have never desired a man as much as you." She traces her finger down my abdomen. "More than the blood, it's you that I crave."

It's her words more than her hand on my belt that send a fire throughout my body. I close the distance between us and kiss her, but it isn't soft and delicate like before, this time it's all passion. I back her into the counter as she pulls the end of my shirt up out of my pants. There is an urgency in her hands while she unbuttons my shirt. I am just as quick to shove the dishes of food back against the wall.

She pushes my shirt open and rubs her hand up my chest and along my neck until her fingers have tangled themselves in my hair, making my heart quicken. Perhaps it is that we can only inhale between kissing that has us breathing so heavily, but I doubt it.

I grab just below her buttocks, gripping harder than necessary, and lift her onto the counter. Running my hands up her back, I arch her body toward me, kissing down her neck and chest as she gasps with pleasure.

My mind is the only part of me screaming to slow down, but I cannot find the strength. Keeping her close, I whisper, "Tell me to stop."

But she doesn't help me. "Keep going," she says breathlessly. Then, clutching the collar of my shirt, she pulls my lips to hers with enough intensity that I know not to interrupt again.

I lift her dress up around her waist, and, grasping her hips, I slide her to the edge of the counter. I can feel her quiver lightly as I guide her thigh up to my ribs and she begins loosening my belt.

A door in the basement slams shut and everything stops in an instant, even my breathing. All at once, I can think clearly, and I am appalled at my lack of self-discipline.

I back away from her, covering my face with my hands as my dismay manifests itself into disappointment. Sliding my hands down to my mouth, I let out a sigh and look up at her. Solid black eyes stare back at me, sending a wave of guilt washing over me.

Dropping my hands, I do not try to hide how badly this makes me feel. "I'm so sorry, Claire."

She stays very still, staring at me, intense and greedy. I know it is not blood she is hungry for. Part of me is relieved that I stopped, but part of me hates that I did as I contemplate what almost happened. I cannot believe I had so little control. How could I have so much trouble being patient? It's true that I haven't had a relationship that wasn't about sex for... well, since I was human. But I thought I would be better at it.

I hear the sound of slow, stomping footsteps coming toward the stairs, and I grab my belt and tighten it quickly as Claire hops off the counter. She begins straightening the food I had shoved aside. I walk back to the counter, buttoning my shirt faster than I think I ever have before.

I look at her, and her eyes are still black. Feeling so very culpable, I take her hand gently, "I am sorry," I whisper. "But I need you to focus on changing your eyes back."

As I slide my hand back, she closes her eyes and takes a deep breath. I button the last few buttons on my shirt when I notice a bit of flour on the back of Claire's dress.

With the footsteps on the stairs moving with a slow, calculated tread, I dust the flour off as best I can.

She smiles softly, keeping her eyes closed. "It's hard to focus on my eyes when you're patting my butt."

I hadn't realized that was exactly what I was doing until she says it, and it takes me by surprise. I drop my hand. "I'm sorry."

"Stop apologizing. I'm a grown woman. I knew what I was doing."

I look down at the counter, not really seeing anything in particular. "You're so young, though. There are certain boundaries that we shouldn't cross. This is my fault."

Her hand moves on top of mine, making me look up at her warm blue eyes. "Biologically, I'm twenty-four years old and you're only twenty-two. So I'm technically older than you."

I smile, but before I can retort with the fact that I'm over five hundred years older than she is, she moves her hand away, and Kate appears at the top of the stairs.

I look over my shoulder at Kate, who, despite looking slightly surprised, also looks very angry. It isn't often that she's mad, so I am instantly concerned.

Without saying a word, Kate stomps out of the kitchen and into the dining room.

I glance at Claire. "Excuse me," I tell her quietly.

I don't know what could have irritated Kate, and I'm hoping it doesn't have to do with Claire.

Leaning against the doorway of the gym, Kate keeps her eyes on the floor as I approach.

I lean back onto the doorjamb opposite her. Waiting for her to look up at me, I watch her for a moment, but when she exhales forcefully, I say, "Do you want to talk about it?"

Pain fills her eyes, but it's quickly replaced by confusion. "Why is your shirt untucked?"

I glance down and see that's she's right, and a quick lie springs from my lips. "I think it will be the fashionable thing to do one day. Everybody will do it."

Crinkling her nose, she replies, "It looks sloppy. And how did you get flour on your shoulder?" She steps closer and begins dusting it off.

I take her hand from my shoulder. "I'm cooking. But quit changing the subject, and tell me what's wrong."

"It's Luther." Of course it is, but before I can say something about how I'm not surprised, she continues, which is just as well. "Where does he get the nerve to tell me what to do? He isn't my father, and even if he was, that doesn't mean he gets to treat me like a child," she huffs.

I grab her shoulders, making her look directly into my eyes. "Calm down," I instruct. But immediately regretting giving her an order, I wince a little and add, "Please."

Her eyes lose the hardness in them, so I slide my hands down her arms until I have her hands in mine. "Do you want me to talk to him?" I ask. As I consider how such a conversation would go, ending in a fight that I would surely win, I pull one side of my mouth up into a mischievous grin.

Seeing where my thoughts are taking me, she smiles faintly and says, "No."

"Can I do it anyway?" I ask.

This time, I get a real smile and a light laugh. "No. Definitely not."

Disappointing as that may be, it's nice to see her smile. But her smile fades when Luther approaches. He stops in the dining room just near us. "Kate, I need to speak to you." Turning to me, he adds, "Alone."

Even though his tone was not harsh, his very presence grates on my nerves. I suppose it's something in his stance. His confidence comes across as conceit. His assertiveness appears brash and pushy. Overall, he exudes an intolerable mix of arrogance and impudence.

Knowing my place as Kate's friend, I let her decide if she wants to be alone with him, though I cannot imagine why she would want that, ever. So when she nods to me, I assure her, "I'll just be in the kitchen if you need me."

Walking out, I can't help but wonder what she sees in him. I'm not even sure why Marcella turned him in the first place.

When I enter the kitchen, I see Claire dipping the chicken into the bowl of eggs and then into the bits of bread, coating it thoroughly. In this moment, she appears very human, and I can't help but appreciate how appealing that makes her.

As she sets the chicken on the plate, I walk over to her. Aching to touch her but restraining myself, I am unable to take my eyes off her.

Feeling my gaze, she asks, "What?"

I respond softly, "You are so very beautiful."

Looking away, she smiles bashfully, and my heart skips a beat. She bites her lip and grabs another piece of chicken. Folding in the ham and cheese, she changes the subject. "Is everything all right with Kate?"

I give a small sigh. "You'll find out that given enough time, things always work themselves out. And since we have time to spare, she'll be fine."

Claire nods and turns her attention back to the chicken. "What do you want me to do with these?"

"We'll put them in the fridge until Lilah gets here, and then I'll cook them. Maybe make a salad and some tea, that way it's all fresh."

Setting another piece of breaded chicken on the plate, she says, "That sounds lovely. Makes me wish I could enjoy with her."

"I'm enjoying this."

She looks at me with a delicate smile on her face. But as she starts to say something, we hear a loud smacking noise come from the direction of the gym.

We both look toward the sound uneasily. "Stay here," I tell her.

I rush to the gym. Stopping in the doorway, I see Luther on his back on the floor and Kate hovering over him.

"We should have left you saying yessa, massa and picking cotton in that damned field!" she screams at him.

In an instant, he lunges at her, and though he moves quickly, it feels like slow motion to me. My stomach drops and a rage rises. With black eyes, I charge, driving my shoulder into his stomach just before he reaches her. It sends him flying into the far wall as I stand up straight, my eyes locked on him, my fangs exposed in a hiss.

As he attempts to fathom what just happened, I say, "Get out of here, Kate," with the thick English accent that I know I am about to use to excess.

"Nicolas," she protests.

But I cut her off abruptly. "I said go," I repeat, and she hurries out. "Get up," I manage through gritted teeth.

"I see," Luther starts as he rises to his feet. "She can disrespect me because of the color of my skin."

"Nobody gives a damn about your skin. People disrespect you because you're an ass." My accent weighs heavy on my tongue as I continue, "And I, for one, am tired of your insolence. It's time someone puts you in your place. Grab a weapon. You're going to need it."

Luther looks around at the weapons on the walls. I can tell by the way his eyes roll over each of them that he is not comfortable enough with any of them to have a favorite, which is laughable considering how old he is.

"Tick tock, tick tock," I tell him. "You shouldn't so cavalierly try my patience, Luther. I have waited eighty years for this moment; I'd like it if you hurried along a bit." I smile sarcastically. "In fact, I feel like a gypsy. I've seen this future. You're about to die, by my hand, and my life is about to improve immensely."

Luther narrows his eyes at me as they glaze over into black. He grabs a maul, and I think to myself, of course he would pick the long-handled hammer. It's heavy and large, but the iron head makes it slow and awkward, just like him.

"Just to be a sporting chap, Luther, I'll close my eyes for three seconds. I suggest you make your move then," I tell him. Standing perfectly still, I shut my eyes, letting my other senses take over. "One," I count aloud.

His clothes swish quietly as he runs toward me, and it helps me envision his every move. He swings the maul to my left. I listen to the way it cuts through the air, judging its distance from me. As it nears my head, I duck down and it passes over me. Opening my eyes, I see him in front of me, his body twisted from following through with the hammer.

I drive my fist into his spine, and he arches back slightly in response. Bracing my forearm in front of his bicep, I strike the palm of my hand into his shoulder, dislocating it. Biting back a painful cry, he drops the maul and places his hand on his injured shoulder.

I hurry to the hammer and pick it up. "The problem with a long-handled weapon is that you can't let your attacker get too close," I say as he glares at me. "You have to get a good swing with this."

In the second it takes for him to pop his shoulder back into place, I swing the maul, making a full circle and building up as much force behind it as possible. The iron head slams into his side, crushing him into the wall and breaking several ribs.

I toss the maul behind me, grab his shirt collar, and roll back, flipping him onto the floor. I sit on top of him and pound my fists into his face relentlessly. He gets in a few good punches to my ribs, but I'm too focused to feel them. I'm not sure how many blows to the face he receives, but when I stop and stand up, blood is gushing from his nose, and the side of his face is swelling quickly, which probably means his jaw is broken along with my hand.

But seeing him like that does nothing to diminish my anger. I pick up the maul and heave it over my head, bringing it down onto his abdomen. His body curls around it as blood spatters out of his mouth.

I drop the hammer near his head with a thud, and, holding my pinky and the side of my hand, I set the bone so that it will heal quicker. As Luther rolls onto his feet, I tell him, "Choose a different weapon." He stares at me, unsure, for a moment. "Go on." I tilt my head toward the wall. "This time make it a challenge."

He walks to the wall, watching me as if he thinks I might attack when he's distracted. He takes the first weapon he comes to, the sai. With its center dagger and two curved prongs on either side, it's an elegant weapon, one of speed and skill, and it's about to be mine. But the sai are meant to be used as a pair and he takes only one, which proves to me that he is, in fact, an imbecile.

He lunges at me, attempting to stab me with the sai, but I grab his wrist and roll my back into him. I smash my foot into his and jab my elbow into his stomach. I take his arm and pull him over my shoulder, tossing him to the floor. He jumps up quickly and comes at me again with the sai, roaring angrily.

I block it with my forearm and slam his head into the wall with my hand. I give him a quick uppercut to the gut just before he raises the sai into the air. As he brings it down toward me, I grab his wrist, stopping him. I slam my other hand into his forearm, hearing the bone snap as I do. He lets go of the sai, and I snatch it out of the air as it falls. I stab him in the cheek, making certain it goes through both sides of his face and into the wall, pinning him. He growls painfully, unable to scream without tearing his skin.

I back up, watching him squirm, until he pulls the dagger out of his cheeks. Overcome with fury, he rushes toward me.

When he's close enough, I flip into a handstand, lock my legs around his waist, and slam his back to the floor. I yank my leg out from under him and kick him in the side of the head, breaking his neck which will not kill him, but it's excruciating.

He lets go of the sai to align the bones in his neck, which is a mistake. I take the sai and hop on him and drive the dagger toward his heart.

Luther grabs the sai, pushing against me. He's strong, but not strong enough. I smile and press the dagger into his skin. Leaning over the sai, I coldly tell him, "When you are dead and your body turns to ash, I'm going to dump you by the steps outside. Every day, I'll walk all over you. And when you're just a smudge on my boot, I won't even bother to scrape you off."

I push down on the sai, slowly letting it puncture his chest. When blood begins to pool on his shirt, I feel a cool hand on my shoulder. "He's had enough, Nicolas," Marcella says softly.

I stop pressing deeper but continue to let him struggle to keep his hands on the sai as it slices into his skin and his blood streams down the dagger. I pause like this for only a moment while I consider whether to finish him or not. I know what I want to do. I know what I should do. But for Kate, I let my eyes change back to green and my fangs recede.

"Just know how close you came," I tell Luther, dropping my accent.

He smirks and says, "Mama's boy."

In one quick motion, I shove down on the sai until I feel the pop of his sternum separating. His screams reverberate inside the gym.

I stand up, pulling the dagger out as I do. I toss it aside, and it clangs and skids across the floor. Writhing and clutching his chest, Luther cries pathetically, moaning and whining as a human would.

Feeling her gaze on me, I look at Marcella. Although my eyes are green, they are cold and hard. I cannot hide the contempt I feel toward her for asking me to stop. Seeing them must cause her a great deal of anguish, because she looks down at nothing, and it takes a moment before her eyes find their way to Luther.

"Stop breathing," she instructs him. "Moving only makes it hurt worse." I keep my eyes on her as I walk out, but her eyes don't meet mine. Once

I'm in the dining room, I hear Marcella muttering something to Luther, some kind of encouragement I'm sure. He doesn't deserve it, and it adds to my frustration.

I go into the kitchen and find Claire standing near the counter. Her eyes widen when she sees me, making me look down at myself. My hair feels mussed, and there's blood on my hands, but otherwise I look passable.

When I look back up at her, she's standing just in front of me. "Are you all right?" she asks. "Did he hurt you?" Concern laces her voice, which confuses me slightly. It occurs to me that perhaps she's never seen a fight.

"I'm fine," I reassure her, taking care not to reveal my current state of aggravation, since it has nothing to do with her.

Sighing with relief, she brushes her hands through my hair. "I was so worried," she says. "I heard the screaming, and I just ..." she trails off, shaking her head lightly.

I take her wrists, pulling them down in front of my chest, making her look me in the eyes. "I'm taking you outside. Tonight."

She stares at me with a blank expression. I'm not sure whether it's nerves or shock, but she says nothing, so I continue, "You have more restraint than that animal in there." I jerk my head toward the gym.

Smiling gently, she asks, "You think so?"

I lean closer toward her and whisper, "I'm going to prove it."

Holding back, she bites her lip to keep a large smile from spreading across her face. I can tell she's happy, but I'm still livid about Luther.

"Listen," I tell her, "I need to be alone right now. For just a moment." Truthfully, I do not want to be alone, but I know myself, and when I'm vexed, I don't always react logically, which I need to do with Claire. "Can you give me that moment?" I ask her.

She nods, so I let go of her wrists and start toward the basement stairs. In my bedroom I can be alone until I collect myself. That way the next time I have to talk to someone, I'll be calm and rational.

I enter my room. All I need to do is lie on my bed and stare at the ceiling until I'm in a better mood. But only moments after I enter the room, Kate bursts in, looking extremely upset.

She stomps over to me and leans in close to my face. "Who the hell do you think you are barking orders at me?" she yells.

I feel my anger rise. "Excuse me?" I ask in disbelief, using my English accent.

I walk to the door and slam it shut, though in a house of vampires, filtering out noise is a mostly useless endeavor.

When I turn back around, she's right in front of me. "I'm not some damsel in distress! Not some weak little human that needs rescuing, Nicolas!" she screams at me.

"I was protecting you," I tell her, my voice betraying my own agitation.

She pokes my chest with her finger as she speaks. "I never asked for your protection! And don't you dare pretend you did that for me. You never do anything that doesn't benefit you somehow."

That did it. "As your best friend, no, scratch that, as a man, I cannot just watch him treat you like that! I have never struck a woman out of anger! Not once in my life!" Which says quite a bit, since I was born in the 1300s. "It's unnatural, unconscionable, and just plain wrong!

And I will be dead before I let anyone in this house get away with it!" I shout. "So tell me why I can't lay a finger on him! You tell me that, Kate! Because this I have to hear!"

By the time I finish shouting at her, my hands are shaking. I have never been as furious with her as I am right now. Knowing that, I walk away. I go to my bed and sit on the edge as I try to slow my breathing.

I see her in my peripheral vision step closer to me, and I tell her abruptly, "Get out. Get out of my room." I look up at her. "Now. Before one of us says something we shouldn't." And by one of us, I mean me.

She doesn't leave. Instead she stands still, watching me. I look at the floor. I close my eyes and pinch the bridge of my nose, but it doesn't help.

"Nicolas," she says softly.

I look up at her again. "Kate, I swear the next time he comes after you, or anybody else for that matter, I will kill him so quickly that no one will be able to stop me. Not Marcella. Not you. And definitely not him," I snap at her, still holding on to my English accent.

"Nicolas," she says again.

"Maybe you're right," I say. "Maybe I do benefit from this, because if I had just sat there and done nothing, I wouldn't be able to sleep. I wouldn't be able to look at myself in the mirror. I don't know how anybody could."

"Nicolas."

"If he could turn on you so easily, that means he's done it to women before and will do it to women after you," I say, running my hand through my hair. "I'm sorry you were hurt by me, but you're asking me to disregard one of the few morals I have left. Do you truly want me to do that?"

"No," she says simply. She walks over and sits on the bed next to me. "All I wanted to say was"—she takes my hand—"thank you. Thank you for being such a good friend."

I shrug one shoulder. "Any time." Thankfully, I've lost my accent.

Smiling, she hugs me around the neck, and I wrap my arms around her waist. "Kate," I say gently, "you're a beautiful woman. You're smart and..."

She leans away from me, smiling. "And I deserve better," she finishes for me.

"You do."

"I suppose I deserve someone like you?" she jokes.

I had never really thought about it before, but Kate and I are great together. The only thing missing is the sexual attraction, so someone like me would be perfect for her. "Yeah."

She giggles. "You wouldn't like him, either."

"Probably not."

She shakes her head, smiling. "Why are we all awake?" she asks, changing the subject. "It's the middle of the day."

I lean over and kiss her on the cheek. "Goodnight, Kate."

"Goodnight." She stands up and walks away. Stopping in the doorway, she looks over her shoulder. "You deserve someone, too, Nicolas." She leaves quietly, closing the door behind her.

I lie back on the bed and sigh. That I deserve someone is laughable. I have never done anything in my entire life to merit such a reward. I do not mean I would refuse such an offer, merely that I would not have earned it.

I close my eyes and see Claire. I imagine her leaning into me, her head on my shoulder, her hand on my chest. My arms are around her, pulling her close. I feel her warm body against me as I listen to her heartbeat. It's not as nice as holding her for real, but it's comforting in its own way.

In my mind, we stay like this, wrapped around each other, letting the time creep by slowly for close to an hour, undisturbed and completely relaxed, until I hear a faint knock on my door. As I open my eyes and sit up, the door opens and Claire peeks in shyly.

"Hi," she says quietly. "I know you wanted some time to yourself, so if you want me to come back later, I will."

My anger had subsided significantly while I was holding her in my thoughts, so I motion for her to come in.

She seems nervous as she closes the door and walks to me, playing with her fingers and darting her eyes around the room. "Was Kate hurt?"

"No. Luther never actually touched her, which is why he's still alive," I answer. Not knowing what has her so anxious, I ask, "Are you all right?"

She locks eyes with me and takes a deep breath. "Look, I know that earlier you were upset and sometimes people don't think clearly and they say things they regret, you know, things they never intended for anyone to hear," she says, her words tumbling out in a rush. "I just wanted to know if you meant what you said. About taking me outside."

Then she mutters something I do not quite catch, but I think she says, "I understand if you don't want to."

Against my better judgment, I take her hand, making her stop murmuring, and say very delicately, "I meant it." I shrug lightly. "I won't be taking you to the city, but you will be outdoors tonight."

She fights back a thrilled smile. I know I've made the wrong choice, but it feels so right. Without hiding the excitement in her voice, she tells me, "I'm not sure if you're in a good enough mood to want to be touched yet, but, just so you know, I really want to hug you right now."

I smile at her. "I'd very much like it if you did."

Without hesitation, she jumps onto my lap, hugging me tightly around the neck. It feels so very nice to have my arms around her for real this time. Her skin is colder than I had imagined, especially against my body, warm from having recently fed. If she would let me, I could hold her like this for the rest of the day.

She brings her face to mine and kisses me. It is soft and supple, and just what I need. There is tenderness behind her lips as they move with mine.

As she pulls away from me, I rub my hand across her cheek, longing to kiss her again. Instead, I pull her ponytail out, letting her hair fall down around her face. I glide my hands through her red locks, feeling the tresses tangle around my fingers. I know what I want to do, I want to tug her hair, pull her head back, and sink my fangs into her neck, but if I do, my teeth won't be the only thing that ends up inside her, so I ignore that temptation.

I toss her hair about playfully, stirring up the aroma of roses. Moving my hands to her hips, I watch her as she straightens out her hair with her fingers. Fascinated by her movements, I cannot take my eyes from her even if I wanted to.

The sound of gravel crunching beneath a set of tires and the roar of a straight-eight engine in the driveway breaks my focus on Claire.

"I have to go. That's Lilah," I tell her as I slide her off my lap. "Give me about an hour for her to eat and settle in, and then you can come up and I'll introduce you to her." By that I mean I will let Claire feed on her.

It does make me feel guilty at times, thinking about what we do to the sheep. But I try to remind myself that they're happy here. Blissfully unaware and involuntarily carefree means they are content, right? I pretend it does, anyway.

One quick kiss and I am out the door and heading for the stairs. The things that happened today begin to fill my head once more. But I don't have time to focus on the mess between Kate and Luther. I have my own relationship to worry about. That's when it hits me: I'm in a relationship. It makes me smile just thinking about it. As I start up the stairs, another thought pops into my head: relationships are monogamous. I stop where I am on the step. Monogamy? I mull over the idea for a moment, and then I shrug, thinking, yes, I can do that.

Chapter 6

It's *difficult to sleep in the* same house with someone you tried to kill only hours before, wondering if he'll retaliate while you're vulnerable, just the edge Luther needs. But listening to him groan for the first two hours until his sternum healed makes me believe he's in no hurry to jump back into that.

Lying on my side, I let my mind wander. Mostly I think of the fight between Luther and me. Was I too hard on him considering that he is much younger than me? No. Would I do anything differently? Yes, I'd break a few more bones. Should I have killed him? Yes.

I should be thinking about how to sneak Claire out of the house and back in without anyone, especially Marcella, noticing. I consider sneaking her back in through the upstairs rooms and trying to convince Marcella that Claire was with the sheep all night. But that won't work. Or maybe I could persuade everyone that I could watch Claire while they left. But Marcella and Kate would be suspicious of me asking to be alone with Claire.

I know in my heart this will never work. I will get caught. Marcella will be furious with me, and I'll be punished.

I sigh to myself. How do I get myself into these predicaments? I roll over to face Claire, her skin still rosy from a fresh feeding. With her hands cupped together as though she is praying, she looks very human, something I really like. And I think, ah, that's how.

"Claire," I whisper.

She opens her eyes slowly and smiles softly at me. "Hello, handsome," she says quietly.

I smile more bashfully than I would have expected. "It's time to go." Torn between what feels right and what is right, I tell her, "Get ready but be quick. We need to be long gone before anyone else wakes up."

She nods and puts her hand on my cheek. "You don't have to do this."

Even though I appreciate her giving me the opportunity to back out, I reassure her, "I want to."

Her soft lips press against mine. Then, keeping her face close to mine, she says, "I won't disappoint you."

"I doubt you could."

She smiles the most amazing smile, genuine and almost shy, sweet and engaging. Biting her lip, she rolls away from me and stands up beside the bed. She glances over her shoulder at me. "What do you want me to wear?"

I think, something that does not show blood well, just in case. I say, "Anything appropriate. It's supposed to be warm tonight, but I have a feeling it will rain, so nothing white."

Her eyebrow rises, hearing a challenge in my words.

"I'm serious, Claire. Do me this favor and wear something dark."

She sighs. "Fine." As she starts toward the door, she says, "I'll meet you upstairs in just a bit. In something white."

I can tell from the way she laughs that she's joking. Though, I admit, I would not be too upset if she did. I smile at her as she leaves.

I take my time dressing, though not as much time as a human would, and still I find myself waiting in the foyer. Sitting on the stairs, I try to figure out exactly how someone who can move so quickly can manage to take so long to get ready. It reminds me of a human woman. While I enjoy most things human, I am not an extremely patient man.

Closing my eyes, I rest my forehead in the palms of my hands. I smell Claire before I hear her enter. I push my fingers through my hair and look up at her, trying to hide from my eyes my annoyance at her lack of swiftness. But she must see it, because she smirks and asks, "Were you in a hurry?"

I shrug. "A little bit."

She sits down beside me on the step. "Why? It's not even dark outside yet."

She's right; it's still dusk. I smile at her inexperience. "Who says we're waiting for the night?"

Confusion covers her face, so I say, "It figures that Marcella hasn't told you." I start toward the door. "Only direct sunlight burns us, and since there are hills to the west"— I swing open the door, letting the dim light pour in, and she pulls herself up a few stairs, back into the shadows—"we're perfectly safe."

Seeing the uncertainty on her face, I step into the light and make a slow spin. "See? I'm fine."

Still unsure, she lingers on the stairs. I know what Marcella teaches: daylight is the enemy. She preached it to me for years before I figured this out on my own. So I understand that it's difficult to accept.

I reach my hand out to her. "I wouldn't ask you to do this if I thought you might get hurt," I say softly.

She hesitates slightly and then takes my hand, keeping her eyes on mine. She inhales deeply but does not resist when I pull her to her feet and into the light. For a moment, we simply stare at each other while she waits to be reduced to ashes.

Finally, I tell her quietly, "You can breathe now."

She exhales her relief, blinking slowly. "Is this really happening?" she whispers, more to herself than to me.

"Wait until you see the sky." Pressing her hand with mine, I nod toward the open door.

Nervously, she looks outside into the illuminated yard. She can see the grass bending in the wind, birds flying to their homes in the trees. Everything she wants to experience, so close. All she has to do is trust me.

She releases my hand and steps onto the porch. Her face fills with wonder when she sees the evening sky for the first time in three years. Dark pinks and oranges streak the clouds, the heaven's blue tint peeking through where it can, emulating a painting by Van Gogh. I could not have asked for a more picturesque view to give to her.

I walk out and stand beside her, looking up at the sky. I keep my eyes on it for only a minute, choosing instead to glance at something even more beautiful. I watch Claire, her mouth slightly parted, tears hanging in her eyes, her skin radiating in the pale light.

"I never thought I would see this again," she says. "It's perfect." She looks at me and places her hand on my face. The warmth of her touch eases my doubts about what I'm doing. She presses her lips to my cheek so genuinely that I forget everything, the troubles of the day, everyone sleeping just inside, even my Ann. In that moment, I want nothing more than to stay with her in this instant, infinitely.

"Thank you," she whispers.

I place my hand so that my fingers are pushing into her hair and my palm is cradling her cheek. I glide my thumb across her skin, feeling the heat that a fresh feeding brings.

I lean toward her slowly, tilting my head as I slide my other hand up to the base of her neck. Brushing my lips against hers, I hear her inhale. Softly, I kiss her, moving her lips with mine. Then, biting lightly, I pull her lower lip gently as I lean away from her.

Keeping my eyes closed, I press my forehead against hers, listening to her breaths for a moment. She slides her hands up to my wrists in a manner that tells me she does not want me to let go of her yet. So I pull her into me and hold her body close to mine, wrapping my arms around her.

It's said that the difficult path is often the right one. Perhaps that's why this is so easy, so desirable, why I feel so alive when I'm with her.

"We should go," I tell her. I take her hand and lead her from the porch.

We hurry across roads, through the fields, and over the river, so that by the time night falls, we have made our way to a cow pasture. Most people would find a pasture to be a malodorous, unromantic place. They would be correct. But that's why no one will look for us here. Besides, it's possible, even here, to find an area that does not smell like an animal, and I soon locate one.

Lying on the grass facing her, I cannot help but wish that I could take her somewhere else, anywhere else, on this, her first night outside in such a long time. But when she looks at me and smiles, I know it's sincere.

"Tell me a secret," she says, rolling onto her side to face me.

I smile back at her. "I don't have any secrets. I tell Kate everything. Except about you."

She shakes her head. "Everybody keeps at least one secret."

She is right. I do have secrets. Most of them are from the two hundred years when I was still bitter from losing Ann, a dark time that I will not share with anyone.

"I'll start," Claire says. "The man that I said I had been with; it was when I was seventeen and he was forty-three. He was my dad's best friend. When my dad found out about it, he was furious. He blamed me, said I seduced him. He called me a whore and never looked at me the same way again. That's when I decided that I would never be with a man again until I was married. It wasn't worth the hassle."

"What did your dad do to his friend?" I know what I would have done.

She gives me a sigh. "Nothing. He never even mentioned it to him. In fact, they played poker the next night." She shakes her head, remembering.

"I'm sorry." And I really am. I know what it's like to disappoint your father.

She shrugs. "I guess none of that matters now. Marcella says there is no heaven or hell for us and I should just worry about making myself happy for however long I have." It's true, she should be happy. "Do you believe that? There's no heaven or hell?"

"There is definitely a heaven and a hell," I reply. "I just don't think we're invited to either."

She laughs, which wasn't my intention, but I like it just the same.

I roll onto my back and look up at the stars. "One night, when I was about eight, I overheard my father talking to someone. We were the only ones home, so I crept to his room, pressed my ear to the door, and listened. He was talking to my mother, though she had already died. He told her how much he missed her, how he still loved her, and how he had been wrong to ask for a son. He said he would take it back if he could, if it meant he could have her again."

I lie there in the grass, silent, trying not to remember the way it felt. A poor little wretched boy, so easily discarded.

"I walked to my room, went back to bed, and never told anyone about what I had heard." I look over at her. "Don't get me wrong, he was a good father. He didn't have to love me to make me love him."

She strokes my cheek with her hand. "I am so sorry, Nicolas." The heat from her fingers trails across my skin. "You deserve to be loved."

"That may have been true once," I say quietly, taking her hand. I point past her. "We should go over there under that tree. It's about to rain."

She smiles, "How do you know?"

Smiling back, I reply, "I just do." The air around us is heavy, thick with moisture, ready for a downpour.

I start to sit up but freeze when I hear her ask, "Who's Ann?"

Such a simple question, yet it stops my heart. With shock written on my face, I look back at Claire. "Where did you hear that name?"

She sits up beside me. "I overheard Kate talking to Luther about her." Of course, it would be Kate. "She said you loved her."

I do. I rub my hand over my mouth, thinking. How do I say that the one woman I compare all other women to, the only woman I have ever loved isn't Claire? "I did," I say, not meeting her eyes. "I loved her very much. She was my fiancée when I was human."

She rubs my arm gently, making me feel guilty for pretending that my feelings for Ann are over. As though I could let them go. "Will you tell me about her?" Claire asks.

I let out a long sigh. If I'm going to tell her, I might as well start at the beginning. "Ann had lost her mother at a young age, but you couldn't tell it. She was very refined, poised, the way a woman would have taught her to be. And even though I was four years older, we had always been close." Keep in mind that this was the fourteenth century. Four years was not that large a gap. "I took a job as a deckhand." I wanted to be a big adventurer, but that never panned out.

"I was gone on the ship for two years. When it finally docked, there she was. When I left, she was just a child, but now she was a woman," I say for lack of a better description. But how could I describe the way she looked on those church steps? Her hazelnut hair pulled back, her blue gown playing off her pale skin, the way her brown eyes sparkled when she saw me. I never thought I would be happy to be on dry land again, but that moment changed me. I saw the adventure I wanted for myself.

"I could have married her." Should have married her. "But I knew her father needed her at home to help raise the younger girls, so I waited two more years until, finally, we were engaged." Now comes the part of the story I typically avoid telling.

I take a deep breath and begin again. "About a week before the wedding, there was a festival in the town square. It was late, and I was walking her home. We cut through an alley and there was a man. He was doubled over as if he was in pain, so I bent down beside him and asked if he needed help. He hit me so fast and so hard."-I put my hand over my heart-"I flew back into the adjacent building. It felt like my whole chest had collapsed. I couldn't breathe. And then I heard her scream." Not just any scream, either. Since then I have heard hundreds of screams like it, but that was my first time. It was the sound of terror.

"I tried to get up, but it was too late. He snapped her neck like a twig." I still cannot figure out why he killed her that way, like it was just for fun. "He walked over to me and jerked me up. He cut his wrist with his teeth and held it up to my mouth." I still remember his cool blood running down my chin.

*   *   *

"I tried to spit out the blood, but I was gasping for air so much that it was useless."

Then he laughed. I will never forget that laugh, because if I hear it again, someone will die, even if that someone is me.

"He left me in the alley alone, thinking I was dying," I continued. "After an hour of intense pain, I turned." Perhaps a part of me did die that night, the best part.

"I went on a three-night killing spree before Marcella found me." I look at Claire and see tears in her eyes. The pain in my voice must be more obvious than I thought. "I know Marcella can be tough and cold, but she loves you."

Claire half smiles and wipes her eyes. "How does she treat the people she hates?"

"I don't know," I say. "If I ever make it to hell, I'll ask them."

She laughs, but then turns serious. "Nicolas," she says, not meeting my eyes. "Do you think it's possible to love more than one person at the same time?"

Guilt fills my heart. I never wanted her to know that I still love Ann. Those feelings only make things more complicated for Claire and me. I wanted to hide them from her, but I failed miserably. I can only hope that I'm not so transparent when I talk to Kate about Claire.

I know she's really asking if it's possible for me to love two people at the same time. "Yes, I do," I say, though it's more a hope than a belief.

Playing with her fingers, she asks, "Do you think you could ever love me?" She looks at me and I see her vulnerability.

I smile softly. "That's the easy part."

Suddenly, thunder booms, shaking the ground beneath us, and the clouds burst into sheets of rain.

Claire screams lightheartedly, covering her head with her hands. I take one of them and pull her to her feet. Together we run past the small pond to the closest tree. Under its branches, we are fairly well sheltered from the rain.

Claire laughs freely as she wrings the rain from her hair. It's nice to hear her laugh as though she's unruffled by anything I may have said or left unsaid.

I shake water from my hands. "Nicolas isn't my real name," I tell her although anyone in the house would have told her if she had asked.

Still smiling, she looks at me curiously. "Really?"

I nod. "I've changed it four times." I had done so for various reasons but mostly because of warrants for murder charges.

She steps closer to me, flipping her hair back over her shoulder casually. "What was your name?"

I lean back against the trunk of the tree. "Promise you won't laugh?" Not that my birth name is that funny, it just never fit me, not even when I was human.

She smiles, intrigued. "Promise."

Exhaling forcefully, I cringe. "Vincent," I mutter and hear her giggle. "You said you wouldn't laugh."

Trying to control herself, she manages to say, "I'm not laughing. This is my 'what a lovely name' chuckle."

Nodding, I let out a small chuckle of my own. "Right. Now you see why I changed it." Truthfully, though, it had reminded me of England and the life that I was meant to live, something I did not want to be reminded of.

She nudges my arm with her shoulder. "It's just that you don't look like a Vincent."

"I didn't think so either."

Turning her attention to the rain, she watches it pour for a few moments. But all I see is the water roll over her collarbone and down her chest until she looks at me with a smirk, breaking my concentration.

"Do you want to know my real name?" she asks.

I smile. "Your name is Claire Weber. Your mother and father are both German. They met in Berlin, where your mother grew up and your father went to law school. But he never finished, which is why he's a shoe salesman. You have two brothers, one older, one younger. Both enlisted as pilots." Unfortunately, her older brother died in combat early on, but as far as I know, her younger brother is still alive. "You have one niece, Sarah. Your red hair comes from your grandmother, Isabelle, which is also your middle name."

Claire puts her fingers together in front of her mouth and bites her lip lightly, which makes it hard for me to think clearly. But somehow I keep going. "Your birthday is April 3 of 1917. You were turned August 9 of '41. And you first kissed me on October 18, '44."

I could say more. I could tell her about how she went to school to be an art teacher, of all things, which drove her father crazy. I could remind her of how she did not get her first kiss until she was fifteen, and she paid the boy to do it. Or how she used to lick spoons and put them back in the drawer when she was angry with her brothers.

I could tell her that her mother cried every night for the first year after she went missing and still searches for her today, which is my fault.

"How do you know all of that?" she asks me quietly.

"I'm interested."

Her hand glides up my neck and to the base of my skull. She pulls my face to hers, kissing me softly. Placing my hand in the small of her back, I draw her to me. Her wet dress drips water onto my shoe, making a quiet tapping sound. But I pay no attention to that, instead I am focused on the way her body conforms to mine, the way her hands pull my shoulders toward her, the way a heat courses through my body as our kissing becomes more passionate.

As she arches her head back, I kiss her chin and then make my way down to her chest, lifting her up slightly as I do. Knowing I shouldn't, I rake my teeth along her neck and to her chin, biting gently. She gasps and presses herself into me as chills form on her arms.

Even with the distraction of my lust for Claire, I have a gnawing feeling that we are not alone. My senses heighten at the potential threat, and I gently pull her away from me. "Wait," I whisper.

I listen intently but hear nothing. I look around but see only cows. No movements. No noise.

"What's wrong?" Claire asks, knowing enough to keep her voice down.

I hush her. I can feel it deep inside, the same way I sense the other vampires that we live with. I can feel their presence, predatory, powerful, and ravenous. But these are not just any vampires—these are nomads.

My heart drops into my stomach. Nomads are the vampires the humans write their horror stories about. Creatures stripped down to their most basic instinctual desires. Animalistic and savage, they have lost every hint of the humanity that tames us. Filling their nights with blood and lust, they leave nothing but death in their wake.

"Hide," I whisper to Claire, keeping my eyes on the trees.

"What do you mean? What's happening?"

Grabbing her shoulders with both my hands, I urge her, "Go to that pond over there. Go under the water and don't come up until I call for you." It will be a challenge, but it is imperative that she hide, and hide well.

Staying under the water will conceal her from sight and mask her delectable aroma. That is, if they have not already seen her.

I'm trying to find the balance in my voice between expressing concern and plain begging, but she must hear my fear because she responds, "Tell me what's wrong."

It is not fear for myself that I feel. Claire would not survive an encounter with a nomad by herself. Not even a young one.

"I don't have time to explain. Just do what I ask," I stress to her. "Please."

She stares at me for a moment, thinking, but we do not have a moment to spare.

"Go," I whisper.

Nodding, she steps back. "Be safe," she says, though she does not know what I am about to do. She turns and runs to the pond. I am sure the water is frigid, but that does not seem to affect her as she wades in until she's chest deep in the murky water. Watching me, she takes a deep breath and submerges herself completely. The water ripples away from where she just was, but otherwise there is no indication that she was ever here.

I turn my attention back to the trees across the field and walk out into the pouring rain. It streams down my face and hands, soaking my clothes and dripping from my hair.

"Come out, come out, wherever you are," I taunt. Then, from the trees, she emerges, slow and creeping. Like a predator watching its prey, she keeps her gaze on me as she walks into the field. Her long black hair hangs over her face, but the part I can see has a pink, rosy glow, meaning she has fed recently. Her large eyes are a piercing green, probably baiting her usual victims.

Her body flows effortlessly across the grass toward me. Stopping near me, she pushes her hair behind her ear, exposing the rest of her face.

"Looky what I found," she teases. She slides her finger from my temple to my chin. "A native. How delightfully quaint."

I grab her hand, moving it away from my face. I suppose it would be easy for some to get lost in her sultry voice, but she does not fool me. I know that drifters like her typically travel in pairs, and if she distracts me, another will swoop in for the kill.

"Where's your friend?" I ask her directly.

She smiles maliciously. "Shouldn't we get to know each other a little before we indulge in a trio?" She walks around me, trailing her hand along my shoulders. "I'll start. I'm Jade. I'm a Capricorn. I enjoy blood, sex, violence, and death." Which is exactly why we cannot have her killing at will here. "And you would be lying if you said you didn't like it, too."

She's right, that would be a lie, and I hate myself for it. As she comes back around to the front of me, I grab both her wrists. "Do you think your friend will come out if I kill you? Would it try to stop me?" I press her back into the trunk of a tree forcefully. "Call it out now," I order her.

"It? Is that any way to talk about a lady?" As if any ladylike part of them remains. She glances toward the trees and calls out, "Kirah, come here."

As I let go of Jade's wrists, a stunning dark-skinned beauty walks toward us. Her short curly hair is weighed down by the rain yet still hangs only to her shoulders. Her solid black eyes are intense and fierce and fixed on me. Stopping a few yards from us, she exposes her fangs in a hungry smile.

I shift quickly into my vampire form, but before I can move, I feel Jade's fingernails slice through my sleeve, cutting into my bicep. I raise my foot up and kick her in the chest, knocking her into the tree. Kirah leaps on me, knocking me down onto my side. She wraps her legs around me and squeezes them together, crushing my rib cage. I swing my arm around and strike her head hard enough to throw her to the ground beside me.

As Jade runs toward me, I grab Kirah by the ankle and swing her around, slamming her into Jade, knocking them both down. I jump on top of Kirah with my fangs exposed. Grasping both of her hands, I lean toward her throat, but Jade flips over my back, grabbing me and tossing me into another tree.

I am on my feet in time to move away from the trunk, causing Jade to punch it instead. A powder of wood chips spreads into the air around her fist. Placing my hand on the back of her head, I shove her face into the tree, breaking her nose.

Kirah brings her leg around, making contact with my abdomen. As I fall backward, she swings her arm behind me, propelling me to the ground on my stomach.

When Jade stomps at me, I roll onto my back away from her. But as I do, Kirah grabs both of my wrists and holds them above my head. Before I can do much about it, Jade sits on top of me. She pushes my head aside, exposing my neck.

I know a way out of this, but I do not like it. I pull my hands through Kirah's tight grip, dislocating my wrists and breaking several of the bones in my hands, screaming through the pain. I sit up and punch Jade in the mouth, knocking her away from me. But as I do, I hear the swishing of water and someone taking in a deep breath.

Without looking, I know it's Claire, and I'm not the only one who hears her. Jade and Kirah look at her standing chest deep in the pond. They leap to their feet. As they start toward Claire, I hit the side of Kirah's knee with my fist and feel a bone pop. She falls to the ground, and I know this is my opportunity to end her life, but I am more worried about Jade going for Claire.

I jump to my feet and vault up into the tree, landing on a branch. Jade runs at Claire as I snap a twig off. With my fingernails, I peel the bark off, scratching the stick into a sharp point in one quick motion. I fling it at Jade and it flips through the air toward her. Just as Claire flinches away from her, the twig impales Jade's heart through her back.

Jade arches her back, falls forward, and turns to ash in front of Claire. All around Claire the stick and remnants of ash from Jade's body float. The look on Claire's face is one I have seen on others before. It is fear and shock.

I cannot dwell on this, because Kirah looks up at me and hisses angrily. I leap out of the tree close to her, put my arm around her neck in a head-lock, and drive my knee into her face. Kirah digs her fingernails deep into the back of my thigh and drags them down, carving gouges in my hamstrings. I throw her to the ground and with a quick kick to her ribs, send her flying into a tree trunk.

She stands up and bounds up into the tree. With the pouring rain making it difficult to keep my eyes open when I'm looking up at her, I lose her in the treetops.

Before I can think about how that is a rookie mistake, she jumps onto my back. Even though I move quickly, her fangs scratch my neck as I pull her over my shoulder.

She scrambles to her feet and swings her fists wildly at my face. I block most of her punches but a few make contact.

Placing one hand on her shoulder, I strike her with an uppercut, except my fingers are extended so they pierce her gut. I thrust them up through her abdomen and diaphragm until I reach what I am searching for. She shrieks painfully and pushes against me, to no avail. Squeezing hard, I crush her heart in my hand and she turns to ash with my arm still inside her.

I wipe the blood and ash from my hand onto my pants and look at Claire as the scratches on my neck disappear. Her hand is over her mouth, and her eyes are wide, but she does not have a scrape on her.

Though the back of my leg is still bleeding and aching, I walk to the edge of the pond without so much as a limp. I sit down along the water's edge, letting the rain run over me.

"Are you all right?" Claire asks, walking through the water toward me.

Excusing the fact that both of my hands and wrists are throbbing and will not heal for about another thirty minutes, I figure I am fine, so I nod and ask, "Are you?"

"I think so." She smiles half-heartedly. "Physically, anyway." She sits down close by, facing me with her legs still in the water. "I was scared there for a while."

I turn her face toward mine. "I won't let anything happen to you. I promise." I immediately regret saying that, as I am not very good at keeping my promises.

She tells me, "I thought you were hurt." I was. "I thought you might lose." I could have. "I thought it would be my fault."

"Claire, stop talking," I say gently, and I take her hand. "If it wasn't for you, I wouldn't be a lot of things. And I'm not sure how happy I would be, either."

She smiles softly and slides closer to me. "So, you getting into fights, is that a common thing?" she jokes. "Because it seems pretty reoccurring."

I smile. It does seem that way, but I say, "Not usually."

She leans her back into my chest, and I feel the heat of her body through her wet clothes. I wrap my arms around her. "If you want to go home, we can," I say, but I'm hoping she'll stay a little while longer.

She sighs. "No. I don't want to."

"Me neither," I tell her. But with her in my arms, I do not just mean now. I mean ever.

We sit there together, talking for hours, before I decide to take her home. Neither of us hurry, stretching the walk back as long as we can.

We finally make it home, and I stop her at the gate. "Listen, regardless of what happens when we go inside, and apart from the nomads trying to ruin our evening, I'm really glad I took you out tonight."

She smiles. "Me, too." Her eyes twinkle when she says it, letting me know it's the truth.

My hand aches to touch her, to push her wet hair from her face, and my lips hunger to taste hers. "I really want to kiss you right now, but someone could be watching," I admit to her.

"Give me a second." She closes her eyes for a moment. Then, exhaling slowly, she moans quietly under her breath. She reopens her eyes and looks at me as though nothing happened.

"What was that?"

She almost blushes. "I was imagining what that kiss would be like. And you were good."

I laugh to myself. "Come on."

I lead her to the house. Just before I open the door, I take a deep breath, trying not to let Claire see my nervousness. I push the door open and step inside.

Suddenly, a fork flies in front of my face and lodges into the door near my head. I look in the direction it came from to see Marcella standing there. Her eyes are cold and distant, but mostly furious.

I pull the fork from the door. "Why would you use a fork?" I ask Marcella. "Surely there's something dull and rusty around here somewhere."

Sarcasm is not the best approach to take with Marcella, and she marches over to me, narrowing her eyes. She has looked at me with that much despise before, but it has been a long time. "Could you go downstairs, Claire?" I say.

"You do not tell her what to do," Marcella snaps at me. "I tell her what to do." She turns her harsh eyes to Claire. "Go downstairs," she orders.

Claire looks to me, and I nod, which only makes Marcella angrier. Claire walks out through the library, and we wait to speak until we're sure she's gone.

"Let me close this door," I say. "We don't want any bugs getting in here."

She reaches around me and shoves the door closed. "I don't give a damn about bugs," she says coldly. "Tell me what the hell you were thinking tonight."

This must be worded appropriately. "I..."

Marcella grabs my throat and slams my back into the door. I manage to stammer out, "I didn't have sex with her." True. "I didn't kiss her. I didn't even touch her." Lie. "I was a perfect gentleman."

Marcella's fingernails begin to cut into my skin. "I just wanted to prove a point," I say.

Marcella raises me up until my feet are no longer touching the floor. "And that was?"

Even though it's difficult to speak, I answer her. "She's further along than you think. She can be outside as long as she's supervised."

Marcella drops me and I fall to the floor. I could have caught myself, but it would not have given Marcella as much satisfaction.

"I decide that," Marcella says. "Not you." She turns to walk away.

I rub the punctures in my neck. "Don't you want to know how she did?"

She stops in her tracks. Somewhat calmer, but still fuming, Marcella looks back at me harshly. "What's all that blood from?"

Looking at the blood and ash on my leg, I respond, "We ran into some nomads. I took care of it." I stand up in the puddle that's forming from my rain-soaked clothes. "I was right, Marcella. Claire did just fine."

She walks over to me. "You put me in quite a dilemma, Nicolas. Part of me is intrigued. But a bigger part has to punish my favorite son for not knowing his place."

It was a stretch to think she would not do something about my disobedience, but what can she do that would make me regret it?

"You have to take Luther out. Teach him something."

She could do that. "What?" I stare at her in disbelief. How can she expect me to teach that dimwit anything?

Unaffected by my dismay, she says again, "Teach him something useful."

Irritable disgust covers my face. "You're kidding, right?" The tone of my voice is angrier than I intend, but I do not care enough to adjust it. "Is this a joke?"

Marcella shrugs. "I don't have a sense of humor that I am aware of."

My pulse quickens, and a heat races through my body. How am I supposed to spend a night with that bastard? I loathe him more now than ever before. This is not fair. This punishment does not fit the crime.

"Do this and bring him back alive or don't set foot in my house again," she says impassively.

I have to flex my fingers to keep my hands from shaking with rage. Afraid I might say something distasteful, I am unable to remain in the room with Marcella.

I need something to distract me. Usually I know what to do. It's a fairly simple solution. But I am supposed to be monogamous and waiting for Claire, so that's out of the question.

I grab the doorknob and swing the door open. I know what I will do instead.

"Where are you going?" Marcella asks.

Still fuming, I respond, "There were wolves in the forest the other day. I'm going to make sure there is not a pack nearby." I try to slow my breathing but cannot.

"Do you want to take Kate?"

"No," I snap. "I want to follow up alone. Completely alone." As I walk out, I slam the door and hear a picture fall from the wall, breaking the glass.

Chapter 7

After another restless day, I wait outside, not so patiently, for Luther. It's colder tonight since the rain had lowered the temperature to the point of it nearly snowing during the day. I wrap my arms around myself as if I'm freezing, but it's all for show. I watch my breath hang in the air as I exhale.

The door swings open, and Luther steps out wearing a heavy coat and boots. If he had on a flannel shirt, he'd look like a lumberjack, but even that thought cannot make me smile.

"About time," I mutter.

He walks toward me. "Was I supposed to be rushing to see you again?"

I ignore his snide comment and start walking, leading him toward the backyard.

"You know, Nicolas, this feels an awful lot like a punishment for me, too," he says. "Do you know how ridiculous that is when I didn't do anything wrong?"

Not in the mood for him, my sarcasm weighs heavy on my tone, "I'm sorry, Princess, is your vagina getting cold? I'm not doing this to listen to you complain all night. So shut your mouth, open your ears, and learn something so that we do not have to do this again."

I suppose I'm still irritated that after not finding any evidence of wolves in the forest, I had to spend the day in Kate's room until I could trust myself to be around Claire again.

I would prefer that he didn't speak for the rest of the trip, but of course he does. "So where are we going?"

It was an innocent question, but I snap at him just the same. "I don't know, Luther, maybe the hospital, since it's the only thing in this direction." I take a deep breath, exhaling forcefully and making a cloud of fog appear in front of me. "We're taking a shortcut through the fields instead of following the highway, which would only prolong our torturous time together."

He looks at me. "You're kind of grouchy tonight, Nicolas. Something wrong?"

I can hear the concern in his voice, which surprises me. I glance at him and consider whether I should tell him the truth. But how do I explain that I started something with Claire that I cannot finish. Or how every time I get close to her I feel as if I'm betraying Ann. How do I discuss how conflicted I am about what I want, what I'm supposed to do, what I deserve, and what I need? It is all so very confusing.

"It's just..." I stop myself and say, "I'm fine, Luther."

I place my hand on the wooden fence that surrounds our property and jump over.

Luther jumps over the fence and lands beside me. "I think it's because you haven't gotten laid in a while."

Define a while. "Don't concern yourself with my sex life."

He continues anyway. "Now me, I have sex all the time. Kate is a minx. Always on me."

Part of me cringes. "Please don't talk about Kate like that." At least not to me.

He shrugs. "Fine. I won't say anything else about her."

He says it like he means it, and I admit it would be nice if he did stop talking for once. Maybe he has changed a little, I think, maybe that fight knocked some sense into him.

Then suddenly he lifts two fingers to my nose. I do not have to catch a scent to know what he's insinuating. I stop and slap his hand away and hit him in the back of the head hard enough to make him nearly trip.

"What the hell is wrong with you?" I snap at him with a thick accent. He looks at me and laughs but I continue, "Grow up. Have some decency. Show some couth."

Smiling widely, Luther asks, "Really? Couth? What grown man do you know uses the word couth?"

Dropping the accent, I reply, "Those of us who can spell it."

His smile fades quickly. "Listen, Nicolas—"

"You listen," I interrupt. "I have had more than enough of you tonight."

"So did Kate," he says and smirks suggestively. He holds his hands about a foot apart and nods.

I know he's only mentioning Kate to get under my skin, but I still lose focus on what I had planned to say.

"Oh," I start. "Is that a reference the size of your..."—I glance down at his pants—"whatever you want to call that?" Let's face it, he is probably fairly large. "Because I'm really happy for you. For some men, size is all they have in their bag of tricks."

I start walking again, and as I predicted, he's right on my heels. "Are you saying you're better in bed than me?" he asks.

Yes, that's what I am saying. "Let's stop talking about this," I say.

He continues, "Because I'm really good."

Everyone thinks they're good. Plus, considering that he hates me, he would more than likely exaggerate his skills, which means his really good is probably more of a sort of good.

"Luther, when you make a woman scream things in a language she didn't even know she knew, then you can say you're good."

He snorts. "You never did that."

I do not mean to brag... all right, I do mean to brag. "Actually," I look at him and see his eyes eager for information and I cannot help myself. "Never mind. I'm not going to tell you about it."

He grabs my arm, but I keep walking. "Don't hold back, Nicolas. Who was she? What did she say?"

"Forget it," I mutter. It was a long time ago, and besides, he doesn't know her, so what does it matter?

"At least tell me what language it was," he pleads.

"I'm not going to tell you about the ladies I've had sex with. I do have a little propriety left in me." Propriety has nothing to do with it, of course. I simply do not want to tell him.

"Propriety? Is that your way of saying you're lying? That the great Nicolas Rider is a sham?"

I will give him this, he knows how to vex me. "There is no sham to it. Sex is about pleasing a person"—or persons, whichever it may be—"other than yourself."

He laughs to himself and says, "And you think you're good at that?"

I know I do not often think about others, but certain occasions, I find it easy. But his spiteful comment provokes me into saying something just to rile him. "If you're so worried about what people say when they have sex with me, why don't you just ask Kate what she said."

I meant "she" as in the other woman but I know what I implied and I know what he heard.

He jerks me by my shirt collar and lifts me off of the ground in front of him. I could have stopped him, but his black eyes don't scare me.

"What did you say?" he asks with a coldness in his voice.

I smile tauntingly. "Touchy, aren't we?" I pull his fingers off of my shirt and drop to my feet. "We're about halfway there, so let's do each other a favor and stop talking."

Without waiting for his response, I turn toward the field behind us. "Kate. Come over here."

I can tell by his expression that he was not aware she was following us and is concerned by what she may have heard. But I know she wasn't close enough to eavesdrop.

Kate runs over to us, smiling. "How did you know I was there?" she asks when she reaches us. Her pale-yellow gown hangs loosely, but I can still make out the shape of her hips through the thin material.

"I'm used to being stalked by pretty ladies," I joke.

She laughs blithely, hugging my upper arm. I smirk at Luther, raising my eyebrows. He narrows his eyes at me, which only makes me feel a certain measure of contentment.

Taking Kate's hand, I lead her in the direction of the hospital. I can feel Luther's hostile glare burning into my back, but I ignore it. "So, Kate, what are you doing tonight?" I ask.

She knows me well enough to know what I'm suggesting. "I suppose that means I'm not invited to join you two."

I reach over the fence and unlock the gate. It swings open and I gesture for Kate to go through first. Luther starts to go next, but I put my hand to his chest, stopping him. Cutting in front of him, I walk through the gate after Kate. "It's not that I don't want you to," I tell her. "It's just that when I'm working with someone who's dimwitted—"

She looks back at me, discouragingly, so I rephrase it. "Thick-skulled? Inane? Asinine?"

Luther hits my shoulder petulantly, and she fights back a smile. I continue, "Whatever word you want to use, when I'm working with someone like Luther, I don't need anything shiny to distract him."

She smiles to herself as she pushes my hair back with her hand. Surely it bothers Luther to see her so attentive toward me, to touch me so casually, to stand so close.

"I'm going to see Caroline then," she tells me.

Caroline, our neighbor's nineteen-year-old daughter, is one of the few humans who knows Kate by name. I cannot explain Kate's interest in the girl. Caroline is plain, has a dry sense of humor, no money, no connections. She probably will not marry well if she marries at all. Yet Kate is intrigued by her.

"It's awfully late, isn't it?" I ask.

Kate shakes her head. "She'll be up." She slides her hands along my shoulders as though she's dusting off some of the mist the fog has left on my clothes.

"All right," I tell her. "Be careful." I kiss her cheek, but it isn't until she kisses mine that I hear a low growl from Luther.

Either Kate didn't hear it or she chose to ignore it, but she blows a kiss to Luther as she walks toward Caroline's house.

I look at Luther. Through the anger, he manages to look hurt. Normally, my heart does not go out to him, and this time is no different. However, I do feel a certain responsibility for his distress.

"Come on," I say quietly. I turn and start toward the hospital again.

I don't know what to say to make him feel better that would sound sincere, partially because I do not want to say it. So I say nothing.

We're almost through the third field before he speaks. "Why does she concern herself with you so much?"

"I don't know, Luther. Maybe it's because I have something you don't—a personality." That was insensitive, and I regret it almost immediately.

His forehead furrows. "You're an ass."

I consider saying something to contradict it, but the truth is, I am. "Yes, but I'm an ass in an endearing and charismatic way. You're an ass in a pigheaded and overly aggressive way, which nobody likes."

Maybe I did not have to add the second part, but he needs to hear it sometime, though perhaps this wasn't the right time.

Watching him try to hide how wounded he is makes me feel contrite. Maybe it's my fault. All right, it is my fault. But sometimes I forget that repressed somewhere inside that absurd excuse for a man is a person with real emotions. That perhaps his stubborn, abrasive persona is just an act to hide how insignificant he feels. If I were him, I would feel that way.

I am not the best at apologizing to people I don't like, so instead of trying, I change the subject. "Listen, Luther, tonight I really need you to focus. This bit of information I'm about to give you could save you a lot of grief, maybe even save your life."

He nods, looking almost relieved that I diverted from what's bothering him. "What is it?"

"There will be times when the healthy are too few and far between to make adequate prey. You cannot dwindle their numbers too much without risking everything." I look to make sure he's listening, and, surprisingly, he is.

"War is nothing," I continue. "Plagues, famine, droughts, these things make life hard for us, too. You have to know who you can pick off and who you cannot."

His mouth twitches slightly before he asks, "Are you talking about children?"

"Definitely not," I state. I'm glad he's questioning me, though; it means he's paying attention. "I'm talking about the sick and dying."

He looks thoroughly confused when he asks, "But I thought Marcella said—"

"She did," I interject. Marcella says, and I quote, *Feed on the sheep, feast on the healthy.* Indulge yourself but keep a sheep for everyday use. The problem is vampires often become bored with sheep. We crave the hunt, the excitement, the fear.

"And she's right," I tell him. "Healthy is preferred. But I have devoted a lot of my time to this, so trust me you can feed on the dying just the same." That is, if you know who you can and cannot bite.

"I'm sure Marcella told you that, contrary to popular belief, you can catch diseases," I say. And I don't just mean those contracted through blood. Most any disease will do. Our metabolisms spread them quickly and severely increase the symptoms. The specific disease will determine how rapidly our bodies burn it up completely, leaving no traces that it was ever in our systems. But I have found nothing that will kill us.

I continue, "She probably convinced you that the sick are a waste of time. But let me correct her; if you want to kill during an epidemic, those are the ones you go for."

It is true, hunting the sick is not the same as tracking and hunting the healthy. It isn't as much fun when they don't run or scream or beg, but it works in a pinch.

As we exit the field, we can see the hospital perched on top of the hill. Lone and dismal, it looks like a place people go to die. It isn't welcoming, the way it should be.

As we start up the hill, I say, "When we go inside, let me do all the talking."

"All right," he says. "But why a hospital? There are sick people everywhere."

I smile to myself at the simplicity of his mind. "A hospital is perfect. It's public, so we don't need permission to enter. There's a plethora of ailments for you to sniff around and really get a feel for this."

Besides, nobody ever questions when patients die here. "Plus, a hospital is like a grocery store for us. You go in, sift through the ripe ones, and select the one you want."

He laughs to himself. "I never thought of it that way."

I want to say something about not considering him much of a thinker anyway, but I resist the urge.

When we reach the top of the hill, we make our way across the parking lot and go inside. The room is not large, and I assume the decorator was inspired by a crypt, because it's unimaginative and dull. The cold white walls, I suppose, were meant to appear sterile, and they do, just not in the way they intended.

Equally drab and sitting at the desk is a middle-aged woman wearing a white uniform. She taps her red, paint-chipped fingernails on a stack of papers with a look of annoyance written across her face. Her brown hair is graying around her forehead, and her brow is wrinkled as she looks up at us through the top of her glasses.

"Can I help you?" she asks in a nasal voice, probably due to her nose being so excessively long and thin.

I smile my lopsided grin. "I hope so. I'd like to know which doctor is making rounds tonight. If you would please tell me, I would be much obliged."

Unaffected by my courtesy, she lets out a sigh before she answers, "Dr. Haddly."

This is going to be difficult with someone who is so unreceptive. I look back at Luther and slap him in the chest lightly. "I told you he worked here," I tell him.

I turn back to her, and as I do my hand hits a cup of pens, spilling them across the desk. "Oh, sorry," I say as though I'm embarrassed. As I pick up the pens, I begin again. "Dr. Haddly is a friend of mine. Granted, I haven't seen him in a while. It's probably been"—I furrow my brow as though I'm thinking—"two years. That doesn't matter, anyway, what I really came here for is because I need to speak to him for a moment. Briefly. So if you wouldn't mind just fetching him for me, I will make it very quick."

She leans back in her chair and crosses her arms, showing me that she believed nothing of what I said, which is not good. "A friend of Dr. Haddly's would know his first name. So why don't you tell it to me."

Clever girl. Time for Plan B. "Maybe we got off on the wrong foot. Let me start over." I offer my hand. "My name is Nathaniel Hager."

"Beth." She reaches her hand across the desk to shake mine, and in that instant, she belongs to me. So long as she is making contact with my skin, I can manipulate what she thinks. Anything I say, she will believe to be her own thoughts. I cannot control her actions, the way an actual enthrallment would allow me to do, but by temporarily entrancing her, I won't have to kill her.

I lean toward her and tell her quietly, "I am a friend of Dr. Haddly's. You will not hesitate to take us to him. You want to help us. You trust us."

I lean back away from her and let my hand slip out of hers. The problem with this type of mesmerizing is that she does not have to do any of what I said. But normally, once a human has thought it, they tend to do it.

She blinks her eyes quickly, not sure of what just happened.

I begin again as though all that occurred was a simple handshake. "It's nice to meet you, Beth. As I was saying..."

She stands up and says, "Right this way, gentlemen." She begins walking toward a set of large double doors.

Dumbfounded, Luther stares at me, his mouth agape. I smile at him, patting him on the shoulder. "Let's go."

I can see Luther trying to process a question, so rather than let him mutter something revealing, I say, "Excuse me, Beth."

She turns around, slowly pushing up her glasses. "Yes?"

"I can take it from here."

Hesitating, she twists her mouth but eventually gives in, "Very well."

She starts back toward the desk not very pleased with us, but I'm not here to make friends. I look at Luther and nod toward the double doors.

"How did you do that? Before, I mean?" Luther asks sounding intrigued.

"The temporary enthrallment?" I shrug. "It's easy." That is, if you know how to enthrall in the first place and have practiced enough to be able to manipulate a human without marking them. All right, maybe it isn't so easy.

"Could I do that?"

Stopping in front of the double doors, I turn to him and shake my head. "Only real vampires can."

I push the doors open and go inside another spacious room with hospital beds along the walls. I'm greeted by the scent of decay, a faint smell that often goes unnoticed by humans but is powerful and odoriferous to me. It isn't death that smells so pungent, rather it is the disease here.

Not all of the beds are full, but there are enough patients to make this field trip worthy of my time. The patients that are here are very ill. Some are pale, with sunken eyes, others feverish and panting. All cling to what little life they have left.

Luther stays close as I make my way toward a doctor and a small group of nurses clustered together at the end of the room. The doctor— presumably Dr. Haddly—is young, which is fortunate for me. He's probably not yet set in his ways, which will make this easier. His dusty blond hair is combed to the left, and he stands slightly slumped, so that even from this distance I can tell he's tired.

Hearing the light moans and raspy coughs coming from the patients, I look back at Luther for a moment and notice him watching the patients intently.

Knowing he has never experienced death like this, I ask in a whisper, "What is it? If you're concerned about something, tell me now."

He glances at me. "It seems like such a waste." His eyes return to the sick man to his right. "So many dying without our help."

I can tell he believes what he's saying, so I correct him. "You only think so because you're young." I grab his arm and stop walking, "The real waste is that we take away a healthy life for selfish reasons instead of settling for the taste of tainted blood."

The sick are always abundant. Some are even in enough pain that they beg for someone to end it, and, like a cruel joke, we will not indulge them. True, their blood does taste different, more bitter, more degraded, but it still quenches in a way that only human blood can. That we do not feed from them more often is a sad testament to our nature.

"It's shameful to value life so little," I tell him as the doctor starts toward us. "Keep that in mind."

He scoffs at the idea. "It sounds like you respect them."

"I do. And you should, too. They do more living in their short lives than you will in a thousand years."

I turn back around to see Dr. Haddly approaching with one of the nurses. Older than the doctor, the nurse keeps her light brown hair pinned up in big curls, probably trying to distract someone from noticing the wrinkles around her eyes.

"Gentlemen, you can't be in here after visiting hours," Dr. Haddly says.

"We're not here to visit a patient. We want something else." I tell the doctor.

His eyebrows come together. "What is it you want?"

Reaching into my shirt pocket, I tell him, "Your discretion." I pull out a folded bundle of money and hold it between us.

I glance at the nurse's nametag, which reads NURSE KLEIN, and ignore the way her eyes widen at the sight of the money. I know it's probably more than she's seen since the war started. Dr. Haddly stares at it for a moment and then looks around to be sure nobody is watching. That's when I know I have him. He brings his hand up and takes the money from me carefully. Then he stuffs it into his pocket. "Walk with me," he says.

"What exactly will you be doing that needs to be discreet?" he asks me quietly as he leads us toward the double doors, with Nurse Klein following behind us.

I look up at the high ceilings and the lights suspended above us. "Observing, mostly."

"Mostly?"

I continue as though he had said nothing. "Preferably alone."

"Why alone?" he asks, and I hear the confusion in his voice.

I meet his eyes and smile. "Dr. Haddly, people die here every day, why would tonight be any different?"

Nurse Klein's mouth parts slightly in shock, and she looks to Dr. Haddly. His puzzled expression melts away as he grasps what I'm suggesting. He stops walking and turns his attention to the floor, but he does not see the bland white tiles. His eyes dart back and forth while he mulls over the idea.

Fearing I might lose him to ethics, I continue, "I'm not saying someone will be hurt while we're here. I'm only preparing you for every possibility. But let me assure you, it would be quick and painless." For us anyway. "Regardless, I assume there is someone here you don't expect to survive the night."

Still not meeting my eyes, he nods, more to himself than to me. "There are a few," he murmurs.

Nurse Klein stares at Dr. Haddly, though he doesn't seem to notice. I can tell she wants to say something but she remains silent.

I let him deliberate for a moment before I add, "I'm prepared to double my offer."

Dr. Haddly looks up at me to judge my seriousness and then drops his head again, still deep in thought. I cannot say that I criticize him for considering this. A painless death for those that are doomed to suffer sounds merciful. At least, that's how he'll justify allowing this.

More so, I believe the real persuasion is in the money. And who could blame him? War makes times difficult for everybody. From families missing loved ones and soldiers that die in the streets, all the way down to a lowly doctor who now works much more shifts for a lot less pay.

Knowing this, I'm not surprised when he looks up at me and offers a compromise. "No children."

"Of course not," I tell him. "I give you my word."

He looks at the nurse. "Nurse Klein, take the other nurses to the pediatric ward." He doesn't trust me, smart man.

Concerned and almost scolding, she begins, "Doctor Haddly." But he cuts her off abruptly, "I said clear the room."

Obviously unhappy about it, she marches off toward the group of nurses.

Dr. Haddly turns to me. "You have one hour." Then he turns away quickly and walks through the double doors.

Thankfully, Luther had let me do the talking, but now that we're alone again, he opens his mouth and out comes more of his inane drivel. "Why didn't you just use your hypno voodoo on him?"

I sigh exasperatedly and shake my head. "One, it's not hypnosis nor is it voodoo. And two, I don't even think those things go together. Besides, it's better to let them make their own mistakes."

I'm not sure if he agrees with me or simply hears the irritation in my voice, but he says nothing more until all the nurses have cleared the room. After that, he says little else that doesn't pertain to identifying diseases that are safe for us.

Like all torture, time moves painfully slow as I explain the differences between the sickly sweet and the bitterly sour scents of various diseases, all smelling of decay in their own way. The way they mix in the air is revolting, and I try not to focus on the unpleasant aroma as I sit on the end of a patient's bed.

Such an odor is redolent of the plague that ravaged its way across Europe when I was young. The humans called it the Black Death. It was blamed for several of my victims. The only positive thing about such an epidemic is that they overlook the quantity of victims that an adolescent vampire consumes. At least, they overlooked me.

Sitting on the railing of the footboard, I try not to reminisce about my past for too long, try not to remember myself in that light, a dark creature bent on making the world feel the pain I had inside me. Bitter and disgusted with myself, I had let my sorrow and thirst drive my actions. I was not pleasant to be around for the first two hundred years. Marcella should not have indulged me the way she did. I wouldn't have.

Luther leans over a sleeping man and inhales deeply. "Is this polio?" he asks.

Until he spoke, I had almost forgotten he was there. Without looking back at him, I separate the smells in the air. "Yes. It will dissolve in your system fairly quickly. It causes paralysis, severe headache, and vomiting. But as I said, it's short-lived in our bodies."

I glance back at him and smile. "If you really want to feed, there's a woman over there with terminal ileitis," I tell him. "You'll be doubled over in pain until morning. But don't worry, the sun will bring you some relief."

He snorts and goes back to smelling the polluted air. Watching him, I begin to feel bad for keeping something from him, something he undoubtedly would want to know—something I would want to know.

"Luther, do you ever think of your family?" I ask him. The family that had escaped when he tried to run from an oppressive plantation owner. The family he told to keep going even as he was being captured. His wife and daughter.

He freezes where he stands and looks at me, unsure where I'm heading. "Of course, I do," he says cautiously. "I wonder what they thought became of me. I wonder if they ever made it North."

"They did," I say quietly. "They settled in Ohio."

In disbelief, he exhales forcefully. "How do you know that?"

"I kept tabs on them." Even though I despise him, I try to say this gently, "Your wife died in 1915 of complications from pneumonia."

He brings his hands up in front of his mouth, "And my daughter?" he whispers.

It's strange for me to be on this side of things. I'm never the one giving news like this. I'm always the one taking lives and never sticking around to comfort the family afterwards. "Abigail died four days ago. She was eighty-six. They think it was her heart."

His lip trembles as tears fill his eyes. "And you are just now telling me?" I can hear the anger in his voice behind the pain.

"Marcella and I agreed that it was for the best if you didn't know about them. We thought that if you knew, you'd go to see them. And we just couldn't risk that."

"Bullshit!" He stomps over to me. "That's bullshit, Nicolas. You hate me, that's all this is about."

True. I do hate him. But would I really keep this from him for that reason alone? That is a rhetorical question, of course.

He continues, "All it boils down to is plain and simple jealousy."

"Jealous?" I jump off of the railing and face him. "What exactly am I jealous of? Is it that you're slower and weaker than me? Or maybe it's because you're the least favorite man in the house, and that includes Harvey."

"Jealous that at my age you didn't have the control I do," he boasts. That gets my heart pumping. My eyes narrow on him and I say coldly, "You think my killing binges were because of a control issue?" Of course, he does, he's daft. "You and I are not the same," I continue.

"That we can agree on. So don't confuse the reason for my actions for one of yours."

I step closer to him, "I wasn't dying in the mud like you. This wasn't my saving grace. I was just beginning my life. I was just about to be happy. And it was stolen from me. My life was stolen. At least you had a family, even though it was only brief. I was robbed of that. All I have left is this shell of a life. So excuse me for being a little upset that I was cheated so badly."

He half-smiles at me. "Like I said, jealous." He places his hand on my shoulder, which only makes my skin crawl. "When you look at me, you don't see a man. You only see a choice. The choice you didn't have. And you hate that about me." He says almost smugly.

"We're done here," I say, shoving his hand from my shoulder. "And for the record, I haven't known about Abigail's death for long. I just received the letter this morning."

I walk away from him toward the double doors. There are still close to fifteen minutes left in our allotted time here, but I do not have even one more minute of tolerance to give him.

The more distance between us, the clearer I begin to think. Maybe he does have a point; maybe it isn't him that I have a problem with. Ah, who am I kidding? It is him.

I push through the doors and am slightly surprised to see Nurse Klein standing there. Leaning against the wall with her arms crossed, she glares at me.

"Leave anyone alive?" she asks.

"Everyone, even my..."-Not partner, definitely not friend-"associate." I reach into my pocket and pull out the rest of the money I owe them.

"Be sure the doctor gets this, will you?"

She pushes away from the wall and reaches for the cash, but I pull it away. "Nurse Klein, please do not condemn me so easily." I release the money to her. "Pretty sure the bible says not to judge others. Of course, I am paraphrasing that."

She shoves the money in her pocket. "It also says something about not killing."

My lopsided grin spreads across my face, "Perhaps we should pray for each other then."

Her eyes soften slightly, and her mouth twitches, and for a moment I think she's going to smile. But before she can, Luther swings the door open and walks past us toward the lobby.

"Goodnight, Miss Klein," I say kindly.

I start toward the lobby when I hear her say, "It's Mrs."

Looking back at her, I respond, "Of course. My apologies, Mrs. Klein."

She smiles softly. "Apology accepted, Mr. Hager."

I nod at her and continue on my way out, through the lobby, past Beth, and outside into the cold night air. I do not see Luther and am thankful for that. He probably needs a few moments to himself, and I would not be the most sympathetic person for him right now.

Taking the long way home, I walk along the edge of the street. Not many cars drive this back road, even during the day, so it is no wonder that I haven't seen any tonight.

As I kick a small stone and watch it bounce away, I hear a child's sharp scream. Normally, a vampire does not concern himself with the troubles of a human, but this scream came from the direction of my neighbor, the same neighbor Kate is supposed to be visiting.

I take off in a sprint, and it doesn't take me long to clear the distance to the house. The smell of blood encircles me as I approach the weathered two- story home, but that isn't what makes my heart drop.

Sitting on the porch swing with her legs drawn into her chest is Kate. Even with her face buried in her hands, the sound of a small child screaming inside, and her own quiet sobs, she feels my presence.

She looks up at me with tears and blood streaking her face. "Nick," she says weakly before she slumps to her knees and cries harder.

I walk across the porch, being sure not to let the boards creak under me. I have been here before, not at this house, but in this situation. There have been times when I was the one crumbling, hating what I had become, hating what I was capable of.

As I come closer to her, I slide my arms out of my coat and wrap it around her shoulders. I know she isn't cold the way a human would be, but the heat left from my body will still be comforting in its own way.

I sit beside her feet on the swing and watch her yellow gown rock back and forth as she slips my coat on. When her eyes finally meet mine, I can see the sadness in them, and it makes a lump form in my throat.

She opens her mouth to speak, but cannot. Her chin and lower lip quiver as she inhales sharply.

Moving her feet from the swing, I slide over to her and wrap my arms around her, pulling her to my chest. I can feel her body shaking against me as her tears wet my shirt.

"How could I?" she mutters. "She trusted me."

Rubbing her head gently, I ask, "What happened?" But I know what happened. The same thing that always does. We overstepped our boundaries. Getting too close means someone gets hurt.

"She cut herself and I wasn't ready. The smell took me by surprise. I couldn't stop myself," she whimpers.

I can hear the child crying inside, young and fragile sounding. Knowing that it isn't Peter, Caroline's brother, I feel wretched that it must be Katrina, the youngest. Six years old is still too old to be left alive after witnessing such a massacre.

"Mommy," Katrina wails. "Wake up. Please."

Kate pulls herself closer to me. "Nick, could you...?" she begins.

I know what she is about to say. "No." I pull her away from me so that I can see her face. "Don't ask that of me."

Tears roll down her cheeks. "Please, Nick, I can't go back in there."

I glance toward the house, "Katrina is just a child." Then looking back at Kate, I continue, "A child, Kate, I can't..."

Watching the heartbreak in her eyes, I realize that she can't either. After a long moment, I sigh. I know what I have to do. It's what Marcella would do for me and what I need to be able to do for Kate.

I kiss her on the forehead. Without another word, I stand up. Walking toward the door, a sickening feeling settles in my stomach. My hand hesitates by the door before I knock firmly. "Police," I say in German.

Small footsteps rush to the door. It opens a crack before a tiny hand, Katrina's hand, grabs mine and pulls me inside the house. "Hurry. Before she comes back."

Although it is my first time in this home, I do not notice the lack of space, the dim lighting, or the limited furniture. I do not see the bodies tossed aside on the floor or the blood smeared across the walls. My eyes are on the darling child in front of me.

Her thin blond hair, sapphire eyes, and round cherub cheeks are only going to make this harder. With a face full of panic, her eyes dart across the room, barely even taking me in. "It was Kate, my neighbor. She's demon. She did this. You have to do something."

Bending down in front of her, I place my hands on either side of her face, making her look at me. Her eyes lose some of their sparkle as she locks them on mine and I enthrall her.

Very softly, I tell her, "You were having a nightmare. There is nothing to be afraid of. Everyone is asleep now. You should be asleep, too."

She nods methodically, "I am tired," she whispers.

Without breaking my contact with her, I take her hand in mine. "I am going to take you to bed now."

We walk down the hallway, and even with the heavy scent of blood in the air, I can still smell which room belongs to her and Caroline. I lead her to her bed. As she crawls under the blankets, I'm careful to keep my hand in hers, as physical touch is the only way to continue my enthrallment of her.

I kneel down beside her bed, and with my other hand, I cover her up. Pushing back the hair from her face, I place my hands on either side of her face again. "Close your eyes and sleep now," I whisper.

She smiles a soft, simple smile at me, which only wrenches my heart more.

Once her eyes close, I close mine, and though I do not think God will listen to me, I make a quiet plea. "God, I am sending a child to you. Please help her find her way into your arms."

Without opening my eyes, I make a quick jerk with my hands and hear a snap, her heartbeat stop, and a light exhale as her last breath leaves her lips.

I slide my hands away and fall back against the dresser, rocking it back and causing a lamp to crash to the floor beside me. But that does not distract me from the crushing pain in my chest, a void that's quickly filling with misery and disgust.

Tears flood my eyes and I struggle to fight them back. I will not allow myself to feel any kind of self-pity for this. It isn't fair to make myself out to be a victim.

I stand up and walk out of the bedroom. Not really looking at anything, I pass through the living room and onto the porch.

"Nick..." Kate begins, but I put my hand up to stop her.

I do not meet her eyes. "I'll send Marcella for the cleanup. Just stay here," I say quietly.

Stepping off of the porch, I ignore the way Kate calls after me, and walk the first half of a mile in a daze. Like a hollow drone, I try not to feel anything, but as I lose that battle, I break into a run.

I attempt to let the crisp night air distract me. I feel the coldness biting my nose and ears, smell the aroma of winter settling in around me, hear owls hooting and screeching as they hunt. But every thought leads me back to Katrina, making me run that much harder.

Finally, I reach the house. Marcella must have felt my presence drawing close, because she's waiting in the foyer.

I am not sure what the expression on my face is but it is enough to make her concerned. "What's wrong?" she asks. "What happened?"

I meet her eyes for only a moment before I look away, trying to hide the pain in them. "Kate needs you. At Caroline's."

Marcella brings a hand to her mouth. There is a brief pause before she says quietly, "Of course." She walks over to me, "Are there any witnesses?"

"I took care of it." I cannot disguise how shaky my voice is.

Softly, she puts her hands on my neck and kisses my forehead. "You did the right thing," she says. But I do not agree. "Stay here with Claire."

I nod and she's gone before her words really start to sink in. Excluding the sheep, I am alone with Claire. Alone. With Claire. Really? Don't get me wrong, I love to spend time with Claire but I know myself. This pressing guilt is crushing me, and I am looking for a way to forget. I know a way, and it only requires one other person. And I am alone with Claire. No, I will not. I cannot. Well, I should not anyway.

I walk through the library and kitchen, stopping only briefly to say goodnight to Lilah, who's oblivious to my inner turmoil. Without making any noise, I go downstairs and into my room.

I sit on the edge of my bed and kick off my shoes. Sighing, I fall back, bouncing slightly on the mattress. Lying there looking at the ceiling, I let myself relish in how easy it would be. Claire is just down the hall, surely wearing something that accentuates her every curve. And she wants me.

Stop, I tell myself. I should not think of such things. I promised I wouldn't. And I won't. As long as I'm in here, by myself, I should be fine. As long as she does not come looking for me, I'm good.

That's when I hear a knock on my door. I sit up as the door opens, and though I'm not looking at her, I know it's Claire that walks in.

She closes the door behind her. "Did something happen?" she asks. "Are you all right?"

I look at her standing near the door. Her red hair hangs freely around her shoulders, the light catches her cheekbones brilliantly. The blue of her eyes has never shone so bright. Everything about her is beautiful.

The thin nightgown she's wearing is just tight enough to make it obvious that she isn't wearing a bra.

I make my decision and damn it, I say it, "Come to me."

She walks over to me, and with every step she takes, my desire for her grows so that by the time she stops in front of me, I have to have her.

I stand up to face her. Placing my hand at the base of her head, I press my lips to hers. There is a necessity behind my kiss that lets her know that this time I do not intend to stop. As I kiss along her neck, she slides her hands down to my belt. Quickly, she has it unfastened, and her fingers work on my button and zipper. She pushes my pants down and lets them drop.

I glide my hands down to her hips and gather up her gown until I have the bottom of it in my hands. I pull it up over her head and toss it to the floor. With my hand on the small of her back, I pull her toward me, kissing her passionately. Feeling her breasts pressed against me makes a heat course through my body. Her hands trace up my spine, bringing chills to my skin.

With one hand, I reach over my head to my back and grab my shirt, pulling it off quickly. Then, taking hold of her hip, I brush my thumb over her birthmark and curl my fingers around her panties. I pull hard enough to tear them off her, and I can feel her smile as her lips move with mine.

I start to tell her that we have to try not to bite when I feel a sharp pinch on my lip and the taste of blood trickles into my mouth. Ah, hell with it. Grabbing her thighs, I lift her off of the ground.

With my eyes black and my fangs out, I lay her back on the bed. I graze my teeth along her neck and feel her breathing quicken. Biting down, her soft, fragile skin offers little resistance to my fangs. Inhaling sharply, she runs her hand through my hair. With her heart racing and my teeth deep inside her, I rock my hips into hers. Arching her back, she moans, pulling me closer to her.

I glide my hand to her butt, and gripping it firmly, I press her against me. I move my mouth away from her neck and press my lips to hers, swirling blood between them.

I push myself up onto my arms so that I can see the way her breasts bounce with my every thrust. Rubbing her hand over the bite mark on her neck, she smears the blood across her chest and neck, moaning. Seeing the way the crimson color contrasts against her pale skin makes me only crave her that much more.

Turning her head, she sinks her fangs into my forearm. The stab of pain and the stream of red that runs toward my hand has my body tingling. I watch her throat for her to swallow my blood, and each time she does, my heart pounds faster.

She rolls her head back, sliding her fangs out of my arm. Reaching up, she grabs me by the curve of my neck and pulls herself against me, kissing me urgently. Dragging my tongue across her lips, I taste the way our blood blends together.

She drops back onto the bed, gliding her fingers down my chest and abdomen, breathing heavily. I pull her leg up beside me and bite into her calf. Moaning, she grabs at her breasts. With a mouthful of blood, I pull my teeth from her leg, letting the blood pour from my lips onto her stomach. She laughs pleasingly, stroking her abdomen with her hands until her belly is smothered in crimson.

I glide my hand through the blood on her stomach and chest, feeling the way her body trembles beneath me as I drive my hips into hers. She grabs beside her, digging her fingernails into the sheet and tearing at the mattress. My tongue slides along her neck and up to her chin, tasting her skin amongst the blood. I muffle her screams with my kiss, crushing her lips with mine.

Her fingernails pierce my shoulder, and I feel the warmth of my blood run down between my shoulder blades and along my spine. She pulls her lips away and bites into my throat. Closing my eyes, I focus on the pull on my veins, the pressure of her teeth, the erotic pain they cause.

Removing her fangs from me, she slides her tongue across her teeth satisfyingly. Her eyelids flutter and she moans, gasping for air, as my hips slam into her. She tangles her fingers in my hair, pulling lightly.

Her breathing becomes more rapid and chaotic. Her grip on me tightens until her screams grow louder, and every muscle in her body contracts around me. Her fingernails scratch down my back as she throws her head back. Then her entire body relaxes. As she attempts to catch her breath, she smiles at me. But I am not done with her yet, and I lean down and kiss her again.

Chapter 8

It's strange to think that only a few hours earlier, I was wishing for the morning to come and release me from a most miserable night. But how things did change. Lying on the fresh linens that cover my bed, I close my eyes.

I can still see Claire sitting on the floor with her back pressed against the wall. Dressed in only my shirt, blood smeared on her neck and cheek, but the most beautiful thing she wore was that smile. The one that was meant for me. The one that was because of me...

I was changing the sheets on my bed, but I couldn't keep my eyes off her, and she knew it. She could see the appeal that she possessed for me. She could see that behind my bashful, lopsided smile I am happy with her.

"So..." she began, "that wasn't exactly the way I remembered sex being."

I should say not, I thought, laughing to myself. "I just hope it was worth the hassle," I said.

Rubbing the dried blood on her arm, she chuckled lightly, "About that. Did you get that good by practicing?" she asked suggestively.

I knew I had to answer carefully. Glancing back at her, I shrugged, "Everyone has a talent."

Leaning up slightly, she laughed so lightheartedly that I had to stop making the bed just to watch her. Her red locks haven fallen forward, her eyes closed, her fingers barely grazed her mouth. In that moment, I was thankful to have lived as long as I have just so I could have the chance to know her...

*   *   *

A door slamming across the hall pulls me from my thoughts. I sit up, knowing it's Kate, and walk to her closed door.

Knocking lightly, I say, "Kate? Are you all right?"

She does not answer so I push the door open and go inside. Lying on the floor near my coat is her yellow gown, spattered with patches of dark red. I am sure that more blood is running down the shower drain this very second.

I fall back against the wall, listening to the water hit the shower floor. What am I supposed to say? It's not your fault? It is. It gets better, easier? It doesn't.

"I know it's hard, Kate, but it's times like this that make us appreciate the good days," I say gently. "And I promise that there will be more good days to come for you."

I walk over to the small waste bin by her desk and toss the gown in the trash. Something tells me she won't want to wear it again.

Luther walks past me, toward his bedroom. I step into the hallway, "Luther."

He turns to me, his face vacant of any expression.

"For what's worth, I'm sorry about Abigail," I tell him truthfully. But I am sorry more for her death than for him missing her life. He does not belong to her world anymore, and one day he will understand that.

His eyes soften. "Thanks, Nick."

Only partially joking, I say, "Only my friends are allowed to call me Nick. You don't have that privilege."

His body relaxes. "Whatever you say... Nick." He smirks at me and goes into his room, closing the door behind him.

Usually he only says things like that to rile me, but this time he is trying to let me know that he will be all right, and strangely enough, it's comforting. As I hear the water stop, I walk to the bathroom door. "Kate?" I try. "Kate. Please answer me." Bracing myself on the doorframe, I lean my weight toward the door. "I understand if you don't want to talk about it. But I would really love it if you would at least say something."

"Something," she mumbles through the door. I can hear from her tone that she's still hurting inside.

Without worrying about whether she is decent or not, I open the bathroom door. Sitting on the floor is Kate with her head in her hands and her knees drawn up to her chest much the same way she had been on the swing earlier tonight.

I lean back against the wall and slide down onto the floor beside her.

"You will get through this. Aside from Marcella, you're the strongest in the house," I tell her gently.

She shakes her head. "I wasn't strong tonight."

I pull her hands away from her face and turn her chin toward me. "You don't have to be strong every second of every day. You just have to try to be. And you do. That's why you're a better vampire than me."

She huffs, "You should give yourself more credit, Nick. You're the best vampire I know."

Chuckling lightly to myself, I cannot believe she's trying to cheer me up. "You must not know very many vampires."

She smiles, but only briefly. Then she looks down at her hands, thinking. Her eyebrows come together and her mouth tightens as she swallows hard. It pains me to see her hurting so much.

As tears fill her eyes, I take her hand in mine. "Do you know why I don't like Luther?" I ask, rubbing my finger over the back of her hand. "I don't like weakness."

I shift my body toward her. "There's a reason I chose you for a friend. When I look at you, I see a strength, power, and intelligence that he just doesn't have. And that's not something that you learn."

She wraps her arms around my neck. "Thank you, Nick. For everything."

I hold her close, letting her long hair wet my arms. With the heat from her skin making its way through her gown, it's hard not to think about the feeding that made her this warm, but I try not to.

"I don't know what I would have done without you tonight," she tells me. "You're the best friend anyone could ask for."

I smile to myself. "Sometimes I have to earn that title." Like tonight, for instance.

Laying her head on my shoulder, she slides her hand down onto my chest and sighs lightly. I kiss her forehead softly and rest my chin against her, keeping my arms around her.

Rocking gently, I sing her favorite song quietly enough that only she can hear me. Her grip on me tightens and she shifts herself onto my lap. She does not have to say anything just yet. I know it helps. It helps just to know someone cares enough to stay with you.

I only make it through one verse and the chorus before she looks up at me with her big brown eyes. Her hand glides up my neck to the base of my head. She bites her lip nervously, which only reminds me of how desirable Claire looks when she does that. Her eyes dart to my lips for a moment before she meets my eyes again, this time with a hunger in them that I have seen with other women before.

I would do anything for Kate. Anything but this.

Taking her hand from my neck, I clear my throat, "Kate..."

"Oh," she says as though she was unaware of what was happening. She pulls herself away from me. "Right. Um, I'm going to go to bed. I'm pretty tired."

Even though I know that to be an impossibility, I agree, "Me, too."

We both stand up and go into her bedroom. "Well," I start, "Goodnight."

As I turn toward the door, I hear, "Nick." I turn around to face her as she continues.

"I don't want to be alone right now. Do you think..." she takes a deep breath, "Do you think you could stay with me?"

I can tell by the way she rubs her arm that she is worried I might say no.

As if that is an option. "Of course," I tell her.

Walking over to her bed, I ask, "Do you want to talk or do you want to sleep?"

Feebly, she responds, "I just want to be held."

I pull back the blankets and say, "Well, I think I can manage that." I smile softly at her, making her smile back as she climbs into the bed.

She scoots over and I slide in beside her. It's different being in her bed.

It does not smell of Claire the way mine does, which only reminds me...

Claire was sitting along the wall while I was wiping a bloody handprint from my headboard when I asked, "Are you all right? You're not overly thirsty, are you?"

I kept my eyes on the headboard, hoping that even if she lied, I wouldn't be able to tell.

"I feel wonderful," she said, and it sounded sincere, but then again, she is good at lying. She walked toward me. "This is the best night of my life. The only thing that could spoil it is you worrying about me." Touching my chin, she turned my face toward hers. "So stop." She kissed me softly and it made me forget all the risks I was setting her up for...

Kate settles into my shoulder, bringing me back to reality. With her body pressed against my side, she drapes her arm over my ribs.

We talk for hours about everything except the events of the night, which is just as well since I do not wish to lie about Claire and me. Not to Kate. Finally, well into the afternoon, we decide to rest.

*　　*　　*

My mind wanders back to Claire as I walk along the tree line of the forest. I wonder what Marcella has her doing right now and if she's thinking of me.

The gravel crunches under my feet, but I pay no mind to that. Instead, I let myself remember her warm hand on my cheek, her body against mine, her soft lips on my neck just before her fangs entered my skin.

"Nick," Kate calls, drawing me back to the cold night and the stench of Luther standing all too close.

I look up at her, half surprised that I heard her at all. "I said, do you want to play a game?" Kate asks.

Anything that could make me stop thinking of Claire and make me more aware of my surroundings would be a good thing. I shrug, "What game?"

Smiling widely, she says, "Hide and seek."

Too easy. All you have to do is smell them out. It's more about tracking than anything else.

"With a challenge," Kate adds.

"Oh yeah?" I start. "What kind of challenge?"

Her eyes dart to Luther. "Show him."

Luther reaches inside his coat and pulls out a brown paper bag with the end rolled up tight. He opens it, and I can smell what's inside before he takes it out. Garlic.

True, we do avoid garlic, but not for the reasons that the humans assume. It overpowers our most sensitive sense, our sense of smell, which we rely heavily upon.

He holds up a necklace made from garlic cloves and thread. I look to Kate. "Is that my garlic? From the kitchen?"

Her grin turns mischievous. "You aren't allowed to cook with it anyway."

True. Marcella hates the smell of it filling the house. But deep down I think she just hates that I can sneak up on her when she cannot smell me adequately.

"All right," I give. "I'm in."

She takes the necklace from Luther and puts it around my neck, blocking all other scents.

"You're it," she says happily.

"Do I at least get to watch which direction you go?" I ask, smiling at Kate.

Luther steps closer to us. "What's the matter, Nick? I thought you would be used to being handicapped by now." He smirks at me as he wraps his arms around Kate's waist.

I admit that was cleverer than I would normally give him credit for, but still just as annoying. "You are my handicap, Luther. Everything about you slows this family down."

Kate hits my shoulder. "Hey," she says disapprovingly.

"Why is he even here?" I ask her irritably. I mean, he does not serve any purpose that I can see. "Honestly, can you tell me one thing—?"

She puts her hand to my mouth as she sniffs the air. "Do you smell that?" She asks quietly.

"No," is my muffled response.

"Shh," she says without removing her hand.

Luther smells the air around him, turning his nose toward the forest. When his eyes turn black, I know it is a human that they smell. "Campers," he whispers.

Kate looks at me and smiles, intrigued. "Oo, I'm calling a timeout."

"Wait." Taking her hand, I start to protest, but I know the taste of Caroline's blood still lingers in her mouth. "Are you sure you want to?"

Her smile fades away into a more serious expression, one that's sad and remorseful. "Yes," she says hesitantly.

Nodding, I slide my hand up to her shoulder, "Be careful out there."

"You're not coming?" she asks, surprised.

Truth is, after feeding on Claire, I shouldn't ingest human blood so soon. It only increases the bloodlust, and though I could control it, why push myself? "No. Not this time."

Luther loosens his hold on Kate and shakes his head. "Always so careful. You restrict yourself too much, Nick. One day you're going to snap."

My eyes narrow on him. "I hope you're around when I do," I tell him coldly.

Kate swats her hand in the air as if that could clear the tension between Luther and me. "That's enough. I've already given the both of you a warning once and I do not intend to issue them all night."

She's right, of course. He should be nicer to me. "You two should hurry up," I tell her, changing the subject. "You can't leave me out here all night wearing jewelry." I pull at the garlic necklace, and joke, "I look silly."

Though Luther could easily twist my last sentence into some petty insult, surprisingly he doesn't.

Kate laughs lightly. "Let's go," she tells Luther and they take off into the woods.

Tossing the necklace beside me, I sit down in the grass. Still unable to smell anything, I lose myself in thought.

First and foremost, I think of Claire. The way she looked when I first laid eyes on her. Her white gown hanging just below her knees, her hair pinned back, her lips painted red. It was enough to distract me from the victim in the alley with me.

I found out later that she was on her way home from temple, and have often wondered what she was praying about so late at night.

I followed her home, watching her the way a cheetah stalks its prey, never seen, never heard. I had to have her. But not for sustenance. And not for only one night either.

I needed her to know me. To want me. The way I wanted her. The way I still do.

Those thoughts begin to dissipate as a scent titillates my nose. Light at first, it grows stronger as my sense of smell returns. But it does not take me long to decipher what it is. The wild, musky human scent makes my heart sink.

Jumping to my feet, I run into the trees. "Kate!" I shout, not caring who else hears me.

My feet pound against the frozen ground, "Kate!" Letting my eyes change to black and my fangs extend, I only hope I am not too late. I can't be.

Making out a large campfire in the clearing ahead and hearing growls and snapping jaws, and I know I'm close. Pushing myself harder than I ever have before, I run through the trees.

When I reach the clearing, I look around quickly, taking in my surroundings. Six werewolves, not a full pack. To my left, Luther is among two rows of teeth. Biting down on his side, a black wolf shakes its head ferociously.

To my right, Kate is backed against a tree. Two gray wolves flank her, ready for the kill. As one leaps at her, she holds onto the tree, curling her body up and jumping forward. She kicks the wolf's head, slamming it into the tree and crushing it against the trunk. A naked human male falls to the ground in the wolf's place as a second gray wolf jumps at Kate. It knocks her down, pinning her to the ground.

As I watch her, a dark brown wolf flies through the air toward me. Grabbing handfuls of fur, I throw the wolf toward Kate. It smacks into the gray wolf, causing it to whine and knocking them both away from her.

As she looks at me, I shout, "Run!"

Without hesitation, she springs to her feet and disappears into the woods with the two wolves right on her heels, but I know she's faster than they are.

The black wolf does not drop Luther; instead, it clenches its jaws down on him harder, making him cry out painfully. Holding my hands out at my sides, I hiss as my fingernails grow out into sharp tips.

The other two wolves run at me. The tan one reaches me first, lunging at my head. Grabbing its throat, I slam it into the ground and stomp it in the side. From its raspy breathing, I know that I not only cracked a few ribs but that one of them punctured a lung.

The red wolf isn't far behind, and it leaps toward me. Swinging my fist through the air, I make contact with its jaw. It whines as it falls to the ground.

The tan wolf bites down onto my forearm, growling and snarling. As the red wolf jumps at me again, I kick it in the chest, sending it through the air. It flies through the flames of the campfire and lands with a thud.

As I pull my arm away from the tan wolf's grip, its teeth shred my skin and muscle. I grab its fur at the shoulder and hip. It snaps at me as I lift it off the ground. Pressing its side against a tree, I push my hands back, folding the wolf around the trunk. It cries and whines loudly as bones snap beneath my hands. I let it fall to my feet.

With it shaking and breathing erratically, I bend down near it. I wraps my arm around its neck and twist until I feel a pop and only a man remains in my arms.

As I start toward Luther, the red wolf lunges through the flames. I roll toward it, placing myself under the wolf. I stand up, extending my hand so that my fingers claw and slice deep into its belly. Blood pours out onto me as the wolf flies over me.

With a heavy thump, it lands on its side, spilling out its intestines on the ground. I walk over and snap its neck, leaving behind only a woman, dead and naked on the cold ground.

I run at the black wolf. Digging my nails into its skin, I climb onto its back. Wrapping my legs around its ribs, I place a hand on both of its rows of teeth. As I pull its mouth open, Luther falls to the ground. But I do not stop there. I continue to pull my hands apart, ignoring the way it bucks and scratches at me and the way it whines painfully. I do not stop when its jaw pops loudly and unhinges itself. It's not until I rip its mandible from its body and it collapses onto the forest floor that I step away from the wolf.

As it writhes in pain, I walk over to it and place my foot against its head. Pressing down, I feel the skull crumple under my weight and see him shift into his human form.

In the distance, a wolf howls. Knowing that more are coming, my instincts are to run. But I hesitate. I look back and see Luther lying on the ground, unconscious. Here is my chance to rid myself of him, but there is no honor in leaving him.

I do not have long to deliberate so I grab his arm and bury my shoulder in his waist, lifting him. As the pounding of several paws grows closer, I run toward my home with Luther folded over my shoulder.

The added weight of Luther slows me down but not enough to make the wolves even come close to seeing me. Careful not to slip on the loose gravel, I speed across the road and through the open fields. Ignoring the way my arm burns and aches from the werewolf's saliva, which delays our healing process, I run hard until I reach our house.

Kicking open the door, I hurry inside. Marcella and Kate are there in time to catch Luther as I let him fall from my shoulder. My arm is burning when I draw it close and the muscles begin to tighten and spasm.

Kate rushes to me. "Are you hurt?"

"I'm fine," I say through gritted teeth.

*   *   *

She looks me over, pushing my hair aside and pulling at my clothes, trying to figure out how much of the blood is mine.

I push her hands away. "I'm fine." I insist. "Just help Luther."

She hurries back to Luther and helps Marcella carry him downstairs.

I follow them as far as the kitchen, dripping blood onto the floor from my elbow as I cradle my hand.

I go into the pantry and look around the rows of shelves. I take down the jug that once held a quart of milk, now holding only water inside. Water blessed by a priest. I take it down and walk out of the pantry, careful not to spill any.

Setting it on the counter, I place my hand in the sink and rip the sleeve of my shirt off.

I take the glass jug in my hand and pour the water on my forearm. It sizzles on my skin, burning its way to my hand. It takes all I have in me not to scream while it feels as if my flesh is peeling. But I know it is necessary. Werewolf saliva slows our healing process, and the holy water cauterizes the cuts.

Wrapping my forearm in a towel, I am glad that Luther is going to sleep through Marcella washing out his immense wounds. Even he does not deserve that much pain.

Because I am not paying much attention to anything other than my arm, I'm not aware of Claire until she puts her hand on my back. "Are you all right?" she asks.

Turning toward her, I grab her face and press my lips to hers urgently.

She pulls her body into mine, arching her back.

I pull my face away but only slightly. "You could've been out there." Her hand is warm on my cheek as she rubs her fingers along my jaw.

"But I wasn't. I was by the hospital. I was nowhere near the forest," she says softly.

Taking her hand, I say quietly, "I can't lose you." I kiss her again, this time softly, letting my lips caress hers.

Placing her hand inside mine, she pulls me toward the pantry, looking back and biting her lip along the way.

She closes the pantry door, grabbing my shirt collar and pulling my face to hers, kissing me passionately. She slides her hand down my abdomen to my pants. I begin to forget about the burning in my arm and think only of the heat left by her trailing fingers.

She loosens my pants and though that was not my intention, I do not stop her.

Chapter 9

I have spent some time, though I know not how much, wandering the streets searching for something. It is not until I see the house from my childhood that I pause. With its straw roof and dark windows staring back at me, I realize that I am dreaming, and I understand who, not what, I am seeking.

I walk across the snow-covered road, leaving my shoeprints in the soft powder. Flakes dance around me, sticking to my shirt and melting in my hair. I walk through my heavy breath as it hangs in the air.

Mere steps from the house, the door opens and a beauty steps out. She is just the way I remember, flawless skin, light brown locks adorned with ribbons, even the way she plays with her fingers is familiar.

"Ann," I nearly whisper.

As a slow smile spreads across her face, she walks over to me and places her hand on my cheek. "My love," she says as though no time has passed. "Why do you look so sad?"

I put my hand over hers, pressing her warm skin against me. "This isn't real. You're not real."

She takes my other hand and lays it on her chest, letting me feel the drumming of her heart. "I seem real, don't I?"

Ignoring the fact that this is surely a dream, I look into her brown eyes. "I miss you." Wrapping my arms around her, I continue, "I want to stay with you this time."

She whispers, "Then don't go," as she nestles her face into my chest. I wish it was that easy. I wish this would not end. But it always does.

I focus on everything about her, the way her hair smells, the softness of her skin, the warmth of her body, how alive she feels. I try to lock the memories in my mind.

"I love you, Ann," I tell her quietly, knowing there isn't much time left. She does not answer, and I know why. Her body, her scent, her warmth fade away slowly. I continue to hold her until she is gone and I am alone in the snow once more.

I stand, watching the snow fall around me, for a moment. When I turn around, I see a crowd of townspeople, some with lanterns, others with torches or pitchforks. Angry and intolerant, the hate in their eyes is something I've seen before.

An older man in the front speaks first. "That's the one," he says to the others, pointing at me. "That's the one who killed Ann."

"No. I didn't," I start to protest. But before I can say anything else, the man raises his lantern. He tosses it at me, and it spirals through the air. It strikes me in the chest, knocking me to the ground, and explodes, spilling hot oil and flames over me.

As the fire consumes me, burning my clothes into my skin, I can only scream...

Letting a small cry leave my lips, I awake with a start, sitting up and sliding back against the headboard. I rub my hand over my chest. My skin still tingles where it had been burning just a moment ago.

I look over, but Claire is not in bed beside me, which is not uncommon. Since Luther was attacked, she has been leaving my room frequently, saying she does not want to get caught, and I want so badly to believe her that I overlook the possibility of another reason.

My door bursts open and Kate rushes to my side. "What happened? Are you all right?" She places her hands on either side of my face.

"I'm fine. It was just a nightmare." More like a dream since Ann was there.

I hold onto her wrist, keeping her hand against me. The way her fingers graze my skin reminds me of Ann's touch, making me close my eyes.

Feeling her weight shift on the bed, I know she is leaning toward me even before she presses her lips to my forehead. "Tell me. What was it about?" she says softly.

Ann. It was about Ann and it was wonderful. To have her holding me again. To see her standing in front of me. It was worth being burned.

I open my eyes to see Claire standing in the doorway watching me. "The sun," I lie. "I was burning in the daylight." Although I'm not looking at her, she knows I am lying and walks away.

Kate knows too and says, "It was about Ann, wasn't it?"

With Claire gone, I can afford to be honest. "I miss her." I say vulnerably.

Kate nods and takes my hand. "Nick, if you're serious about starting something with Claire next year, you're going to have to let her go."

She's right, of course, not about waiting until next year, but still. "What if I can't?"

"You mean won't," she corrects. "It's not fair to ask someone to share you with a woman who has been dead for more than five hundred years."

I give her a sharp look. "You can stop talking about Ann now." Defensively, I add, "We're done here."

"Well, I'm not," she snaps. "She's dead, Nick. It wasn't your fault. You couldn't have saved her. And you sure as hell can't change it." She stands up so that she's looking down at me. "You've grieved long enough. It's time to get over it."

I stand up to face her. "Get out of my room," I tell her coldly.

"Nick—" she starts, but I interrupt her.

"You know where the door is. I suggest you use it."

Irritably, she huffs and stomps away. When she reaches the door, she sighs and her shoulders relax. She turns toward me, and there is kindness in her eyes. "I know you think you can love two people at the same time. And maybe you're right. But between loving Ann and loving yourself, that doesn't leave much room for anyone else," she says.

She walks out as I sit down on the edge of the bed. I know Kate means well. I know she cares about me.

"Kate," I call softly.

I hate lying to her. It eats me up inside. I'm supposed to be her best friend. Best friends don't keep secrets from each other. At least they shouldn't.

Kate steps back into my doorway with her coat on, and it distracts me from what I intended to ask. "Are you going somewhere?" I ask instead.

She nods. "Marcella and Luther are already training. I told them I'd meet up with them. We'll probably only be out for another hour or so."

"Oh." They are leaving me alone with Claire. They really trust me all too much. That will only make mine and Claire's secret seem that much more deceitful. "When you get back, there's something I need to tell you."

I do not believe that telling Kate about Claire and me is the best decision. But really, I don't base the majority of my choices on good judgment.

"Do you want to tell me now?" she asks. "I don't have to leave. I could just stay with you."

In no hurry to disappoint Kate, I shake my head. "We'll talk later," I insist.

I see the hesitation in her eyes. She's unsure whether she should leave me, so I smile, making her feel better about going.

Smiling back, she blows me a kiss. "Goodnight."

I pretend to catch her kiss in the air. "Goodnight."

After she's gone, I get out of bed and go upstairs. I find Claire reading a book in the library with her legs draped over the arm of the chair. I watch her swing her feet for a moment before I walk over behind her. Placing my hands on her shoulders, I kiss her neck gently.

"Mm," she moans. She twists around to face me, dropping the book from her lap. "I love the way your lips feel on my skin."

"I don't exactly hate it," I tell her.

She smiles at me, biting her lip and grazing my cheek with her warm hand. "Are you going to tell me about your dream?" she asks.

Reluctant to answer, I sigh lightly, keeping my face close to hers. "People were blaming me for Ann's death." That may not be the only thing that happened, but Claire does not need to know everything. "They did in real life, too, but this time they said it to my face, and they burned me for it."

"Oh, my poor baby," she says seductively. Her hand slides down my chest. "Surely there is something I can do to make you forget all about that bad dream."

I won't forget it. I'm not sure I even want to. But I like where this is going. "I can think of a few things," I say. And trust me, I can. "But you'll have to give me a minute first." I haven't fed much these past few weeks, and the burning in my throat is becoming unbearable.

I press my lips gently to hers. "I'll be right back," I tell her. Then I kiss her one more time before I stand up.

Taking my hand, she says, "Hurry."

I give her my lopsided grin, "I definitely will." Although I do not want to, I walk out of the library, and start upstairs toward Lilah's bedroom.

As I reach the top of the staircase, I smell two separate aromas in the air. The first is a very distinctive form of roses, which I know to be Claire. She was up here recently, and the second scent tells me why.

Faint but unmistakable, it grows thicker as I approach the bedroom door. Knowing what I will find, I grudgingly knock, "Lilah."

Nobody answers, much as I expected. I push the door open. Lying on the bed as though she had simply been tossed there is my Lilah. Cold and lifeless, her heart does not beat, no breath leaves her lips, and her thin frail arm is draped across her face.

Sighing, I walk to her limp body and slide her arm away from her face so I can see the hollow paleness of her skin. Her mouth is slightly parted, and her hazel eyes are beginning to haze over.

I push her hair away from her neck, exposing the fang marks just below her jaw line. There is a bitter taste to accompany the scent of death that lingers around me. Not enough of her blood is left to make the air sweet or satisfying.

Claire lost control; this I know. But I tell myself that it does not mean anything. She lost control before we became involved too. She is young. It happens. Everything is fine.

I continue to push away any thoughts that link Claire's lack of restraint to me until I notice a puncture on Lilah's wrist peeking out from under her shirtsleeve.

I shove her sleeve up to find the other half of the bite mark that has already begun to heal, and I know, deep down, that this is not a solitary incident.

Pulling at her sleeve, I rip the material up to her shoulder. On her arm are six sets of fang marks, some of which are several days old. This is only one arm; I know that much of her body will have a similar appearance. There is no reason that Claire should need to feed every day. Well, there is one reason. A bloodlust. One that I caused. One that will get worse.

My stomach churns with distress. Part of me is sickened at what I have done to Claire, and part of me does not mind her appetite so much. I could hide this from the others, pretend that I killed Lilah, which in a way, I did. But that wouldn't help Claire in the long run.

I start down the stairs quietly, fumbling my fingers around each other. I wish I could forget what I just saw and take Claire in my arms as I had planned to. But I cannot.

Waiting at the bottom of the stairs is Claire, smiling as though there was nothing to see upstairs. But her smile fades as I approach seriously.

I stop in front of her. I place my hands in front of my mouth for a moment before I ask, "Why didn't you tell me?"

She can hear in my voice that I am not talking about Lilah's death so much as I am asking about the numerous bites over the last few days. I could have helped her, taken care of it before it became a problem.

"It would have changed things between us. It doesn't have to though." She rubs her hand up my chest. "We could just go on as before."

Tempting as that sounds, and believe me, it's tempting, I take her hand in mine. "This bloodlust, it's progressing," I say, unable to meet her eyes.

She puts her other hand on my cheek, making me look at her. "I can handle it," she insists.

I wish that were true, but it is obvious that she cannot. Leaning my forehead against hers, I say the hardest thing I can think of, "I don't think I can do this anymore."

"Shh," she tells me gently. "Of course, you can." Taking my hands, she wraps them around her waist, and strokes my cheek with her fingers. "I know you want me. Like I want you." She leans her mouth close to mine. "I'm yours for the taking," she whispers, sending a heat through my body.

For a moment, I let her kiss me, losing myself to my desires. I long for this moment to last, but it doesn't. My thoughts circle around what is best for her and, ultimately, for all of us.

Holding her shoulders, I push her away gently. "No," I say, though it does not sound as strong as I intended.

Her eyebrows draw together and she shoves me away forcefully. "I want blood, Nicolas," she snaps. "I want yours, but Harvey's will do in a pinch." She steps closer to me, closing the distance between us, and pokes her finger in my chest. "His death will be on your hands, not mine."

There is something about her strength and power that pulls me toward her, weakening my sense of right and wrong, making it a struggle for me to tell her, "I can handle that guilt."

She leans close to me, trailing her finger along my jaw. "We'll see about that." There is a chill in her voice that wasn't there before, proving that it is her thirst driving her now.

Walking away from me, she lets her hand glide across my chest. I could stop her. I know I could. I am stronger and faster than she is, and, let's face it, I know more about being a vampire. But I also know how much she wants to drink. I have been there before. No real control, no conscience telling you to stop. Raw animalistic desires propelling your every move. It is not something I wanted for her. But here we are.

I grab her hand, making her look at me. "Be gentle," I try.

Pulling away from me, her eyes change to black. She scoffs at my request and starts up the stairs.

I slump down onto the step, listening to the stillness of the house. Two humans will be dead because of me. That normally does not bother me so much except these are not just any humans. They are ones that we somewhat care about, our sheep. Harvey is, or was, Kate's favorite. So kind and caring, like a child.

After a brief moment, I hear a light thump on the floor above me. It's the sound of Harvey's body hitting the hardwood. I should go upstairs and place him on the bed as though he was not so thoughtlessly discarded. It may help lessen Kate's inevitable anger toward me. But I don't want to see him like that.

I sit patiently, waiting for Claire, until she walks down the stairs effortlessly.

"Oh, Nicolas," she says. "Why do you make me do such things?"

"I didn't make you do that," I say, though I know it's mostly my fault. "You chose to hide this from me when I could've helped."

She stops in front of me. Rising her dress, she slides onto my lap, straddling me. "Wouldn't it be easier just to give me what I want?" she asks, running her fingers along my chest.

Yes, that would be easy. It would be so very easy. "Claire, you need to go downstairs," I say.

She places her cheek against mine. "Why?" she whispers.

Her tongue slides along my ear. She bites gently on the lobe, making me close my eyes as my breath quickens. I am losing my willpower. Losing to her. My only resort is to lie. "I want you to wait for me."

She leans away to look at my eyes as I open them. "I have to get rid of the bodies, and then I will be down," I say. "Because you're right, I do want you."

She smiles, thinking that she's won. "Don't take too long." She presses her lips to mine.

She stands up and walks away, watching me over her shoulder and making me wish I could follow her.

I listen to her footsteps as she goes through the kitchen and down to the basement.

Sighing, I drop my head into my hands. What a mess I've created. I know I was planning on telling Kate anyway, but not Luther and definitely not Marcella. Now, with Claire's growing bloodlust, it will only make this harder to explain. I knew the risks and chose to ignore them, doesn't have a very nice ring to it.

I know I should remove the bodies and bury them in the backyard. But I sit very still on the steps with my guilt and wait for the others.

Time goes slowly as it often does when one waits for something. But after nearly an hour, I hear Marcella's laughter outside.

Sitting up straight, I ready myself. They will all be angry. Marcella will mostly likely forgive me and Luther will be easily disregarded. Those I can handle. But Kate will be hurt. Hurt by me.

Nervousness takes me over. My stomach churns and twists. My chest grows heavy. If I could sweat, my palms would be.

As the door opens, I swallow hard, but it does not help to clear the lump in my throat. Marcella walks in, followed by Kate and Luther. They're holding hands, which if I weren't already queasy would have made me nauseous anyway. The air in the house is unsettlingly still, and they feel it as soon as they enter.

"Where is Claire?" Marcella asks, and I can hear the concern in her voice which is seldom present.

"Downstairs," I say.

She walks over to me and bends down so that her face is inches from mine. "Where are the sheep?" she says coolly.

Kate steps toward us with worry in her eyes, and I have to look away from her. "I messed up," I tell them quietly.

"Harvey?" Kate calls with a shaky voice. She hurries to the stairs. "Harvey?"

As she pushes past me, I stand up, grabbing her hand. "Don't."

She jerks her hand away, knowing what she will see upstairs, and slaps me in the face. "Why would you do that?" she shouts as tears fill her eyes.

"Harvey was mine. Mine, Nick." She shoves me back against the railing. "You had no right."

Clearly she is hurt and angry which she should be, "I didn't kill him. But I didn't even try to stop Claire." Exhaling forcefully, I run my fingers through my hair, "I'm sorry, Kate."

I try to take Kate's hand, but she pushes mine away as she tries, unsuccessfully, to hold back her tears. I hate to watch her cry, knowing it could have been prevented.

"What did you do?" Marcella asks with accusation in her tone.

Exactly what I promised I wouldn't. Neglected to think of anyone but myself. "I think you know." I tell her.

In a flash she is in front of me. Grabbing my face and lifts me off of the ground, she slams my back into the wall. With black eyes, she hisses, exposing her fangs. Her fingernails dig into my cheeks, and I can smell the blood before I feel it run down my skin.

She tosses me to the floor, making me tumble down the steps.

I land on my back on the cold foyer floor with Luther leaning over me, smirking. "Figures you couldn't keep a promise."

Getting up, I push him away. "Stop talking, Luther. This doesn't concern you." I order as my cheeks heal.

"Like hell it doesn't," he snaps.

I grab him by the collar and drag him to me. "Watch your mouth. There are ladies present." If there's one thing I can't stand it is disrespect. "And I will not tell you again."

"I'm a part of this family, too," he insists.

I let go of him and he backs up slightly. "You're right, but until you contribute, you haven't earned your place."

Marcella walks to us, graceful as ever. "That's enough. I've had it with the bickering." Turning to me, she says, "Nick, Luther may not help us," Finally, she admits that. "But at least he doesn't hurt us." Ouch.

He smirks at me, making my eyes narrow on him.

"Now," she begins, "We all know how to fix this," Marcella says.

My heart sinks just a little more. "No, Marcella," I plead. "There has to be a better way."

"Either we starve it out of her or we end her life, Nicolas. You should know better than anyone. You went through this once yourself, remember?"

How could I forget? The countless nights coiled in pain. The endless hunger taking over my every thought. The burning, a fire worse than any flame, searing my throat.

She continues, "Which is why I am surprised you could be so callous."

A knot begins to form in my stomach. "How long?" I ask weakly.

She places her hand on my shoulder, making me look up at her, "At least a month."

A month is miserable even without a bloodlust driving you, much longer than any of us prefer to go without drinking and considerably more difficult for a young vampire. But if Claire has to do it, so will I.

I nod slowly. "I'll tell her."

Marcella's grip tightens on my shoulder, pushing her fingers into my muscles. "You will say nothing to her." She orders, "If I even catch you in the same room with Claire over the next year, I'll kill her." She leans close to my face, "It's either you or her, and I'm not about to lose my son, even though you disappoint me." She walks away, leaving me without solace.

Luther slaps me on the back, knocking me forward. "You know, Nick, you always say that all vampires are selfish. But have you ever stopped to think that maybe it's just you?"

Damn. I hate when he's right. I glare at him, but Kate is by his side in a flash. She takes his hand and leads him out of the room without so much as a kind look my way.

Exhaling miserably, I sit down on the steps again. Alone with my despair and anguish, all I can do is think of everyone I've let down, including myself.

*   *   *

Even though a week has passed, we seem to be no closer to an end. Claire's painful screams have become continuous, broken only by her whimpering. The fire inside her must be insatiable. Her ravenous hunger is pushing her to feast, but she cannot let her control falter.

Sitting in the hallway beside her bedroom door, I listen to her constant cries, knowing I can do nothing. I keep my head in my hands and my knees drawn to my chest.

Focusing on my breathing, I try to ignore the way my guilt eats at me, the way the remorse in the pit of my stomach nauseates me. I would rather be anywhere than here, listening to her screams.

Not even the light footsteps that stop close to me distract me from my anguish.

"Let's go for a walk," Kate says softly.

I look up at her, hiding the pain in my eyes. "I deserve to hear this."

She bends down next to me and places her hand on mine. "Yes, but unlike you, I don't deserve this and I need a break. So please take me for a walk."

Kate should not have to listen to this, I know, and the thought of escaping the sounds of Claire's agony is tempting. I stand up and take her hand. "Come on."

We make our way outside, into the snow that falls around us. We walk across the yard, leaving tracks in the thick white blanket, before Claire's shrieking finally fades and the silence is relieving to us both.

"Nicolas?" Kate starts. I glance over at her but she keeps her eyes on the ground. "Do you love Claire?"

I look away, biting my lip. Truthfully, I'm not sure how I feel about her, but I know I must take care how I answer. Kate has a way of telling people things they weren't meant to hear. "I think I could," I respond, and I look at Kate again, trying to gauge her response. "It's like you said, I just need to let myself love her."

Keeping her head down, she exhales forcefully, letting the heat from her breath cloud the air. "I wasn't talking about her the other night." Confused, I watch as she rubs her arm nervously. "I'm thinking of ending it with Luther."

Although I do not really see the connection between her comments, I tell her, "You should. He's an imbecile. A complete waste of your time."

She does not meet my eyes, and I begin to feel guilty about being insensitive. "I'm sorry. What happened?"

Looking at me, she says, "I fell for somebody else."

"Really?" Finally, she wants to rid herself of him. Smiling, I nudge her with my elbow, "What's he like?"

She blushes, "Well, he's usually considerate, especially about me. He, um, always knows how to make me feel better."

Sounds like quite a catch. "He must be great. He really should be considerate to you all the time, though."

She smiles at me, "Everybody has flaws." But her smile fades quickly as she looks toward the ground again. "And I'm prepared to overlook yours." I stop walking.

Surely, I misunderstood her just now.

She turns toward me. Taking a deep breath, she says, "I'm in love with you, Nick."

Nope, I didn't misunderstand. "Don't say things like that, Kate. Once they're out there, you can't take them back."

"I don't want to take it back."

I sigh. I really do not want this for us. "Don't leave Luther for me."

She takes my hand. "You can't be with Claire for at least a year. I'm here now."

"This has nothing to do with Claire." And it doesn't. "This is about us. We're perfect the way we are."

She places her hand on my cheek. Her touch is so natural that I do not even shy away from it. "We could be so much better."

I can tell by her tone that she believes it.

"You don't have to love me," she says. "You could pretend I was someone else when you kiss me."

I put my hands on her neck with my fingers grazing her jaw line. "I would never pretend that. I wouldn't have to. You're more beautiful than you'll ever know." Even though I'm not attracted to her, what I said is true. "You're smart and cunning, the perfect vampire," I continue. "But if you spend your time with me, you could miss the man you're meant to be with. This isn't a rejection. It's me saving you. Saving you from me." I pull her close and wrap my arms around her.

I kiss her on the top of her head. "I care about you, Kate. That's why I can't do this."

Her arms tighten around my waist as I hear her sniff quietly. I do feel bad knowing that it hurts her, but in the grand scheme of things, it's better this way.

I hold her for a long time, as long as she needs me to, until she looks up at me. "Take me home," she says quietly.

Nodding, I take her hand and lead her toward the house. I wait for her to speak, but she says nothing. She only leans her head against my shoulder, letting me know that she'll be all right.

As we approach our house, I begin to worry. It's much too still, too quiet. Where is the incessant screaming, the deep scratching of fingernails along the stone walls of the basement?

I quicken our stride as much as I can without making Kate aware that I'm concerned about Claire.

When we finally go inside, Luther is pacing the foyer. He looks at me with apprehension in his eyes. "Claire's missing."

A heat charges through me, and I shove him back. "You idiot. You had one job to do, which you only had to do for five minutes. But I guess that too much for you."

Five minutes, that's it and he failed. Failed at something that we could not afford for him to screw up. I knew I shouldn't have left him alone with her. I knew he was incapable of even the most simple of tasks.

"Don't start with me, Nick," he snaps. He steps closer to me with his face in mine. "We wouldn't be in this situation if it wasn't for you."

"That's true," I shout back. "Because if I had let those wolves kill you, someone else would have been watching Claire and she would never have gotten away."

Before he has time to respond, Kate's hands are on our chests pushing us apart. "This isn't helping," she says.

I take a deep breath, trying to control my fury.

"I'm sorry, Nick," Luther says. "We all make mistakes."

He would know that better than anyone. "Don't talk to me." I snap and point to the door. "Just find her."

Kate nods and takes Luther's hand. "Stay here, Nicolas. In case she comes back."

That's a terrible idea but I nod anyway.

They leave together but split up not far into the yard. As soon as they're gone, I go, too. There is no way I am sitting out on searching for Claire. It's too important that we find her. If Claire exposes herself, not only will the humans try to kill her, but they will look for more vampires, putting us all in harm's way.

It takes longer than I expect to catch her scent. She had attempted to cover it up by using Marcella's perfume, and she was better at it than I would have suspected.

With her scent mostly masked, it's no wonder the others could not pick it up. I, on the other hand, am not only the best tracker in the house, but I know the way she smells better than anyone else.

Once I have her trail, I bolt across the yard, jump the fence between our neighbor's field and ours, and sprint as hard as I can. I can't help but wonder why she went this direction. There isn't much out here, and there are quicker ways to reach the city. But perhaps she is not heading for the city. Perhaps she's heading for...

I see it at the same time I think it. The hospital. Of course. Marcella showed her where it was. It's the only place Claire knows.

If my legs could burn and ache, they would be as I charge up the hill to the vacant-looking building. I burst through the doors unsure of what I expect to see.

Slumped over the desk is the night clerk, Beth. I walk over to her and push her hair aside to see her neck. Fresh puncture wounds stare back at me. Claire was here.

A piercing scream grabs my attention, forcing me to look toward the double doors as they swing open. A young blond nurse rushes down the hallway toward me with fear and panic scrolled across her face. She runs past me without even slowing to tell me what she is afraid of. I guess, Claire is still here.

I dart to the doors and push them open slowly, careful not to add to the excitement in the room. Blood streaks across the stark white walls. Beds are flipped over and tossed aside, bodies discarded on the floor. A woman crouches in the corner with her hands covering her face, shaking and weeping violently, too frightened to run.

In the center of the room is Claire, eyes black as night, fangs exposed in a hiss, fingernails dripping with the blood of her many victims.

As an older patient starts to run past her, she grabs him by the hair, jerking him back. Opening her mouth wide, she goes for his throat.

"Stop!" I shout.

With her fangs close to his skin, she pauses. Although her eyes are black, I can tell she's looking at me.

"Drop him," I order.

She stands up straight and lets her fingers slide out of the man's hair. He scoots away as fast as he can, but in reality, he is not fast enough to escape a vampire.

I walk over to her urgently. Placing my hands along her jaw line, I tell her calmly, "You have to stop this, Claire."

Her eyes change back to the soft blue I'm used to as tears fill her bottom lid, "Help me," she says weakly.

My heart goes out to her. How couldn't it? I did this to her for my own selfish reasons and now she stands in front of me, vulnerable and rampant. "You're sick, that's all."

She wraps her arms around me, and for a moment everything else is forgotten. We are not standing in a room painted red with blood. Not listening to the scared sniveling and whimpering. Not able to smell the fear around us.

I haven't felt her in so long, and I don't want to let her go, but that does not change the circumstances. The longer we stay, the more danger we put our family in.

"We need to go," I whisper.

She looks up at me from a tear-streaked face and nods.

I lead her toward the double doors, but something catches my eye. I stop, letting her hand slide out from mine as she keeps walking. On the floor next to a patient's bed is a small, brown teddy bear. I do not see its ragged appearance or its missing ear, the mismatched button eyes or faded pink nose. I only see the stains of crimson splattered across its chest and a small, human hand outstretched toward it from under the bed.

Not wanting to think about the pale, unmoving child that hand belongs to, I look away, keeping my eyes to the ground. I hear footsteps coming from the other side of the double doors and shout, "Claire, wait!"

But I'm too late. She pulls the doors open and the human on the other side of the doors is waiting with a broken chair leg raised in the air. She looks up at him as brings it down toward her. Deep down, I know she could stop him, but she does not even try.

He drives the stake into her chest and she begins to fall back just as I reach them. I slam his head into the door hard enough to make him slump over, unconscious. I turn as Claire's body hits the floor and shatters into ashes.

I drop to my knees, my mind unable to accept what my eyes have just witnessed. She is gone. She is really gone. I scoop up what is left of her, just a handful of ashes, nothing more, and let them slip through my fingers as tears fill my eyes. But the funny thing about pain is that sometimes it makes you angry.

Making a fist around the ash, I let my eyes phase to black. My fangs extend and press into my lips. I drop the ash beside me and stand up. I'm not sure how Marcella is going to clean this up, but I will do my part by shortening the list of witnesses. I walk to the unconscious man. Placing my hands on either side of his face and twist quickly, separating his head from his body. I hurl the head into the far wall and let out an angry scream but it doesn't make me feel any better. I kick his body, sending it down the hallway and into the lobby.

Just then the elevator doors open, but before the three nurses can make a run for it, I'm in front of them. I step into the elevator and slice one nurse's neck open with my fingernails, spilling blood onto the floor. As she falls, I slam another nurse's face into the wall hard enough to hear her skull crack. That just leaves the middle nurse. Rightfully afraid, she backs against the wall and screams as I step closer to her. But mercy has left me. Grabbing her hair, I pull her head to the side and expose her neck and sink my teeth in her soft flesh.

Her blood cools my burning throat, easing some of my physical pain, but my thirst is never fully satisfied.

I let her body fall to the floor when I hear someone running in the hallway. Reaching out of the elevator at just the right time, I grab the woman who had been crying in the corner by the throat and pull her to me. I slide my fingers to her chin and twist, listening for the break and feeling nothing when I hear her neck snap. I open my hand and let her lifeless body to the floor.

I walk out of the elevator to see a young boy standing in front of the double doors. With his eyes opened wide and pupils dilated, I can smell his fear.

Wiping the blood from the corner of my mouth with my thumb, I stare at him with black eyes. I want to tell him to run, but knowing that I would chase him if he did, I say nothing. Someone exits the stairwell beside the boy, and it takes me a moment to realize that it is Nurse Klein.

Startled by my appearance, she steps in front of the boy to shield him. "Nathaniel," she says to me, and I remember that's the name I used here. "I know you don't want to hurt anyone." Wrong. "And you're going to let us walk out of here." Wrong. "I trust you." Mistake.

"It's all right," she whispers to the boy, who's peering around her hip at me.

She walks toward me, trying to appear confident, but I can tell by her erratic breathing that she's nervous. She keeps her eyes to the ground, either because she believes making eye contact would only provoke me or she simply finds it unnerving.

I stand very still, watching them until they're beside me. Grabbing her upper arm, I make her look at me and give her a cruel, cold smile.

Letting go of the boy's hand, she shouts, "Run, Alexander!"

He does not hesitate and takes off down the hallway. But lucky for him, I am distracted by another. I press Nurse Klein's back against the wall. Leaning close to her, I inhale the smell of her cold sweat.

Between her uneven breaths, she says, "If you're going to kill people, you should kill the right ones."

I look at her, intrigued. "Every human sins. What makes one better than any other?"

"Nothing. A life is a life, but"—she pushes my hand from her arm and I let her—"some lives are not worth living."

I place my hand on either side of her so that she will not attempt to run. "Some lives hurt others," she says.

By her tone, I suppose she has someone in mind. "I know better than to play God. It's not my place to pass judgment," I tell her.

"There is a man upstairs. Eighth bed on the right." Here it comes. "He's a rapist. He doesn't deserve to live." She lays her hand on my chest lightly. "Promise me that you'll take his life after you take mine."

There is something in her voice, though I'm not sure what it is. It could be deceit, but I do not care if it's a lie. She wants someone dead, and so do I.

Dropping one of my arms, I nod toward the exit, "Go."

She must know that my offer will not last long because she slides along the wall away from me and hurries toward the lobby.

I walk up the stairs, listening to the panic above me. My inability to smell Claire here proves to me that she never left the first floor which is why there are so many footsteps scurrying across the floor.

When I reach the second floor, I see a surprisingly empty hallway. A wheelchair is flipped on its side, blocking the stairs. There is a doctor and nurse I don't recognize holding what appears to be a rope made from bed sheets that's hanging out of a broken window. But other than that there is not much to see.

Two patients and an orderly run past without noticing me in the stairway. I grab one of the patients, digging my fingernails into his neck. His blood streams around my fingers and the smell tickles my nose delightfully.

My teeth are in him before he even realizes what's happening. I toss his body, and as it tumbles down the stairs, I look to my right at the makeshift rope. The orderly hurries the other patient onto the rope as I walk toward them slowly, letting their fear resonate in the narrow space. As the orderly climbs onto the rope, I rush to them, making him nearly lose his grip. Grabbing the doctor's white jacket, I slam his body into one wall and then the other so violently quick and hard that I do not need to throw him out of the window to ensure his death but I do it anyway.

The nurse, a young brunette, lets out a scream but does not take her eyes away from the broken window. Without the help of the doctor, she struggles with the weight of the rope. I stop next to her quivering body where her soft sobbing is more than apparent and glance out of the window. Hanging onto the knotted sheets below are three patients and the orderly, attempting to make an escape. Looking back at the nurse, I watch her fight to keep from dropping the rope. Her feet slide across the floor slowly toward the window, but still she does not let go. Placing my foot in front of hers to stop her progression forward, I lean close to her terrified face, forcing her to glance at me. When she does, her crying increases, making the vein in her neck push out further. Just the sight of it makes my mouth water and my pulse quicken.

As a tear rolls over her lip, she pleads, "Please."

I have said it before, humans will never understand how their fear entices us. How her begging only makes me want this so much more. "Don't say that. It tempts me," I tell her.

"What should I say?" she stammers out between sobs.

With a chill in my voice, I tell her, "Nothing."

I move my foot and she slides across the floor once more, making her cry out again. I make my way back down the hallway, listening to her relentless battle with the rope, and stop at the wheelchair.

It is true that I do not care if those people live, but she could have dropped them to save herself, or at least attempted to save herself. But she didn't. Even now as she can feel the inevitability of losing her battle with the heavy load she bears, she tries to help them.

Picking up the wheelchair, I walk back to the nurse. I set the chair down in front of the window, and motion for her to hand me the rope.

Still weeping, she shakes her head. "Just let them make it," she tries. But she is mistaken as to what I intend to do. Prying her fingers loose, I take the rope from her gently. She only cries harder, probably feeling as though she has failed them. But I do something she did not imagine from me. Putting my foot on the chair, I tie the end of the bed sheet to it tightly.

Worry and confusion smear her pretty face as she watches me. I remove my foot from the wheelchair, and it flies up, thumping into the window frame with a loud crash from the weight of the people on it. One or more of them may have been jolted off, but really I wasn't trying to help them.

Without the chair between us, I step toward her and lean my face close to hers, "Run."

She pushes past me and sprints for the stairs. I could catch her, but I let her go. No sooner than she is gone, I turn to the makeshift rope and slice through it with a fingernail, sending the wheelchair colliding into the floor, and the people on the rope, well, they fall too.

Hurrying down the hallway, I push through another set of double doors and walk into a room similar to the one downstairs except there are fewer patients and the walls are still crisp white.

Letting my fingers trail over the railings of the beds, I count them to myself until I reach the eighth bed on the right. I take the chart from the foot of the bed and look at the name. Noah Peterson. Doesn't look like a rapist. But I am already here, I might as well finish it. I read further for the diagnosis. Pneumonia, not something I need to worry about catching. I toss the chart behind me.

An older man, he sleeps with one hand draped over the edge of the bed, clenched into a fist. He must be very ill not to have noticed the chaos around him. I pull back the blanket, revealing his neck and bite into his flesh.

His blood burns my throat when it should cool it, but the taste is sugary so I ignore that and drink until the sweetness of it sours in my stomach. Clutching my abdomen, I drop to my knees from the burning inside. My vision begins to blur until I see hazy doubles and my muscles grow weaker by the second. I am not sure what is happening until the man's hand relaxes and a rosary falls to the floor. A priest. I should have known.

My breathing becomes difficult, and I feel as though I am choking on what little air I'm able to suck in. With pain cramping my stomach and my hands trembling, I collapse, smacking my cheek on the cold tile. I can feel warm blood begin to trickle from my nose, but I am too feeble to wipe it away.

As I strain to keep my eyes open, I see three people walk toward me. The one in white bends down near me and it is easy to recognize her voice. "Guess you should have run, too," Nurse Klein says coldly.

As my eyes close, I hear her address the two soldiers. "Those wolves said we only have a few hours. Get him in the truck. And make it quick."

Then everything goes black.

Chapter 10

Damp and stale, the air smells of mildew, which only adds to the unrelenting pounding in my head that makes me leery of opening my eyes, afraid that any amount of light would only make it worse. But with the musky, wooded taste on my lips, I know I have to. After all, there are werewolves nearby.

The light does not disappoint my expectations, sending a sharp pinch of pain straight through me. I try not to move, knowing it would draw attention to me. My body feels unusually heavy and weak as it presses into the bars of a not so comfortable cot.

"What a shame," I hear a deep voice say. "The leech lives."

Knowing my cover is blown, I look around the large space. Cold block walls line the perimeter, giving way to only one doorway. A heavy oak desk sits nearby along the wall, alone and rigid. Bars surround me, separating me from the other prisoners. From what I smell, they are all werewolves, so I do not mind the partitions. There are four wolves, two women, two men, all staring at me.

I sit up, moaning from the stiffness of my body and holding the back of my throbbing head.

I know which direction the voice came from but still I ask, "Which one of you dogs just called me a leech?"

A low growl ripples through the room. I thought that might make an impression.

The deep voice booms again, "That'd be me."

The prison cells make an "L" shape in the room, and I turn my eyes to a large man that is diagonal from me. With broad shoulders and well-defined muscles straining against his shirt, he reminds me of Luther, except his skin is pale white and his curly black hair is messy and out of place.

I shrug. "Figures. You're such a big guy, I'm sure you have a small"—I pause for effect—"mind." I give him smirk to just rile him and it works.

He grabs the bars and points to me. "You're dead, little man."

I laugh to myself. Surely, he does not realize how many times I've heard that before. But the chuckle only hurts my head, and I lay my forehead in my hands as a young human walks into the room.

Dressed in a German private's uniform, he sits down at the desk and looks at me with a sly smile. "Hope you're comfortable. You'll be here a while."

I lean back against the wall. "You should probably come in here and fluff my pillow then."

His eyes narrow but he says nothing. Looking down at a stack of papers, he begins shuffling through them aimlessly. I look around my cell more closely. It's reasonably small, with only the cot, a blanket, and a flat pillow.

In the cell to my right, an Irish-looking man is doing one-handed push- ups, perhaps in an attempt to intimidate me, which it does not.

His red hair and freckled skin give him a soft appearance even without the hint of kindness that's visible in his eyes.

To my left, a lovely woman glares at me with pale bluish-gray eyes. Her hair, so light that it appears almost white, hangs to the middle of her back. Her grip on the bars between us has her knuckles bleached.

"Easy, girl," I whisper to her, only making her clench her jaw.

I lie back on my tiny cot and stare at the ceiling and think of Claire. I remember the way she felt in my arms, the taste of her lips, the sound of her voice, her scent. Oh, what a wonderful scent. Delicate and airy, it lingers on my clothes even now.

As I lie there longing for her, a tear rolls down my face toward my ear. Keeping quiet, I let another tear fall.

"Ugh," I hear. "Stop that. You look like a baby."

I ignore the impulse to glance at the light-haired woman and keep looking at the ceiling.

She huffs. "Unfortunately, they don't plan on killing you," she says.

So that is what she assumes saddens me.

"I wish they would," I murmur, not intending for her to hear me.

I hear her body shift toward the bars, "Me too."

I look over at her with sadness in my eyes. "Please stop talking to me," I say, and then I roll onto my side to face the wall and pull the blanket over my head to further express my disinterest in the conversation. And she takes the hint.

Hearing the wolves moving around and murmuring to one another, it's hard to forget I'm not alone, even though I feel like I am, alone with my memories of Claire and my quiet guilt, knowing I could have done so many things differently. Had I changed just one, she would still be alive.

The blanket is thin enough to see the solemn block wall in front of me. I rub my fingers across the rough surface, imagining Claire beside me. Letting myself miss her. Letting myself feel the pain I have caused. Allowing the tears to come freely and stain my shirt sleeve.

I lie very still for some time before I begin to hear a whimpering near me. Wiping my face, I pull the blanket away and glance over to the next cell.

The light-haired woman is sleeping on her cot, dreaming of something unpleasant from what I can tell. Her muted whining noises resemble those of a puppy. She wrinkles her brow, and I wonder if it's me she's dreaming of.

Looking around the room, I notice that none of the other werewolves are sleeping instead they look slightly annoyed by her sounds. Even the Irish man to my right is staring at the ground and focusing on his breathing. Sighing, I get up and walk to the bars. From this distance, it's easy to pick apart which scent is hers. A blend of the forest and honey, it smells vaguely familiar, yet I know I have not encountered it before.

The Irish man watches me closely as I reach through the bars toward her. "Hey!" he yells. "What do you think you're doing?"

Probably nothing, as I am not sure this will even work in my current state. Putting my finger to my lips, I tell him to be quiet and with my other hand, I grab her ankle.

The Irish man and the other two wolves are on their feet no sooner than my skin touches hers. Despite the tension surging through the room, I let my mind roll over my faded memories of the sunrise.

"You see the daybreak up ahead," I whisper, giving her a new dream to imagine. "The glow warms your skin, making your unease melt away." I feel her body begin to relax. "Look at the way the dew on the grass gleams and reflects the colors in the sky." I paint a picture for her, and she does not fight my assistance. Her whimpering ceases. Her breathing calms.

"Stop that!" the shorter, dark-haired woman snaps at me.

Her sharp shout wakes the light-haired woman, and she kicks my hand off of her quickly. I pull my hand back into my cell as she walks to the bars.

"Don't. Ever. Touch me," she says harshly.

Rubbing my wrist where her heel dug into me, I tell her, "I was helping."

She leans her face toward me, "Nobody asked you to."

That burns through me, and I stand up to be level with her. "Just so you know, when you have a nightmare, you whine like a puppy and nobody else can sleep because of it. That doesn't bother me so much since I don't require sleep, but the rest of your pack was suffering through it. But don't worry your pretty little head over it, because it won't happen again."

As I walk back to the cot, the Irish man says, "I don't mind the whining, Tara." He is lying, but that isn't what I notice. The light-haired woman is named Tara. Since he is groveling to her, she's probably married to someone high in the chain of command. At least, higher than the Irish man.

The werewolves' hierarchy of positions is archaic. Single females are at the bottom of the pack, unable to give orders to anyone else. It is only when they marry that they are given a title by assuming as much power as their husband.

The respect the other wolves show her suggests that she's probably married to the alpha, and since he is not here, she's the leader, even if they don't like it.

Sitting on my cot, I hear, "I don't like to not be in control of myself," Tara says to me, not with kindness but with understanding. "So I would appreciate you not doing that again."

I smile softly at her. "Now, was that so hard?" She looks at me curiously, "What?"

"Playing nice."

Rolling her eyes, she exhales forcefully and walks to her cot as three guards walk in carrying bowls. Two of the Nazi guards give their bowls to the werewolves and then leave as quickly as they entered. The other Nazi stops in front of me.

The wolves begin to eat whatever is in the bowls, though it does not smell appealing while the Nazi in front of me stirs a spoon around. "Want some?" he asks mockingly.

Not really, I think. But I walk over to him anyway and peek into the bowl at the lumpy porridge, or what's supposed to be porridge.

I reach for it and he moves it away. "What's the magic word?" he asks.

I drop my hand. There is no way I am saying please to this joke of a person.

"He doesn't even need it," Tara tells the guard.

"Shut your mouth, bitch," he snaps.

I don't know if he meant a female dog by that or not, but it does not matter. Before he can react, I grab his collar and slam him into the bars, making him spill the porridge on his pants.

Putting my feet on the bars so that I can put my weight into it, I pull myself toward him. "That's not a very nice thing to say." I state coldly, "Apologize."

Even without taking my eyes away from him, I can see the look of confusion on Tara's face.

Though he struggles with his face pressed into the bars, he still manages an attempt to say, "Sorry."

I let him go, hopping off of the bars and he wipes off his pants with his hand, irritably.

I smirk at him and say, "Guess you should learn some of those magic words, too."

He looks up at me sharply and spits in my face.

Oh, what pleasure I will have teaching this man about respect. Wiping the saliva from my cheek with my shirt sleeve, I tell him, "You just made my list."

"What list is that?" he asks.

The list of people I will kill if given the chance. "You'll see."

He walks to the desk and motions for the young Nazi to move. "Get up," he orders, though both seem to be privates.

"No, Joseph," the other private says.

Since they're soldiers, Joseph is probably a last name, but at least it is a name to attach to that dark hair and those beady eyes.

"Come on, Butler. You've been sitting all day."

It is obvious they haven't been around vampires much, because if they had, they would know better than to give their real names, especially to one as vengeful as me.

Their bickering stops when a captain walks in. Jumping to their feet, they come to attention. But the hard-looking captain is not watching them, his eyes are on me. "It's time," he states.

Butler hurries to my cell door with keys jingling in his hand. My mouth waters at the very thought of him getting close enough to kill.

But before the key is in the lock, the captain speaks again. "Let the wolves out first."

"Yes, sir," Butler stammers out, embarrassed by his simple error. He starts toward Tara's cell but then stops. "Finn or Tara?"

"Both," the captain tells him harshly.

Butler opens the cell door, and Tara emerges slowly, as though she does not entirely trust him. Then he walks to the cell of the Irish man, or Finn, and lets him out as well before coming to my door again.

Leaning close to the bars, I roll my tongue over my teeth expecting to feel fangs, but finding none. "Your blood smells light and sweet. My favorite," I whisper with a chill in my voice.

He looks at me with fear in his eyes, but he shoves the key in the lock anyway and turns it, grinding metal against metal. As Butler opens my cell door, Finn grabs something from the desk, though I do not see exactly what it is. Before I can step out, Finn walks in, stopping a few feet away from me.

"If you so much as sniff at me, I will not hesitate to bring you down," he says.

"Well as long as you don't try to mark me as your territory, we shouldn't have a problem," I say sarcastically.

He huffs and walks up to me, bringing the object he took from the desk between us. With a better view, I can see that it is a long pole with a thick leather strap on one end, and I know what it's for.

Taking the strap by the buckle, Finn wraps it around my neck, and tightens it. The leather pulls, twisting my skin. I grab at the strap. "Easy," I tell him.

He fastens the buckle, and as he pulls his hands away, I snap at him playfully. He yanks his hand away quickly, making me laugh to myself.

But he isn't laughing. He takes the pole and jerks me forward roughly. "You don't listen very well." He leans close to me, "But you will."

I doubt that. "I think you've forgotten who's on the top of the food chain. Here's a hint, it's not you," I say to him with more assertiveness than he expected.

"That's enough, ladies," the captain states as he walks toward us. "You can have a pissing contest all damn day, but you're on my time now." He nods his head toward the door. "Get moving."

Finn pulls me out of the cell, and I have to put my hands on the pole to keep the strap from digging into my neck. He moves quickly, going faster than is comfortable for my slower, weaker body.

At the door he stops abruptly, letting the pole push into my throat, hard, and I can hear him chuckle to himself as I let a hiss slip from my lips.

I am sure the dim lights do not make it easy for the humans to make out anything in here. Not that there's much to see, just more gray stone and mortar, a dirty floor, and a few wooden doors.

I walk along, struggling each time Finn jerks me forward. From the corner of my eye, I watch Tara. Keeping her head down, she walks quietly, thinking of something that seems to me to be almost sad.

"Tara?" I whisper to her, but she doesn't respond. I glance at Finn, but he didn't hear me so I try again. "Tara?" Still she ignores me. "Are you okay?" I ask.

Her eyes dart side to side, and she purses her mouth as though she wants to say something but does not.

"You're probably not supposed to talk to me," I tell her. "You don't have to say anything. Just listen."

I readjust my hands on the pole before I continue. "I can help you. I can help us both. You want to get out of here. So do I. All I need is fresh blood." She glances at me briefly. "If you help me, I will set you free."

I'm not sure if I mean that or not, but I sound convincing. "I promise," I add.

Finn pulls me, but this time I am not expecting it and fall forward. A warm hand grabs my arm, keeping me from hitting the floor. Without looking, I know that it is Tara holding me. When she realizes what she's done, she drops me. Luckily though, the delay allows me to catch myself.

I stand up and dust my pants off as we start again. "Thank you," I say to her.

Finally, she speaks, "It was only a reflex. Don't read too much into it."

I smile to myself. "I thought maybe it was because you're having a hard time hating me."

She huffs, "Hard time? It's the easiest thing I've done since I came here."

Even though she's saying she hates me, I'm glad to have someone to talk to.

"Why?" I ask quietly. "What did I ever do to you?"

"Your kind kills my kind. It makes us natural enemies," she says sharply.

Well, that is certainly true. "Oh, I see. Because you were born one way and I was made another, we shouldn't form our own opinions of each other." She looks at me with her eyebrows drawn as I continue, "Sometimes it's hard to think for yourself. I understand why you don't want to."

"Excuse me?" she says harshly and loud enough for even the humans to hear. I guess she is not used to people being so blunt to her.

Finn looks back at her. "What did he say?"

She stares at me for a moment before shaking her head. "Nothing."

I don't say anything else to her as we walk up the stairs and through the maze of hallways. I only keep my eyes on her somber face.

By the time we stop in front of a large oak door, I've almost forgotten that I shouldn't feel bad for her. Forgotten that the werewolves were the ones who helped the humans trap me. If not for them, I'd be home right now.

The captain opens the door and steps aside, allowing Finn to drag me inside. Along the wall are two young soldiers standing at attention. The one with blond hair swallows hard when his eyes meet mine.

The man smiles as I come closer. "Welcome, Nathaniel." I almost laugh when I realize the only information they have is what Nurse Klein has told them about me. "My name is Ulrich," he continues. "I have a few questions for you."

Of course, he does.

Finn shoves me into the chair, and the two soldiers hurry to strap my wrists and ankles tightly. As soon as they have me secured, Finn loosens the strap around my neck and takes the pole away. He walks over to stand next to Tara along the wall.

Ulrich pulls up a chair in front of me and sits in it with his arms crossed over the back, facing me. "Are you comfortable?" he asks.

"I'm sure my level of comfort matches your level of compassion," I tell him with a smirk.

He smiles a fake grin back at me. "Let's get to know each other. I would describe myself as a go-getter. Smart and cunning. How would you describe yourself? Strong? Fast? Immortal?"

I assume this is his roundabout way of learning about me without being obvious, or at least he is trying not to be obvious.

"Humans often describe me as nefarious," I tell him.

He tips the chair toward me. "What words would you use?"

I look at him sarcastically and say, "Strong. Fast. Immortal."

Seeing that he is not getting anywhere with his questions, he lets the chair rock back onto all four legs. "Why don't you tell me about the girl, then?"

Hoping he is not talking about Claire, I shrug. "What girl?"

I look to my right at the large windows and see the night sky staring back at me.

"The one who was at the hospital with you," he says. "The one that got away."

Got away? Just because there was no body, they assume she made it out. How very naïve.

My eyes meet his briefly before I let them proceed around the room. Behind the other two soldiers, I can see a long table, but from this angle, I can't make out what is lying on top of it.

"Oh, that girl," I tell him nonchalantly. But I still have to take a breath before I continue. "I don't travel with her." Looking at Ulrich, I lie, "Vampires tend to like solitude."

From my left, I hear Tara say loudly, "That's not true." Wishing she had not interrupted, I glare at her.

"Vampires are pack creatures, same as us," she tells Ulrich.

Pack creatures? Like we're some kind of animals. Like we aspire to be as primordial as the werewolves.

I do not try to hide my annoyance with her when I tell her, "Some do prefer companions. But make no mistake, I am alone in this world."

As I turn back toward Ulrich, I notice the large clawfoot bathtub in the corner, filled to the top with water. With its silver feet and tall, flowing back, it does not seem to belong in this drab room, but there it is.

Irritably, I tell Ulrich, "Why don't you just tell me what it is you want to know so I can refuse to answer and get this over with?"

This time his smile is genuine. "Tell me how to find more like you."

I thought that was probably what he wanted. "You can't. Lightning doesn't strike the same place twice. You will never catch another vampire."

He stands up. "Perhaps not." Sliding the chair aside, he leans towards me. "But I will try." Firmly, he says, "Now tell me where they are."

Giving him a smirk, I say, "You really are daft, aren't you? Did you not hear me? I said I was alone. That means all by myself, without anyone else around. Does that clear it up for you?"

With the back of his hand, he slaps me in the face, and Tara flinches at the sound. Maybe it startled her, but I doubt it.

Chuckling, I tell him, "Listen Ulrich, you might as well kill me because there is no way I am going to tell you anything." He is delusional if he thinks a petty slap will do much at all.

"Rest assured, there is always a way to make someone talk," he says coldly. "I can always find something worse than death."

I smile sarcastically. "That's right. You found me."

With hard eyes, he leans back and looks to Finn. "Get him up."

While Finn walks toward me, I have to wonder why a werewolf would ever take orders from a human. Whatever would possess him to be submissive to someone so inferior?

Kneeling in front of me, Finn loosens my ankles. The pity I see in him makes me think he knows what they have in store for me and that it must be dreadful.

As Finn moves on to my left wrist, Ulrich starts toward the bathtub in the corner.

"I know leeches like warm water, but you'll have to make do with cold." He holds his hand above the tub and closes his eyes. His lips move quickly in a silent prayer, and he lets his hand make a cross over the water.

Finn is not ready when I jump out of the chair. Trying to run, I jerk against the strap still holding my right wrist. There is no point trying to hide my fear of holy water. Soon enough they will all see the pain it brings me.

Finn grabs me by the collar and lifts me up to him while the blond soldier loosens my right wrist. "Try to stay calm," Finn tells me quietly. "Maybe it'll hurt less."

Hurt less? Is he serious? Has he ever been set on fire? I don't think so.

With both hands, I push against Finn, but to no avail. He isn't as weak as me, not by a long shot. He pulls me toward the tub even though I struggle.

As my feet drag and kick at the floor, I scream, "No! Stop! Tara, make him stop!" But she does not give the order.

With my back to the bathtub, I brace myself against the edge of it and plead with him, "Please, Finn, don't do this."

Ulrich smiles at me. "It's me you should be begging."

"Don't hold your breath," I manage as I fight to stay out of the water. "On second thought, do."

Ulrich knocks my arms out from under my weight, sending me crashing into the tub. The water boils around me, burning into my skin. The bubbles from my screaming make their escape, leaving me to scald alone. My fingers dig at Finn's arms, but without my vampire nails, I cause little harm to him through the long sleeves of his shirt.

Thrashing about as wildly as Finn's tight grip will allow me to, my clothes feel as though they're melting into my skin. If I didn't know better, I would expect my flesh to liquefy and pull off of me in large masses, like boiling fat from an animal.

My body twists in agony. My skin, now bright red, sizzles in the water. My only comfort is in knowing that this is surely what Ulrich will experience in hell, when I send him there.

The intense pain makes it difficult to focus on anything other than the way the water blisters my skin. The way my muscles contract in response. The way the fire on my flesh overshadows the burning in my throat.

Finn tugs me up and pulls me over the side of the tub, dumping me on the floor. Gasping, I try to calm my erratic breathing. I focus on stopping the uncontrollable trembling of my body and quieting the overwhelming need to whimper.

As I lie on the floor shaking, Ulrich bends down toward me. "Where are the others?"

I look up at Tara, asking for her help with just a glance. But her eyebrows are already drawn together painfully. Holding back tears, she looks away from me.

"You're not really alone, are you?" Ulrich asks mockingly.

"No." Turning my eyes to him, I continue, "There is a coward with me right now."

His smile fades. "Put him back in," he tells Finn coldly.

But before Finn can grab me, I use every ounce of energy left in me and leap at Ulrich. Knocking him to the ground, I make a fist with my quivering hand and pound it into his face. I manage two good strikes before one of the soldiers slams the stock of his gun into my nose, sending me backward onto the floor. Tara is there when I land, holding me back from attacking again.

"Mark my words, Ulrich, I will watch you die," I tell him as he is helped up from the floor.

"I want that parasite restrained," Ulrich barks at everyone.

Finn tosses Tara a rope and she wraps it around my wrists tightly. "Why did you stop me? I could have gotten us all out of here," I whisper to her.

She looks up with her eyes briefly. "You could've killed us all."

The rope is rough and cuts into my already sensitive skin. But I ignore that and tell her, "I wouldn't have killed you. That's not in my current plans."

She knots the rope forcefully. "I know your kind. You don't need plans to hurt us, only opportunity."

I say nothing. After all, she's right.

Glancing up at me, she smiles. "If I knew that would shut you up, I would have said it a long time ago."

Even though she pulls at the rope, testing her knot, and it scrapes at my wrists, I smile anyway.

"Pick him up and put him back in the water," Ulrich snaps at Finn, redirecting my attention away from Tara.

My smile disappears when Finn jerks me to my feet. He picks me up and shoves me back into the water. Again, I scream, feeling the fire around me. Scorching my flesh, the water boils against me. It is worse this time, as my skin is still raw from before.

But I am not in the water long when I hear the muffled sounds of an argument and Finn pulls me out of the tub. Dripping water onto the floor, I stand weakly in front of him, supported only by the strength of him holding me as my body trembles in his hands.

I hear Tara snap, "He's had enough."

Looking over at her, I see her standing in front of Ulrich with a light red handprint on her cheek. As angry as that makes me, there is little I can do.

Ulrich narrows his eyes on her and says, "Finn, put him back in the water."

Pushing past Ulrich, she steps toward Finn. "You take orders from me and me only. And I say drop him," she says firmly.

And just like that, I am on the floor, watching her glare at Ulrich.

"If you want to torture him, you do it without our help," she says bluntly to Ulrich.

He steps close to her, putting his face near hers. But when she does not back down, he looks at the blond soldier. "Smith, tie him down. And Pierce, bring the werewolf over here."

The younger soldier, Pierce, takes Finn by the arm and leads him to Ulrich as Smith takes the rope that is tied around my wrist. He drags me to the center of the room near a large drain.

While Smith loops the rope through the holes in the drain, securing me to the floor, I hear Ulrich tell Pierce, "If either of them move, put a bullet in Finn's head."

Ulrich walks to the table and takes what resembles a black rope in his hand. "There's more than one way to skin a cat," he says. As he walks closer to me, I can tell that it is not a rope in his hand but a whip. "Or in this case, a leech," he adds.

I do not struggle. There is little reason to. I know that I cannot pull myself loose, and fighting will only make it harder for Tara to watch me. Besides, I do not plan on giving Ulrich that satisfaction when I can help it.

He walks behind me, and I hear the tip of the whip hit the ground. Sitting up, I put my legs beneath me and hold my head high. The pain of a whip is something I have handled before and surely this will not be my last time.

There is a crack and I feel skin rip from my back. Sucking in a sharp breath, I clench my teeth to keep from crying out.

Again, the whip slashes me, cutting deep into my back. I can feel the first wound begin to heal and Ulrich pauses for a moment.

"Isn't that interesting," he mutters to himself.

Sarcastically, I tell him, "I'm glad you like it. I'm sure you will get to see it a lot more."

He answers me with another snap of the whip. I close my eyes, try to take myself somewhere else. With someone else. But every time I begin to see her silhouette in the sun, the whip slices through me, bringing me back to the here and now.

I lose count of how many strikes I receive once my shirt is just strips of material draped across my back. Thin streaks of blood weave their way from one shoulder to the other without a noticeable pattern.

By the time daylight is nearing, I am lying on the floor with my hands in front of my face, keeping my eyes closed until I hear Ulrich drop the whip.

Panting, he orders, "Take them back to their cells."

Pierce takes the rope in his hands and I jerk it, pulling him closer to me. "You should get out while you still can," I say weakly. "There will be no mercy this time." And I mean that. Every time I show kindness to an adult, it ends up coming back against me. I will not make that same mistake here.

I cannot hold him near me for long, though, before my muscles give out and the rope slides through my fingers.

I haven't experienced tiredness since before I was turned, but now I am physically exhausted. Although the wounds have healed, my body aches. My muscles feel as though they are weeping, longing for the blood that would restore them to their former strength.

Pierce does not wait for me to get to my feet. He drags me across the floor toward the others. He stops near Smith, who puts a strap around my neck. I don't need to focus my eyes to know that it is the one attached to the pole.

He pulls me up. I never thought my body could feel as heavy as it does now.

"Move it," Pierce says to us. We meet Joseph and Butler outside the doors and make our way back toward our cells. This time, however, I say nothing. I only concentrate on not letting my legs give out and not falling, as I am not sure I would be able to get up again if I did.

The strap pulls at my neck and twists my skin, leaving a raw, red strip in its wake. It feels like an eternity, and I know what an eternity is, before we reach the room and I see the other werewolves. But I am happy to see my uncomfortable cot again because sleep will be a release from this pain.

I do not even mind when they essentially toss me into my cell, because it brings me that much closer to the bed. I grasp the bed frame with my hands and pull myself up, and then I crawl onto the cot. But feeling the bars through the thin mattress only hurts my tender back.

Rolling over onto my side to face the wall, I ignore the sounds of Tara and Finn being placed in their cells until I hear her say, "Nathaniel?"

Surely, she isn't talking to me.

"What happened to the girl from the hospital?" she asks quietly.

I guess she is talking to me. "She died." I find that harder to say out loud than I thought it would be.

"Oh." She slides closer to the bars separating us. "I know you probably hate me for telling them how to catch you. But you have to know, I never meant for it to turn out this way. I never thought it would work. You shouldn't be here. It's my fault that you are. And for that, I'm sorry."

As I think about what she is saying, I hear her start to slide away.

"It's Nicolas," I tell her. I roll over to face her, and she looks confused. "My name is Nicolas Rider."

She smiles softly. "I'm Tara Brooks." She points to the big werewolf in the corner. "That's Abel." Then, gesturing toward the female wolf, "Lydia. And you know Finn." She reaches her hand through the bars. "It's nice to meet you. Officially."

Abel jumps to his feet. "Tara, don't. Are you crazy?"

She looks at him harshly. "Do not talk down to me," she orders.

Turning her attention back to me, she keeps her hand outstretched toward me. It would be so easy to bite her, and her blood would suffice. It would give me enough strength to kill my way out of here. Scooting across my bed, my mouth waters and my throat burns with thirst.

Taking her hand, I smile my lopsided grin. "It's nice to meet you, too."

Chapter 11

Humans often believe they are the preeminent species. That if given the choice, werewolves and vampires would choose to be like them. But the longer I lie here, the more I find that being human would be my last option.

After a dismal attempt at sleeping through the aching of my muscles and the heavy scent of werewolves, I find my body is still as weak as that of the soldier who watches over us.

I look at Joseph sitting at the desk. He glances up at me from the top of his eyes and smirks. "How do you like your dinner, leech?" he taunts.

Dinner? I suppose he thinks that the cold potatoes and dry piece of chicken are dinner.

At least the roll is somewhat entertaining, as I have been tossing it up and catching it just to pass the time. With each sweep of the air, it grows more stale and hard. More like an actual ball.

"Why don't you come in here and let me tell you?" I ask, although I do not honestly expect him to.

He smiles sarcastically. Flipping a pencil back and forth, he goes back to ignoring me.

I throw the roll above me and catch it again. "Hey, Tara?" I say as I lean up on my elbows, "Why are you here?"

She sets down her plate. "Someone told the wrong people about us." Playing with her fork, she continues, "They went to the school and took some of our kids. Said if we didn't cooperate, we'd never see them again." She looks up at me with sadness in her eyes. "Our kids are somewhere in this building, I know it. But I've been here for eight days and haven't seen my son yet. I'm going to get him out of this. I'm not sure how."

Sitting up, I move closer to her. "Why don't you phase? You and your wolves could tear this place apart." It's only logical that if she wants to get her son back, she should take him.

Smiling, she tells me, "For a number of reasons. They keep injecting us with wolfsbane."

"I thought that could kill you."

She shrugs. "Apparently not in small enough doses. It represses our wolves so that we can't phase even if we want to. But more importantly, werewolves do not kill humans."

I lean back against the block wall. "I remember stories of when they did." Of course, I also remember when we used to frame werewolves for slaughtering a village and they would hunt us down for it.

"So do I," she mutters. "But that was a long time ago."

"It's not natural for you to be so passive," I tell her. "I know a way to get your son back and you wouldn't have to kill anybody." All she would need to do is help me get fresh blood, and I would do all the work.

"That would require my trusting you." She smiles. "Which I don't."

I smile back as Butler walks in carrying a plate of what appears to be a much better-looking piece of chicken.

He sets the plate down in front of Joseph. "Enjoy," he says sarcastically.

"I will," he sneers back.

As Joseph begins eating, Butler leans his back against the wall, crossing his arms over his chest, and I turn my attention back to the wolves.

I assume Abel and Lydia were talking about me because when I look at them, they are both staring in my direction. Abel glares, which is not surprising, but Lydia looks uneasy. She tries not to meet my eyes. Perhaps it is a wolf thing. Perhaps she's trying not to intimidate me.

I look away, almost feeling sorry for her. I cannot imagine what it must be like to have my extent of power be determined by the one I marry. It seems unfair. I would never assume a woman to be below me. Yet werewolves have done it for centuries. Funny thing is, they think vampires are the savage ones.

My eyes trail across the room, making their way to Tara, who is sitting on her cot eating her miserable meal. She doesn't seem to take pleasure in her food, and I presume that if she didn't need to keep up her strength in order to bust her son and her pack out, she would not even touch it.

"What's your son like?" I ask her.

Just thinking about him makes her smile. "Well, he looks a lot like his father and acts like me. He's a good kid, but don't tell him that."

I smile at her. "What's his name?"

"Roderick. But everyone calls him Roddy."

I am fairly certain that Roderick is a German name, which makes me ask, "Is your husband German?"

"Yes," she says almost as a challenge. "And a Nazi."

Interesting. Perhaps nobody willingly told the Germans about the werewolves then. Perhaps someone found out about him and beat it out of him. But Tara has probably thought of that scenario.

Curious, I ask, "How did you meet him?"

She sighs, hesitating to tell me. "It was arranged by my father."

Arranged? Wolves haven't arranged marriages in a long time. "And you've only had one child after all these years?"

Smiling, she asks, "How old do you think I am?"

Werewolves, unlike humans, are not as concerned by the number attached to their age. Why would they be? They stop aging the first time they phase, which is usually in their early twenties. "Just a guess, but I would say at least three hundred."

"Good guess," she says without revealing her actual age to me. "And yes, I only have one son." She shifts on her cot. "Werewolves that are with child are not permitted to phase. With each call of the full moon, it becomes harder to deny your wolf. Then, when you're in pain from labor, you must fight against your instincts to phase, because if you become a wolf, it could kill the baby."

I lean toward her, interested.

"Labor is extremely difficult for a werewolf. It isn't uncommon for a wolf to die during childbirth. So it was not something I was going to jump right into."

She looks away, mumbling to herself. "And to think that I could lose him now..." She trails off, and I hear a catch in her breathing.

After a moment, she looks back at me. "What about you? How old are you?"

Too old. "I was born in 1387 as a human. Which means technically I have been alive for five hundred fifty-seven years. But I was turned into a vampire when I was twenty-two, so that's how old I really am." Or at least, that's how old I tell everyone I am.

She smirks at me. "And you've not found a wife in all those years?"

While normally her sarcasm would make me smile, this time it only serves as a reminder of the love that I have lost. I shift uncomfortably. "No."

Seeing my distress, she apologizes. "I'm sorry, Nicolas. I didn't mean anything by that."

Even though I can hear the guilt in her voice, it does not change how badly those memories sting. "I know," I tell her quietly.

"Do you want to talk about it?" She slides closer, taking the bars in her hands.

"That would require my trusting you." I look up at her and smile. "Which I don't."

She smiles back at me softly.

Looking to my right, I see Finn lying on his cot watching a small mouse eat the crumbs left on his plate, which gives me an idea.

Moving to the edge of my bed, I crush the roll in my hand. Sprinkling the pieces in the floor, I place my feet in front of me on the railing. I wait patiently, never moving, for the mouse to catch the scent of the roll, and eventually it does.

It scurries over, cautiously running between the bars and into my cell. Finn leans up, watching it, and laughs. "He'll never eat with you sitting right there."

Still, I do not stir, not even to contradict him. I keep my eyes on the remnants of roll beneath me.

It nibbles on the smaller pieces, further away from me at first. Then it creeps closer. Honestly though, animals are not afraid of vampires anyway. It's not like they're prey to us. We cannot even attempt to drink their blood without becoming ill, and we have all tried it. But only once.

Finally, the mouse makes its way close to me. It dines on a large piece of bread, holding the roll to its tiny mouth.

Slowly, I hover my foot just over the edge of the bed. Then with one swift move, I cram the heel of my shoe down on the mouse, snapping its fragile bones and killing it.

"Why would you do that?" Finn asks almost aggressively.

Placing my finger to my lips to silence him, I pick up the little mouse carcass by the tail and walk over to the bars between Joseph and me. Butler watches me curiously as I stretch my arm through the bars.

With a flick of my wrist, I toss the lifeless body toward Joseph. It lands on his plate with a slight thud, and he snaps his head up at me.

Pulling my arm back into my cell, I say with a smirk, "How do you like your dinner?"

"You son of a bitch!" he shouts as he stands up, knocking the chair back into the wall.

"Now, now," I start, "you shouldn't talk about my mother like that. Better men have died for a lot less."

He stomps over to the cell. "You're going to be a dead little prick when I get through with you."

Smiling, I rub my hands together. "Come and get me then," I taunt.

Joseph reaches for the keys but Butler grabs his shoulder. "You know you're not allowed in there," he says quietly.

I can see that Joseph is mulling over Butler's words, so I tell him, "He is not your superior, is he Joseph?"

Pushing past Butler, Joseph takes the keys and walks over to Abel. "You want to do something for me?"

Abel pounds his fist into his other hand. "Gladly."

As Joseph walks Abel to my cell, Tara hops to her feet. I hear the metal scrape as the key slides into my lock and the tumblers roll into position. Joseph pulls the door open and Abel steps in.

I have to admit, Abel is much bigger than me, and in my weakened state he looks as though he could do a number on me.

"Abel. Wasn't that the weaker son?" I tease.

He steps closer to me, and I hear Tara order, "Abel, do not touch him unless provoked."

From this distance, I can smell Abel clearly, and his scent is familiar. It reminds me of someone. But whom? It was recent. I was in the woods. Oh, no. I know who he is. He is one of the wolves that chased Kate out of the woods that night.

Not sure if he remembers me or not, I try to pretend to be unconcerned about him. "You need provoked? Then I will make it easy for you. I will make it so you cannot resist tearing me apart." I smile insolently. "Meow."

Before I have time to react, his fist is in my gut, doubling me over. He is stronger than I assumed. Another fist slams down onto my back, knocking me to the floor.

"Stop it!" Tara shouts, holding onto the bars between us with a tight grip. But the problem is that she can't give him an order that will allow him to be injured. So as long as I'm fighting, he can attack me back.

Leaping up, I tackle him by the knees and pull him to the floor. I jump onto his stomach and pound my fist into his face twice before he shoves me off. As he stands up, I drive him into the bars with my shoulder and punch him in the ribs with all of my strength.

He cries out slightly and grabs my throat, pulling me up until my toes are barely scraping the floor. He tosses my body onto the ground near my bed, and I feel my shoulder pop as it dislocates.

I start to push myself up with my other arm when I feel him kick my ribs, lifting me into the air slightly. When I land on my sore shoulder, he kicks me again, this time in the stomach.

He punches me in the face, and blood trickles from my lower lip. With my tongue, I lick the corner of my mouth, tasting it. Putting my hand up, I tell him weakly, "Okay. You win."

Even though I can tell he wants to hit me again, Tara's order forces him not to, and he starts to walk away.

Shoving my shoulder into the railing of the cot, I push my arm back into place. Then, quickly, I grab the pillowcase and let the pillow fall out onto the bed and rush toward him. With his back to me, I whip the pillowcase around his neck and pull with all my weight, jerking him back. Putting my knees in his spine, I keep the material taut as he grabs at it.

Unable to grip it, his face begins to turn blue, and Tara screams at me, "Nicolas, stop! You're killing him!"

Maybe she does not realize that is what I intend to do. He drops to the floor, still trying to choke down any amount of air.

"Stop!" she shouts. "Please! For me."

I have no reason to stop for her, but I do. I let the pillowcase slip from my hands, and Abel gasps for air, rubbing his neck. I spit the blood that has accumulated in my mouth onto the floor near his head. "Get out of my cell," I tell him coldly.

He stands up and points at me. "This isn't over."

I do not bother to watch the way Abel scowls at me all the way back to his cell. Instead, I look at Tara, who shakes her head at me in disbelief.

"What?" I ask her defensively.

"Vampires are all the same," she mutters quietly as she walks back to her cot. Sighing, she sits down and crosses her arms over her chest.

A hint of anger stirs in me. How can she be upset with me? "You can't really blame me for fighting. I have no reason to be submissive like you do." It's not my child locked in here somewhere. "I just want out of here. What they did to me last night is going to happen again. In here, I'll lose what little compassion I have left for humans."

Having no humanity makes you a vile person. I should know. I was like that for two hundred years, killing mercilessly just to appease a growing hunger. It is a dark place that I do not intend on going back to.

She hears the honesty in my voice, and the tension in her face begins to ease. "You have to understand," she starts calmly. "My pack is diminishing very quickly. We have five men fighting in this war. Some for Germany, some not. Some of our wolves were killed recently, and I'm supposed to be protecting them. I'm supposed to keep them together."

She sighs, placing her head in her hands. "I am the acting alpha right now. I can't lose any more wolves. It doesn't invoke much confidence in me from my pack."

I know she said a lot of things, but the only part I heard was that her wolves were killed recently. Could these wolves be the same ones that I killed in the forest? I hope not, but the lump in my throat tells me they probably were.

"When were your wolves killed?" I ask, attempting to sound casual.

Her eyes meet mine, and she looks more tired than I would ever expect a werewolf to appear. "A few weeks ago. We were all meeting in the woods. They were attacked by vampires for no reason." Sounds like us. "Finn, Lydia, and I heard them but by the time we got there, the vampires were gone. Abel and Donna went after the female, and Donna was killed in the process." Definitely my family. "But Abel remembers all three vampires, and he's going to help us track them down when we get home."

My stomach churns wildly with nervousness. Should I tell her it was me? That I killed those wolves? Would she hate me if I did?

"Right," I manage to whisper.

I glance over at Abel, who's smiling at me. "I got a good look at those bloodsuckers," he says.

He knows it was me. I do not doubt that.

"I guess that's one reason I told them how to catch you," Tara begins. "I was just so angry at vampires in general that it didn't matter which one I hurt." She looks over at me. "Honestly, though, what would be the odds that I could trick the right ones?"

She laughs to herself, just thinking of the unlikely chance of coming face to face with her wolves' killer. But all I can think is the odds seem pretty good, actually.

Before she has a chance to see my uneasiness, the captain walks in. Joseph and Butler jump to their feet and salute.

"At ease," he tells them. Then, leaning close, he whispers something to Butler.

"Yes sir," Butler tells him.

Then, just as quickly as he entered, the captain is gone. Butler walks to my cell with the keys jingling in his hand. "Captain says to take you to the showers."

Relief sweeps over me. Finally, I can wash the old blood from my skin. Butler walks toward Abel but says to me, "And you will have an escort."

He unlocks the door and lets Abel out. While I really do not want to be more or less alone with Abel, I jump at the chance to have a shower.

I walk over to the bars, waiting for Butler to open my cell. When Abel reaches for the pole and strap, I tell them, "I won't try anything."

They both look at me disbelievingly, so I continue, "It's daylight outside. Where would I go?"

Still not trusting my obviously logical reasoning, Abel grabs the pole. After the door opens, he tightens the strap around my neck, making it difficult to swallow. Then, following Butler, Abel jerks me out of the cell and down the hallways until we reach the shower room.

Dingy, white tiles line the walls and floor. Sitting on a chair near the far wall are a towel, bar of soap, and a set of fresh clothing. Well, fresher than what I am wearing, anyway.

Abel drags me to the middle of the room and starts to loosen the strap. "I'm the only one who knows that it was you in those woods."

"I figured. I'd like to keep it that way, too," I tell him. "You don't need to tell anyone. You can still try to kill me when we get out of this."

He takes the pole away, and I rub my neck, which is red from the leather. "We'll see," he says. "About not telling anyone, that is."

Close by, Butler turns on the water and lets it run. "Better hurry. You only have five minutes," he informs me, and then he walks over and leans back against the wall.

Abel smiles at me. "Tell you what. I can keep your secret, but..." he starts, "you have to treat me like your own personal alpha." He leans closer. "That means when I say jump, you do it."

A heat begins to course through my body. Nobody tells me what to do. I keep my eyes focused on the wall in front of me when I hear the pole slip out of Abel's hand and clank against the tiles.

He starts to bend toward it but stops when I coldly say, "Those wolves weren't ready for me."

Abel stands up straight, and his eyebrows come together angrily. "You better watch those next few words," he manages through gritted teeth.

I smile to myself and look at him. "They were young, which made it so very easy. And when I was finished, I could still smell their stench on me."

He brings his fist at my head like I knew he would. But because I was expecting it, I am able to block his hand with my forearm. With my foot, I flip the pole up between us and grab the end of it.

Before he can react, I swing the pole as hard as I can, striking him just above his ear and knocking him to the floor. His breathing does not stop but relaxes as he loses consciousness.

I look up at Butler, who is now standing with wide eyes and pointing his gun at me. Tossing the pole toward his feet, I walk over to the water that's pouring onto the tiles. Placing my palm in the shower, I say, "Really, Butler? Cold?"

The gun trembles in his grip but he does not lower it. "The captain said to only let you use cold."

I reach over and turn the hot water on. While the water warms, I go to the chair and start undressing as I tell him, "By the way, my five minutes doesn't start until I'm in the water, and it's going to be more like ten."

I pull my shirt over my head and smell the faint hint of roses clinging to it. It saddens me to know that this shower will wash away what little scent of Claire still lingers on me.

Stepping into the water, I wash as quickly as I can. Not because I'm worried that Butler will actually cut my shower short, but it is more that I want to just stand here and let the water run over me, taking with it some of my problems and melting my tired muscles back into a renewed relief.

The water brings with it thoughts of Claire. The memories flow, starting with the first time I saw her bathing in my shower, letting the lather run over her pale, milky skin. Her hungry glance made it hard for me to breathe, and my hands ached to touch her.

I hang my head, letting the water pour over my forehead. It drips from my hair and splatters on the tiles below, but still I think of Claire.

Closing my eyes, I can see her soft eyes looking into mine. The gentle way she bit her lip, sending chills along my skin. I can feel her warm arm draped across my chest as she slept.

But it was the first time I kissed her that makes me cross my arms over my chest, holding onto my shoulders, trying not to let the tears fall. I can feel her lips pressing into mine, reminding me of the way I knew in that moment that I was not alone. That there was something worth living for. Something I had forgotten, and now I have lost it again.

I stand like this for a long time, lost in my memories, until I hear Butler's heavy steps coming closer.

"I know," I tell him with a sigh. "Time's up."

Looking up, I shut off the water and walk to the chair. I dry off and dress quickly but still manage to notice Butler looking at Abel curiously.

"What do we do about him?" Butler asks to himself.

"I'll take care of it," I say, nearly startling Butler. I slip my shoes on again and walk toward Abel. Kneeling next to him, I trail my fingertips on the wet floor. Flicking the water from my fingers onto his face, he begins to moan.

"Wake up, Abel," I say, and he opens his eyes. He blinks a few times, trying to focus. When I know he sees me, I lean closer. "I'm not one for taking orders. So let me explain to you exactly how this works. You keep your mouth shut, or I will tell everyone that you were the wolf that led the soldiers to them."

Still groggy, he mumbles, "They wouldn't believe that."

I lean back away so that he can see my smile. "They don't have to believe it. They only need to consider it."

He knows I am right. If they even wonder if it might be possible, the pack will begin to unravel.

I stand up and walk to the pole. Picking it up, I hold it out toward Abel as he slowly moves toward me, rubbing the side of his head.

He snatches it from my hand roughly. Then he tightens the strap too snug for comfort and jerks me forward. "Come on," he says to Butler. "Let's get this leech back to his cell."

We are back shortly, though my neck feels like the strap has been around it for hours. Red and raw, my throat burns inside and out.

In my cell, I simply lie on my cot, staring at the ceiling and thinking of all the things the Nazis are surely dreaming up for me.

After a few moments of quiet, I hear Tara whisper, "Nicolas?" I look over at her. "You can't enthrall me like you do your human drones, can you?"

Sheep, she means my sheep. "No. Not even if I wanted to." I lean up onto my elbows. "Why?"

Shrugging, she continues, "It's probably one of the reasons you hate wolves, huh?"

"On the contrary," I tell her as I sit up the rest of the way. "I like werewolves quite a lot."

Placing my feet on the floor, I slide over toward her. "If I had to choose what I wanted for myself, I would have chosen to be a wolf."

She half-turns her head to the side, much the way a puppy would when it's confused, so I continue, "Wolves are remarkable. The perfect blend of raw animal power and human existence. You're beautiful, dangerous, and immortal, yet you still live your life as a human would." I lean my back against the bars between us, keeping my eyes on my cot. "I'm a little envious of wolves, actually."

"But you're stronger and faster than I will ever be." She starts, "You..."

I finish her sentence for her. "Want to kill every human I meet."

Looking over my shoulder at her, I say, "Every one of them."

"I'm not a human. Do you want to kill me, too?" she asks.

I tell her honestly, "Sometimes."

She scoots closer, taking hold of the bars beside me. "Do you think you will try to?"

I could say yes. But then she would not allow herself to get any closer to me. I could say no. But that might be a lie. "I hope not," I tell her quietly, almost ashamed of my answer.

Reaching through the bars, she touches my arm gently. "Me, too," she says softly.

I look down at her hand on my elbow and smile to myself. She will never know how much her kindness means to me, especially right now.

She moves away and goes to the other side of her cell by Lydia. I watch them as they both sit on the floor, facing one another. Tara puts her hands out with the palms up, and Lydia hovers her hands with her palms down just above Tara's. Without taking her eyes away from Lydia, Tara brings her hands up quickly, attempting to slap the backs of Lydia's hands, but Lydia moves just in time. Laughing, they position themselves to do it again.

I turn back around and pull my legs up onto the bed in front of me. Resting my head and arms on my knees, I sit, listening to the occasional smacking sounds of hands against hands in the next cell and wait for the hours to pass.

Fifteen minutes after the sun is gone and the darkness has settled outside, I hear the captain walk in and Joseph and Butler jump to their feet.

"Bring Lydia to guard this time," the captain says sharply. As Butler hurries to let Lydia out of her cell, the captain turns his eyes to me. "On your feet, leech."

Even though it is not in my nature to obey others, I know there is little point in resisting.

Standing up, I walk to the center of my cell. "You shouldn't call me leech. It'll end up costing you your life," I tell him.

"I'll take my chances." He smirks at me. "Leech."

Somehow, I knew he would say that. I keep my eyes on him as Lydia enters my cell and even when she puts the strap around my neck. Generously, she does not tighten it as much as the others had. How very compassionate of her. I will have to remember that when I am choosing who to kill.

"Ready?" she whispers.

I look over at her softly. "Whenever you are."

She starts walking but does not pull me fast enough that I feel as if I'm being dragged, which is a nice change.

After the maze of hallways, we reach what I am calling the torture room, where Ulrich plays God and picks on a temporarily weaker species. Again, Butler and Joseph wait outside near the door while the captain and Lydia walk me inside.

The captain waits until Lydia has me secured to the heavy chair to make his exit. This time, however, one arm of the chair has been modified slightly. Instead of the standard angle where the arm meets the back, there is a triangular block with its tip in the corner and the flat side keeping my right elbow straight. They have also added two new straps, which appear to be nothing more than leather belts, one above and one below my elbow.

Lydia stands along the wall quietly while the two soldiers, Smith and Pierce, flank the chair behind me. With his back to me, I watch Ulrich near the long table. He keeps whatever he's concentrating on in front of him so that I cannot make out what it is. But I am sure to find out soon enough.

"I've been thinking about what you said," Ulrich tells me in his thick German accent.

"Was it about your haircut making you look like a penis? Oh, wait, I didn't say that out loud, did I?" I ask.

He looks over his shoulder at me briefly and then nods to one of the soldiers. I can hear his hand cutting the air before Smith slaps me in the face. Ulrich begins again, "I may never catch another vampire." He turns around, holding a needle with an empty syringe attached. "But you cannot stop me from making my own."

As he steps towards me, I warn him, "You should stop this. You have no idea what you're about to do."

Smiling at me, he comes closer. I continue, "Don't. A new vampire is not a joke. It will kill everyone in this building. You don't want that kind of blood on your hands."

He stops and leans toward me. "I would sacrifice more than that to win this war."

I could tell him that he is crazy, but I get the feeling he already knows. He puts the needle close to my skin. Struggling against the strap, I try to at least make this difficult for him. But the belts are tight enough that I cannot even feel my fingers any longer and am completely unable to move my arm.

He slides the tip of the needle into my vein and pulls back the plunger, drawing my dark red blood into the tube. "You can't do this!" I scream at him.

He slides the needle out and lets my blood trickle down my arm. "Watch me," he says.

The puncture from the needle heals quickly enough, but I am not so much concerned by the blood on my forearm as I am the blood in the syringe. "No soldier here deserves to be turned," I tell him. Nobody anywhere ever deserves it.

He walks back toward the table. "Who says I'll waste a soldier when there are perfectly good werewolf children downstairs?" I can tell by the way the pitch in his voice changes that he's bluffing. "After all, nobody wants to shoot a child."

He sets my blood on the table and picks up a metal cup. As he carries it toward me, I can smell old, dead animal blood, probably from a rat. "Lydia, come here," Ulrich says.

She walks over to them, and he hands her the cup. "Make him drink it," he orders her.

Hesitating slightly, she puts the cup to my mouth. Keeping my lips tight, I thrash my head from side to side. I know what animal blood will do to me, and that's when it's fresh.

The blood in the cup swishes around inside and splashes onto my shirt "Stop spilling it!" Ulrich shouts at her.

"I can't help it," Lydia says timidly. "He won't drink." She pulls the cup back enough for me to spit some of what is on my lips onto the floor.

Ulrich holds his hand out toward Pierce, who then hands him his handgun. Ulrich places the gun to Lydia's head. "Drink it, leech. Or you will be wearing her skull fragments all over your face."

I look at Lydia, who's shaking and afraid. "Please," she whispers to me. "My daughters need their mother."

Damn it, why did she have to say that? Ulrich cocks the gun. "Fine," I tell him, though, honestly, I should just let him shoot her. "But untie my hands and let me do it myself."

He stares at me for a moment, holding the gun to her head and debating with himself. Finally, he lowers the gun and says, "One hand. But no tricks."

Gesturing with the gun, he motions for Pierce to come to me. The young soldier hurries and unties my left hand.

Ulrich snatches the cup from Lydia's hand and holds it between us. "Bottoms up," he says to me.

Taking the cup, I lick my lips, tasting the cold, stale remnants of the animal blood, and my stomach twists in disgust. Glancing at the blood, I see that it's only filled halfway to the top, which it a slight relief.

Looking at Ulrich, I see him grinning at me, and I know there are so many things that I used to be able to do that would wipe that smirk from his face. But I would need to be my formidable self again to do them.

Tipping the cup up, I drink the blood as fast as I can. Bitter and revolting, it does not even start to quench my thirst. My muscles begin to cramp as the nutrients are robbed from them. My throat rages in defiance of such a poor excuse for a meal, and my stomach aches and knots in an attempt to refuse the pathetic offering.

Clutching my abdomen, I drop the cup, letting it crash to the floor. I close my eyes and slump forward, doubling over in pain. Sharp and penetrating, it cuts through me, stabbing me to my core. Through gritted teeth, I try not to cry out but cannot stop the painful exhale. Holding my breath to keep from moving my stomach any more than necessary does not seem to help, but I do it anyway.

My mouth begins to water, but not from hunger. "I need a trashcan. Or a bucket. Or anything else," I manage through ragged breaths.

Only Lydia realizes that she must hurry, and she rushes toward the clawfoot tub where there is a silver bucket on the floor.

She runs toward me but isn't fast enough. My stomach contracts, and the animal blood surges up my throat, pouring onto me and the chair. But it isn't over that easily.

I curl my body as much as I can, since one arm is still tied, and retch again, knowing that the blood will burn my throat even more. Like fire, it pushes its way out, splattering mostly on the floor before Lydia shoves the bucket in front of my face.

Ulrich steps back and tries to shake some of the drips of blood from his shoes. "Stop that," he tells me as if I was putting myself through this for fun.

"He can't," Lydia snaps at him. "His body is purging. He can only digest human blood, which you already knew."

Ulrich narrows his eyes at her, and she stops talking which would not have worked on a more dominant wolf.

After a long while of vomiting until I can barely breathe, the pain and nausea ease some. I lean back in the chair, still trying to catch my breath.

"Thank you, Lydia," I say faintly.

She takes the bucket from my hand with little effort and dumps the blood onto the drain.

Ulrich wipes his shoe on my pants leg, saying, "Tie him back up."

Pierce walks around, and I do not fight him when he takes my hand. He starts tightening the leather strap around my wrist when something slams into the fingers of my right hand hard enough for me to hear them snap. Even with the sudden intense pain, I do not scream. I look over at Ulrich, who is holding a hammer.

He smiles coldly. "We need to see how fast you heal."

Managing to unclench my jaw, I tell him, "You should have asked."

He nods. "This is better."

I pull my left hand loose from the still not completely tightened-down strap and grab my fingers. Pierce reaches for my hand, but I shove him away, pushing him back onto the floor. "If you want me to heal quickly, I need to set the bones," I tell Ulrich.

Smith comes toward us, but Ulrich puts his hand up to stop him. I pull and compress my fingers, feeling the bones shift inside. It is painful but I am fairly used to breaking my hands.

"How long does it take?" Ulrich asks.

I know what he's asking, but still I raise my eyebrow. "To set? Longer than whoever fixed your nose did. I want my hand to look decent," I say sarcastically.

He leans toward me, putting his face close to mine. "To heal?" he clarifies in a harsh tone.

Without backing away from him, I answer, "It's different for every body part. But a fractured finger? Maybe thirty minutes." Or at least that's what it used to take. Who knows what this inadequate body will do?

"Tie him," he tells Pierce without looking away from me.

When Pierce takes my hand, I do not fight him. A struggle is just what Ulrich wants from me.

It does not take long for Pierce to secure me this time. As Pierce steps away, Ulrich reaches behind his back and pulls out a dagger. He presses the tip of it into my cheek, turning my face to the side "And just how long does it take to heal if you are stabbed?"

Not long. "Same as it would take you," I lie.

But he does not believe me and slides the knife down my cheek, slicing through my skin. I can feel the blood trickle on my cheek, rolling toward my jaw and dripping onto my shirt as the cut begins to seal itself.

Ulrich backs up and smiles. "Liar." He flips the dagger over his fingers. "This will be easier for you if you're honest with me."

Right, like I believe that.

Suddenly, his smile fades. He holds the dagger by the blade and hurls it at me. Attempting to slide back as much as I can as the dagger drives into the chair between my legs, I let out a startled cry.

"Watch it," I tell him. "I don't regenerate. I'm not a lizard, you know?" Though that is not entirely true. I mean, I am not a lizard. But I can regenerate most parts, the ones my body deems necessary. Problem is, the parts that my body considers optional, I consider very necessary.

He pulls the knife from the chair and jabs it into my thigh. My face tightens, and I swallow back a painful scream, refusing to give him that pleasure.

"Now what happens?" Ulrich asks.

I look up at him. "You pull it out and watch me heal."

"And if I don't."

Is he serious? "I won't be able to mend myself with a knife in my leg," I tell him matter-of-factly.

Apparently, he does not appreciate my tone and leaves the dagger where it is. As he walks back to the table, he says, "Beat him."

Pierce and Smith walk around to stand in front of me. They raise the stock of their guns up and pound them into my stomach, chest, and face repeatedly. It hurts, but mostly it makes me angry that there is nothing I can do about it. A broken rib, a busted lip, and, I am pretty sure, a swallowed tooth later, Ulrich walks back over to us.

"Enough," he tells the soldiers.

As Pierce lowers his gun, I spit the blood from my lip onto his boot. He brings his gun up again, and Ulrich snaps at him, "I said enough."

I smile at Pierce, ignoring the way my grin pulls at the cut on my lip as it begins to heal. "That goes for you, too," Ulrich tells me sharply.

He reaches down and pulls the dagger from my leg. The relief nearly makes me sigh, and I begin to heal quickly. Reaching into his pocket, he pulls out a lighter. Looking at its shiny silver with an eagle embossed on the front, I feel as if I have seen it before, though I'm not sure where.

He strikes the flint, and the flame ignites. Ulrich holds the lighter close to me. "Let's see how you recover from a burn."

Then, from behind him, I hear Lydia say, "It will kill him."

Ulrich and I both look at her as she continues, "Fire kills vampires." She grabs her necklace from under her shirt. "If you want to burn him, you have to use something like this," she says, holding her cross pendant in front of her.

Ulrich puts the lighter back in his pocket and walks over to her. He snatches the necklace, breaking the chain. Letting it dangle so that I can see it, he walks back toward me.

The pendant makes me nervous. My heartbeat quickens in anticipation of the burn. My breathing becomes heavy and hard. My skin crawls with his every step.

Part of me thinks about praying for this to be quick, but the rest of me knows that God will not listen to my prayers. Because no matter how much I believe in him, he does not believe in me. Not anymore.

Ulrich presses the cross to my cheek, and it sears into my skin like a hot branding iron. I can smell my flesh burning. I can hear my skin sizzle. I hold my breath, trying anything to stop the fire, but nothing seems to help, just as I knew it wouldn't. Jerking in the chair does not help, either; it only makes him push the pendant against me more.

When he finally pulls it away, it rips the flesh from my cheek, leaving behind a raw and blistered cross-shaped burn. The pain is intense, but I don't get to focus on this long before he presses the cross onto my neck.

The burning of the necklace far outweighs the fire in my throat, and it makes me twist my face with pain. But he does not hold it there long, and once it's removed, I can think of something other than the scorching it brings. I can breathe again, though only in jagged breaths.

We go on like this for hours. Beating, burning, and then beating some more. Watching me heal. Watching me bleed.

But like a saving grace, I can feel morning growing near. They know it, too, as they come to the end of their persecution for the night. Pierce and Smith flank me from behind again, waiting for another chance to beat the sarcasm from my lips.

Ulrich walks toward me from the table with a needle in his hand. This time is different, however. This time there is something in the syringe.

If only I could wipe the blood from my face, then maybe my vision would not be so hazy and I could make out what's in the syringe. But I cannot.

He stops in front of me. "One more thing," he says as he puts the needle next to my arm and feels for a vein.

Focusing my eyes on the small scratchy handwriting on the label stuck to the syringe, I blink a few times, which seems to help. Slowly I can begin to read it: men-, mening-, meningitis.

My heart drops into my stomach. I inhale sharply, jerking as much as I can, trying to free my arm. "No!" I shout at him. "No!"

Meningitis is no stranger to me. It is a terrible infection to have, even for a human, and worse for vampires. With some of the most painful and long-lasting symptoms, it is one of the most dreadful things we can catch.

"Please don't," I try, but it does not come out weak and frail as I was hoping to make it sound.

He pushes the needle into my vein. "Stop!" I order, and though it nearly kills me, I add, "I am begging you."

That makes Ulrich look up at me with a hint of satisfaction in his eyes, but it doesn't stop him. He pushes the plunger down, and the liquid inside the syringe enters my body.

It isn't instant. He has time to take the needle away before my stomach begins to cramp. A long, hard tightening in my abdomen that nauseates me. I breathe through it, but it's followed shortly by a more concentrated abdominal spasm. Hanging my head and gritting my teeth, I try not to cry out.

Ulrich watches me for a moment, and then, realizing the time, he tells Pierce and Smith, "Get him up."

With my eyes closed tightly, I do not see them but know they must have motioned for Lydia, because she walks over with her light steps. She wraps a strap around my neck, I assume the one that's attached to the pole, but I do not open my eyes to confirm that. Then the soldiers release my wrists and the blood rushes into the numb fingers of my right hand, causing the standard pins and needles feeling. But that is the least of my concerns right now.

I grab my stomach with both hands and double over in the chair as they loosen the ankle restraints. They try to pull me to my feet, but there is a sudden sharp pain in my head that causes my knees to buckle. I drop to the floor with one hand on my forehead, feeling my head pounding inside. Drawing my knees to my chest, I let out a small whimper of a moan.

The pressure inside my skull grows with each passing second. So much so that I am able to count my pulse from the throbbing. My stomach churns and wrenches, twisting into knots. I retch, and what little blood was left in my stomach ends up on the floor.

Both soldiers step away from me as my spasmodic vomiting continues, but Lydia kneels down beside me. Her soft hand rubs my back gently, and I am sure if there was anything she could say to make this better, she would have said it by now.

I can feel the sky begin to lighten, and for once I'm willing to let the sun make me succumb to ash.

"Get him out of here," Ulrich snaps.

I'm not sure who grabs the pole, but one of the soldiers drags me out into the hallway, and I hear Butler's voice say, "What happened?"

"Take him back to his cell," Smith orders.

I heave again but nothing will come up anymore. There is nothing left in my system. Nothing left to boil in my throat or spoil in my stomach. Nothing but pain fills me now.

Joseph chimes in, "Do you want us to drag him the whole way?" he asks sarcastically.

If my head did not feel as though it is about to explode, that may have made me smile.

"I don't give a shit what you do. Just get him out of my hallway," Smith says harshly.

I hear the door slam as, I assume, Smith and Pierce return to Ulrich. Joseph sighs and picks up the pole where the others had dropped it. "Come on, leech."

"Just be easy when you drag me down the stairs," I say weakly, exposing my bloodstained teeth.

"Fat chance of that," I hear Joseph say under his breath. He starts to pull me down the hallway, letting the dirt on the floor cut into my shoulder. "Wait," Lydia tells them. I feel her kind hands on me again, this time under my arms, lifting me to my feet. She wraps my arm around her neck, supporting most of my weight.

I open my eyes to look at her face, but the dim light in the hallway pierces through my head and I close them again painfully.

Smelling her so close should remind me of how thirsty I am, but with my stomach churning, I would rather have nothing in my stomach for now. Besides, her blood would not help make this illness dissipate any faster.

The walk back to my cell seems to take longer than it ever has before.

Lydia lets me down gently onto my cot and takes the strap from my neck. But honestly, with all the pain in my head and stomach, I had forgotten it was there.

She covers me with my thin blanket and I grab her hand. "Thank you," I tell her quietly, since I don't think I could stand anything loud at this moment.

Sensing my pain, she pats my hand to let me know she believes I am being sincere, and walks out. Joseph, however, is not so caring and slams the cell door shut, adding to the pounding in my skull.

My stomach spasms again and I pull myself into a ball. I slip my pillowcase off and hold it close to my mouth. My body tries to vomit, and after several failed attempts, somewhere, somehow, more blood comes up. It stains the white pillowcase, making one end a deep red.

I hear Tara whisper, "What's wrong with him?"

"Meningitis," Lydia tells her quietly. "Tara, they said they were going to make more like him."

Tara shifts, but without opening my eyes I can't tell if she moved closer to me or farther away.

"They even took his blood," Lydia continues. "We have to do something. Our kids aren't safe here. Not with those... things in the same building."

At least she is right about that. None of them are safe around a new vampire.

They say nothing else as my vomiting proceeds. After several hours the nausea stops, but the migraine grows worse. My body temperature spikes, and if I could break into a sweat, I would.

Shivering, I lie under the blanket, holding my head, while Joseph bangs a metal cup against the bars just to make it worse for me.

With my hands trembling, I wish I had my strength just so that I could puncture my fingers through my skull in hopes of relieving some of the pressure inside, but I know that would never work.

Moaning, I try not to move, since every twitch of a muscle causes my head to pulsate. My neck feels as if any movement of it could break it into a million pieces, and part of me thinks that could be an improvement over my current condition.

Suddenly, I hear Ulrich's voice, which is slightly surprising. "Let me in," he tells either Butler or Joseph. But I do not open my eyes to find out which.

The heavy metal door grinds open, and I hear his footsteps draw closer to me. He takes my hand and pulls my arm straight.

"What are you doing?" I ask him with a feeble voice. He presses to feel for a vein. "I'm making you better."

I feel the pinch of the needle as it enters my skin, and I risk a glance.

The light causes my brain to thud against my skull even more, but I see the syringe through blurry eyes. Ulrich pushes the plunger down slowly, letting the light amber fluid mix with my blood.

"Why?" I wonder. Why would he help me? He's the one who did this to me.

He stands up. "I'm a scientist and you are nothing more than my experiment." His footsteps leave and the door is closed again.

Slowly, I do begin to feel better. Not completely cured, but at least I am able to open my eyes again.

Still, my body aches and my fever keeps me shaking. My head aches every time I try to lift it from the pillow, but it's an improvement nonetheless.

I do not move, not even to look at the soldier who walks in when he says, "Captain wants to see you." But I don't recognize his voice. It sounds very young, though, probably another private.

I keep my eyes on the ceiling as Butler, Joseph, and the other soldier shuffle out of the room, leaving me alone with the wolves.

"Nicolas?" Tara says quietly.

"Yeah," I say without looking at her.

"Did you mean what you said?" She slides closer to me. "You'll get us out?"

Her question is unexpected, and I can't help but to sit up, though my head protests it severely.

She reaches her arm through the bars, and my mouth waters. Surely, she is not suggesting what I hope she is.

Finn jumps up. "No, Tara. You can't do this."

"Silence. All of you," she orders them. Then, looking at me, she says, "Take only what you need."

She is serious. I know this offer may not last long, so I get out of bed and start toward her. My legs do not want to make the trip to her, but my thirst is more persuasive. I sit on the floor near her arm and take her wrist in my hand.

Too afraid of her answer, I don't ask if she's sure about this. Instead, I simply tell her, "This is going to hurt."

I raise her wrist to my lips and hesitate there. I know how bad this will be for her, how much trouble she could get into when her husband finds out, but I also know there is no other way. At least, not for me.

I bite into her soft flesh, cutting her with my human teeth. But once her blood hits my tongue, my dormant vampire self is awakened. My fangs extend, puncturing into her vein and flooding my mouth with her delectable blood.

Sweet and thin, it streams down my throat smoothly, cooling the insatiable burning. Not even her sharp inhalations, her painful moans, and her struggle against my strengthening grip can take away the pleasure this moment brings me.

Her blood feeds my once starved muscles, restoring them to their former power. It fills my empty stomach, easing the pains of hunger. My eyes glaze over into black, soulless mirrors reflecting the hollowness inside. My fingernails grow and dig into her wrist, dripping blood onto the floor.

Pulling my teeth from her, I lick the remaining blood from my lips and teeth. Slowly, I loosen my grip on her wrist, and she pulls her arm back into her cell.

Nearly drunk with indulgence, I smile a genuinely gratified smile. This is it. I am almost free. I laugh to myself quietly. These pathetic humans do not know what is in store for them when night covers the earth.

I hear Tara sigh lightly, and I look at her. She holds pressure on her wrist with a pained look on her face.

Reaching through the bars, I start to take her hand, but she jerks it away from me.

"I'm sorry," I tell her softly. "I didn't mean to be so rough." I pull my hand back through the bars to my cell again. "You should hold your hand above your heart. It'll stop the bleeding."

Standing up, I step toward my cot when I hear, "It's okay. I'll heal soon enough."

Turning around, I meet her eyes and she leans back. "Could you, maybe, change your eyes?" she asks.

Until she said that, I had forgotten that she could be intimidated by them. Until this moment, she has not truly seen me as a vampire. I was not a threat. Not something she should fear.

"Sure," I tell her, closing my eyes. I let them change back to my soft green, and my fangs and fingernails recede until I look just like the human I used to be.

As I open my eyes, she smiles at me. "I've never been bitten by a vampire. I didn't really know what to expect."

Expect pain. Because that is all vampires cause. "I've never tried to stop with a werewolf." I didn't really know if I could.

Still feeling my brain beat against my skull, I tell her, "I'm going to lie down for a while."

"Really?" she asks, almost shocked. "You're not going to start massacring everyone?"

Chuckling to myself, I tell her, "Not during the day."

She nods and I crawl back onto the cot, covering up with the flimsy blanket.

"If you can help it, please try not to kill anyone," Tara says.

I look at her to gauge her seriousness, but she just stares at me sternly. "I don't want that guilt on me," she tells me.

I sit up, though my body still does not want me to. "Then I absolve you of all responsibility for my actions."

Lying back, I do not wait to see if she accepts my response. I roll onto my side, facing the block wall. Rubbing my temples, I try to focus on something other than the pounding of my head and wait for the night.

Chapter 12

Hours pass quickly as I imagine all of the things that I could do to the soldiers here. Ways that they should be killed. Torture I could implement on them. But Tara's words keep ringing in my ears, distracting me from this simple pleasure. She wants to spare the humans, which is neither possible nor probable.

Lying as still as possible, which for me is very still, I listen as the three soldiers shuffle in and surround the desk. Joseph whistles loudly. "Hey leech," he calls. "I got something for you."

"You mean you *have* something, not you *got* something," I correct him without taking my eyes from the ceiling.

He snorts to himself. "Your head still hurting?" he asks snidely.

"I'll live," I tell him.

"Unfortunately," Joseph mutters under his breath. Then, more clearly, he continues, "Come here and get these."

I look over at him as he holds some clothes through the bars toward me. "Captain wants you to have them," Butler says.

Sweeping my eyes over them, I can see the younger soldier standing behind Butler. His blond hair is combed to the side neatly. His fair skin is flawed only by a faint scar that runs along his jaw. He reminds of a child I once met, Caleb, so that is what I will call him.

Rolling over slowly, I sit up in bed. As I make my way to the bars, Joseph drops everything but the shirt, which he holds by the corner. When he pulls his hand back, taking the T-shirt with him, I stop walking and watch, knowing he's about to do something just to irk me. Balling it up in his hand, he snorts hard, making a wet gurgling sound in the back of his throat. Then he holds the shirt up to his mouth and spits into it.

I let out a heavy sigh. I swear I have killed children who were more civilized.

I could do it. I could kill him right now. Pull these bars apart. Grab him by his scrawny neck. Tear his limbs from his body. And just watch him bleed out. It would be easy. So very easy.

Instead, I sit down on the edge of the cot as he shoves the shirt into my cell. "Try not to get any blood on this one," he says with a smirk.

"That would be like you trying not to look so idiotic," I tell him as I lie back down.

He tosses the shirt at me, but it only goes about halfway before it lands on the floor. "You missed," I inform him.

I ignore the way he stomps off toward the desk, disregarding his grumbling to himself, and stare at the gray ceiling above me, waiting.

It isn't long before I sense the night settle around me. But that isn't the only thing I feel. There is something else, too. Something not so pleasant. Something that makes me uneasy. Somewhere close by, a new vampire has awakened.

Hungry and feral, it lurks in the shadows. Hoping someone crosses its path. Hoping a lot of people cross its path.

The heavy steps of military boots enter, and I hear the captain bark, "Get him up." The three privates scramble to their feet to salute him.

As Butler hurries to Finn's door, I walk to the center of my cell. "Good. I'm glad it's Finn and not Abel," I mutter quietly, though I make sure it is loud enough for the captain to hear.

"Wait," he says, as I knew he would. "Take the big one instead," the captain tells Butler, referring to Abel.

Slightly confused, Butler stands still for a moment before he goes to Abel and unlocks the door. Making his way toward me, Abel snatches the pole and strap from the desk irritably. But that's good. I need him to hate me. It makes this look more convincing.

Butler opens my cell, and I let Abel put the strap around my neck. It is tight, but I am not paying attention to that. I'm only thinking of the blood I am about to spill.

The captain leads us out, with Butler and Caleb following closely behind. Down the hallways and up the stairs we walk in silence. I drag and stumble over my feet the same way I have on previous nights, but this night is different. This night, I will get my revenge.

Seeing only Ulrich in my mind, I imagine the way his blood will taste. Whether it will be loaded with iron, sweet or bitter. Whether it will be thick and heavy in my stomach or thin and slide easily down my throat.

My mouth is watering even before I see Pierce standing in the doorway waiting for us, unknowingly only waiting to die.

Abel shoves me in the chair and tightens the wrist restraints before removing the strap from my neck. Keeping my head lowered, I inhale the rich aroma that is Ulrich's sweat and pretend that it is me making him nervous.

Standing at the table, Ulrich fumbles with something in his hands, not worried enough about having his back to me. With Pierce taking his place behind me, Butler and Caleb close the door to wait outside.

As Abel bends down to strap my ankles, Smith slaps his hand away. Huffing to himself, Abel walks away, leaving Smith to deal with the restraints. Smith kneels down in front of me, and I raise my head just slightly. His eyes meet mine and I smile coldly. His face becomes blank and pale as I let my eyes phase to black.

Inhaling sharply, he reaches for his gun, but he isn't quick enough. I rip my hands from the straps and pull the armrest from the chair. As I jump to my feet, I shove the post of the armrest into Smith's chest. Blood fills his mouth and trickles down his chin as I grab his Astra 600 from his holster. Smith stumbles backward as I point the gun at Pierce and pull the trigger, dropping him to the floor.

Bursting through the door, Butler and Caleb raise their guns, but I fire before they even have them halfway drawn. They collapse onto each other, making a small pile on the ground.

Hearing the commotion, Ulrich turns around quickly with a vial in his hand, and his back pressed against the table. I step toward him. Grabbing his neck, I sink my fingernails in the soft tissue and tear through them in one flawless motion. Dropping the vial, he clutches his throat with both hands as he gasps for air. With a stunned look on his face, he falls to his knees.

"You can't just kill everyone!" Abel snaps at me.

Yes, I can. As Ulrich topples over, I check the bullets left in the gun. Knowing I fired three rounds, I am hoping the weapon was fully loaded and I still have five bullets left, which I do.

Without looking away from the gun, I say, "You're right, Abel."

I raise the gun and fire a round into his forehead. "You *are* the only one who knows."

Or should I say, knew. That is about me being the one in the forest that night.

I crouch down close to Ulrich and roll him onto his back. I look into his terrified eyes as he stares at me, seeing only death in my eyes. He struggles for air through his shredded trachea, trying to cover the holes with his hands.

Bringing my fingers to my mouth, I taste the blood on them. His blood. It is saltier than I expected, but still very drinkable. I consider biting his wrist so that he could watch me kill him. But then again, I don't want to hurry his death along.

Taking his hands, I move them away from his neck so that his panting becomes more raspy and jagged. The blood on his throat bubbles with his breaths, and I can hear it gurgling in his lungs.

A slow smile spreads across my face. This was definitely worth waiting for. This is the real reason I did not attack during the day. I was afraid he would slip from my grasp. But I was patient, and now he is dying alone on a cold floor while I watch.

In the distance, I hear several men running down the hallway, and I know my time with Ulrich is drawing to a close. Unfortunately, I will not get to see his death. Not if I let him suffer.

Pressing the gun to the right side of his abdomen, I pull the trigger. Pouring from the exit wound on his back, a thick black blood puddles on the floor. I know I hit what I was aiming for. His liver will bleed out in less than five minutes even if he puts pressure on it.

Standing up, I leave him in the pool of his own blood that is saturating his shirt and clotting in his hair. I leave him to his wretched remaining minutes, dying painfully without so much as a hope that someone will stop me.

I walk to the window and look down. It's only a three-story drop. I could jump. I could leave right now. Nobody would be able to find me again. This is the smartest option for saving myself. But what about the wolves? I promised them. I sigh.

Leaving the window, I hurry to the door, stepping over Butler and Caleb. As I walk into the hallway, four soldiers charge around the corner, and it couldn't be more perfect.

Three bullets and three quick shots mean that three soldiers drop to the ground. Lifeless, their bodies fall limply and without grace.

Hurling the gun at the fourth soldier, I lodge the barrel into his skull with enough force to knock him off his feet and make sure he never gets up again.

Walking down the hallway, I drag my fingernails in the walls on both sides of me, cutting into the block and leaving the gritty remnants of it hovering in the air.

Moving quickly, I start down the stairs when I hear more soldiers approaching. As soon as I see them at the base of the steps, I leap toward them, landing in the middle of close to ten men. Pounding one man's head into the blocks, I kick another soldier back into the adjacent wall, crushing his ribs with my foot. With my arm, I strike one soldier in the back, knocking him forward onto the steps. Then, just as quickly, I stomp his neck, extending his head back until it meets his shoulders.

Knowing he cannot fire at me without risking hitting his own men, one soldier pulls out a knife and swings it at me.

Grabbing his wrist, I snap his forearm with my hand and pull the knife from his grip. I flip it around my fingers and bury it in his gut. Pulling it out, I swipe the blade across another soldier's throat, spilling blood on the floor.

One soldier turns to run, but I grab his shoulder, pulling him back. I glide his spine onto the knife and break off the handle.

Clawing into an older man's chest, I steal his gun away from his white- knuckled grip. He falls back and slides down the wall.

I fire a Luger into another soldier's head but do not stop to watch him drop before I pull the trigger two more times, taking out the last two standing soldiers.

Tossing the gun down, I pull the older man to his feet. Shaking and whimpering lightly, he reeks of fear and I cannot help myself.

With a handful of hair, I jerk his head to the side and bite into his neck. Smooth and seemingly limitless, the warmth of his blood cools my aching throat. His raspy, muted screams only make my heart beat faster and my greed rage further.

Trying to keep the fleeting time in mind, I slide my teeth out and discard his body to the floor. I wipe my mouth with the back of my hand, smearing blood across my fingers. Reaching down, I take a gun and a knife from one of the fallen soldiers. I check the gun. It's fully loaded.

I start walking and am mostly down the hall before the next round of soldiers emerges. Fewer this time, there are only four men. They run into the hallway and line up, blocking my way, but not for long.

Without stopping my approach, I shoot one man in the knee. Clutching his leg, he falls to the ground, and I unload a round into his skull. The next man has time to begin to raise his gun before I fire into his chest, killing him.

Now close to them, I stab the third man in the lower abdomen and slide the knife up to his sternum, spilling his intestines onto the floor.

A shot is fired by the remaining soldier, and I feel the pierce of pain in my shoulder.

Grabbing the end of his weapon, I jerk it from his hand. I flip it quickly and jab the bayonet up through his neck into his head and pull the trigger. Bits of skull and flesh are blown into the air as his face explodes in front of me.

Scraping chunks of bloody skin from me, I hear the rapid breathing of somebody. I turn to find the man with his abdomen sliced open panting wildly, his eyes fixed on the ceiling.

I bend down near him and watch him until he turns his eyes to me. "Kill me," he pants out.

I could say no. I could let him die slowly, painfully. But his death means nothing to me.

Taking my gun, I place it to his temple. "Have you made your peace?" I whisper to him.

He nods as his body begins to shake. "Then may God be with you," I tell him.

With a trembling hand, he reaches up. Touching his head, chest and both shoulders, he makes a cross over his body.

I wait until he finishes, then I pull the trigger and his chaotic breathing stops.

Getting up, I hurry down the hall, turning the corners and killing the soldiers I meet until I reach the room where Tara is waiting.

As I run in, Joseph jumps to his feet, reaching for his gun. But I grab his head and shove it down onto the desk. I put my gun to his head and Tara cries out, "Don't kill him!"

Surely, she does not think I have been listening to her. The blood and flesh on my shirt make it obvious to me that I have not. But still I sigh and slide my gun into the small of my back, feeling the warm metal through my shirt. Taking Joseph's gun, I toss it to Finn in his cell.

"Stick your tongue out," I order Joseph, and he does.

I grab a pencil and jam it through his tongue, lodging it into the wooden desk and pinning him down. Of course, he could get up, but it would be excruciating, so I doubt he will try.

I take the keys from the desk and walk over to Tara. I can tell she isn't pleased by my actions, but at least he is alive.

As I unlock the cell door, she asks, "Where's Abel?" Right, Abel. I shake my head. "He didn't make it."

I can see her processing what I said, but knowing she doesn't have time to grieve, she refocuses. I open the door, and as she walks out, I hand her the keys. She goes to Lydia's cell and unlocks it. "We'll search the lower level for the children. You two search this floor. We'll meet downstairs in fifteen minutes. If you're not there, I'll assume that you're dead."

Walking over to Finn's cell, I hear Tara say, "I want my son, Nicolas." I look over at her as she stares at me sharply. "Try not to kill anybody else."

I know what she's really saying, try not to get Roddy killed, and I won't.

I nod to her as Lydia steps out of her cell. Without another word, Tara and Lydia rush out. I look at Finn in his cell. With part of me thinking that I should just leave him, I grab the bars and jerk the door off its hinges.

As I toss it aside, he walks out. "Let's go," he tells me.

I let him lead the way, but as he goes out of the room, I stop. I walk over to Joseph, who's still moaning. Balling my hand into a fist, I raise it up and bring it down on his head, caving his skull in around my hand.

Finn steps back in as I shake the fragments of bone from my hand. "Tara said not to kill anyone," he snaps at me.

Looking at him with my black eyes, I say, "I'm not really a follower."

I walk past him back into the hallway, and after a moment, he joins me. "I didn't think you would come back for us," Finn admits quietly.

Truthfully, I didn't either.

Sighing, he asks, "Where do you want to start?"

I look down the hall in front of me, which is the way I just came from.

There's nothing that way but death. I glance down the hallway to my right. "This way."

Rushing down the hall, I pass several doors, listening and smelling for signs of a child but finding none. Suddenly the alarm sounds. Tara and Lydia must have been seen. Now more soldiers will be looking for us, which is what happens when you let humans live.

Two soldiers rush out of one of the doors ahead of us. They see me but aren't fast enough to draw their weapons before I take aim on them. With two quick shots, they both drop.

Finn and I hurry to the bodies. I bend down and pick up the handgun. I can smell the silver bullets without looking at them but still I take one out and show it to Finn.

"It's silver," I say holding up the bullet. "If it hits you, you'll die, so you might want to try to kill them first."

I hold the gun toward him. After a brief moment, he nods and takes the weapon.

"Are you a good shot?" I ask him as I stand up.

He shrugs. "Decent."

Decent will do. "Just try to hit the Nazis and nobody else," I joke.

He smiles lightly, though I can tell he does not like the idea of killing the humans.

When we start down the hall again, I catch a whiff of pure blood. A child's blood. The smell is captivating, but I clear my mind of the hunger inside me and hit Finn's shoulder lightly. I nod toward the door that I assume the children are behind.

Finn nods and takes his position beside the door. I kick the door open and quickly assess the room. The four soldiers to my right are standing near a card table with their weapons drawn. Without really looking at them, I can see three small children huddled in the corner of a tiny cell.

Too quickly for the soldiers to keep up, I run toward them. Pressing my gun to one man, I shoot him point blank in the chest. Swinging my hand in the air, I slice open another soldier's neck, pouring blood onto the wall and floor.

The two other soldiers open fire, but I leap behind them. I shove my gun against the head of one man and blow the front of his skull out with one bullet. Then I break the leg of the table with my foot and kick it up into the air. Catching it in my hand, I thrust the splintered end through the last soldier's back.

As his body drops, I hear the screams of two small girls. The scent of the soldiers' blood is heavy in the air, but I smell someone I have met before. A boy. The one I frightened while he was looking for his father on the battlefield.

I turn my eyes only to have it confirmed. Staring back at me are the hazel eyes of a scared little boy. He looks just as I remember him. With his shaggy blond hair and weak frame, he stands in front of the girls, protecting them from me. His eyes widen with recognition.

"Hello, Roddy," I say quietly, finally understanding why Tara had smelled so familiar to me.

"I did what you said," he stammers out. "I didn't tell anyone about you." Of course he didn't. Only a fool would have.

Finn walks in and looks around. "Did you have to kill all of them in front of the kids?" he asks irritably, putting his gun in the small of his back.

I simply shrug at him. I probably didn't have to. But I can't change it now. Dropping my now-empty gun, I walk to the cell and pull the door off.

Finn steps into the doorway and holds his arms out. "Come here, girls." Two six-year-old twin girls who resemble Lydia run into his arms. He closes his eyes with relief while he holds them. As he kisses their cheeks, I realize something I should have seen earlier. I realize that Lydia's daughters are also Finn's.

"Where's mom?" one of the girls ask.

Taking their hands, Finn tells them, "She's waiting for us, so we need to hurry." He looks at Roddy. "Come on. Your mom wants you with us."

But Roddy does not move. Instead, he looks at me nervously. He doesn't trust me, nor have I given him a reason to, so I step into the cell. As I walk over to him, he backs against the wall.

I kneel down close to him. "Roddy, I promised your mother that I wouldn't let you die tonight. And I have to admit, I'm a little afraid of her," I lie.

"You should be," Roddy says defiantly.

I smile because this is how I remembered him, full of arrogance and pride. "We don't have time to become friends right now. But I'm still going to get you back to your mom even if you don't want me to."

I reach for him and he pulls away. Grabbing his arm forcefully, I put my face closer to his. "Let's move," I say coldly so that he knows I am serious.

I lead him from the cell while Finn checks the hallway and takes the girls out. They start down the hall as I pick up a gun from the floor.

Hearing gunfire in the hall, I rush to the door, keeping Roddy behind me. I look and see two soldiers dead on the floor in front of Finn with clean shots to the head. I smile to myself. Decent, huh?

Several more soldiers run around the corner into view and raise their guns at Finn. Without hesitation, I fire at them, killing two.

"Run!" I shout at Finn. He does, but I have the feeling that if it were not for his girls, he would not have left me. Crouching in the doorway, I unload my handgun into the soldiers. Turning to Roddy, I urge, "Hand me another gun."

He listens and gives me another Astra 600, which is good since there are six soldiers standing and eight bullets. They shoot at me, hitting the door and frame and shattering the wood fragments into the air. Again, I fire into the crowd, making sure every shot is a deadly one.

When the last one falls, I grab Roddy's hand and pull him into the hallway with me. I know others would have heard the gunfire, and we don't have much time to make our escape. We run as fast as Roddy's legs can move and make our way to the stairs.

I can smell Finn in the stairwell, which is a good sign. At least he made it this far. When we reach the bottom of the stairs, I get an overwhelming sense of dread. The new vampire is nearby.

"Stay close," I whisper to Roddy, and he steps beside me. Figuring I can protect myself without the gun, I ask, "Do you know how to shoot?"

He nods eagerly. I hold the gun out toward him. "Aim for the heart," I tell him, not only because the chest would give him a broader area to hit but also because he would need to shoot a vampire in the heart to kill it.

Reaching for the gun, Roddy licks his lips anxiously. I start to think that maybe this isn't such a good idea when Roddy grabs the gun and trigger. It goes off and the bullet strikes my stomach.

Placing both of my hands on my abdomen, I hear him cry out, "Oh, no! I'm sorry. I didn't mean to."

The pain of a bullet ripping its way through my organs is intense, but nothing I haven't felt before. I pull the gun from his fingers.

"Let's get something straight," I say, leaning close to his stunned face. "You don't know how to use a gun."

I rub my sore stomach and start down the hallway.

"How are you all right?" Roddy asks. "I mean, I shot you in the belly. Shouldn't you be at least limping?"

Pulling him along, I try to hurry him as much as I can. "I'm a vampire," I tell him. "Vampires don't limp. They either die or they get back up."

He smiles. "A vampire," he whispers to himself. "I knew it."

I cannot fathom what else he would have thought me to be. But then again, a child's mind is full of imaginative things. I am sure, though, that whatever he believed me to be was not a good creature.

Grabbing Roddy's shoulder, I stop. The feeling in my gut is growing stronger. We are not far from the vampire now. It is in one of these rooms, with only a door separating me from it.

Stepping close to a door, I let myself focus on the new vampire, feeling for its hunger and intemperance. I go to the next door, placing my hand on the wood. Its greed is strong and draws me in.

Twisting the knob, I push the door open, not knowing what I will find. Sitting in the floor of another cell is a young Nazi. He looks at me with soft blue eyes. "Please help me," he says weakly.

I trail my eyes over to the corner of the cell. A white–haired man wearing a black robe with blood smeared across the small white square in the collar lies dead. Another priest.

"Please," the Nazi says again. "I'm a prisoner here." He walks over to the bars. "They'll kill me if you don't let me out." He reaches through the bars toward me, but I stay back from him. "Please. I don't want to die in here," he pleads.

He sounds convincing. He must have been a good liar when he was human too.

"Too bad," I say as I raise the gun. A new vampire is dangerous. They need a leader to teach them restraint, among other things. Things I do not want, nor have time, to teach him.

Roddy steps inside the room. "You can't shoot him!"

The Nazi's eyes widen, and his breathing quickens with the scent of the boy's blood.

"He's just a prisoner. You should let him out," Roddy urges.

But I am not listening. I aim for the heart and pull the trigger. As the bullet hits him, the vampire shatters into ash. It hangs in the air for a moment before settling onto the floor.

I look at Roddy. "You thought I was human once, too, remember?" Tossing the gun down, I turn to leave and notice a small box labeled, trinitrotoluene. It's probably only here as a safety measure in case the vampire escapes. I pop the lid from the box.

"What is it?" Roddy asks.

Looking at the red sticks lining the box, I say, "TNT." I take four of the sticks and show them to Roddy. "It's an explosive. It's highly unstable, so we need to be careful with it."

Standing up, I slide the sticks in the small of my back and grab Roddy's wrist. I pull him back into the hallway, and we hurry, though I am not sure if we're going the right direction or not.

As we turn the corner, I see Tara, Lydia, Finn, and the girls standing near a door. Roddy sees her, too, and takes off running for her. "Mom!" he shouts.

She drops to her knees as he leaps into her arms. She presses him against her, smiling with relief while tears roll down her cheeks.

I walk the rest of the way to them as she stands up. Smiling at me as though she didn't believe in me, she wipes her face. "You're late," she says.

I smile back at her. "I didn't think you would leave without us."

Her smile fades. "We may not be leaving at all." Pointing to the door, she continues, "There are ten soldiers in there, and their guns are loaded with silver. It's the only way out. I've looked."

But I did not come this far to stop now. "Then I guess it's good that silver is not poisonous to me." Sighing, I take the four TNT sticks out and hand them to Finn. "If I die, blow the whole place up."

"Right," he says sarcastically. He starts to hand me his gun. "I only have two bullets left."

I put my hand up to stop him. "I don't need it."

He looks at me curiously, but I only look at the door. Standing on the other side are ten soldiers. Ten soldiers who do not know what is coming for them.

I kick the door, and it flies across the room, knocking two soldiers down. They open fire as I bolt forward, leaping up and running along the wall. Pushing off the wall, I kick the closest soldier in the head, snapping his neck.

I make a fist and punch the next soldier in the throat, collapsing his trachea. He drops to his knees, gasping for air that he will never inhale.

Grabbing another soldier, I lift him in the air and bring his back down on my leg, breaking his spine and letting him roll onto the floor.

A bayonet stabs my bicep, and I shove the gun away so that the blade snaps off in my arm. Still holding the gun, I jerk it out of the soldier's hands and shoot him in the chest.

Sweeping the gun around, I knock another soldier's feet out from under him, and he lands on his back. I slam the stock of the gun into his head, killing him.

I continue to move quickly so that the soldiers do not know where to shoot, though they still try. The two soldiers from under the door get up and start toward me, but one is hit by a bullet that was meant for me.

Bracing my gun with my shoulder, I fire two rounds, killing two more soldiers. I don't slow down enough to think of how very young they are. I do not concern myself with pity or remorse. I want them dead, and I will not stop until they are.

Dropping the gun, I pull the bayonet out of my arm. Stepping behind another soldier, I grab his hair and slice his neck. He falls forward, and I pull the last soldier to me, stabbing the blade through his eye.

I stand still for a moment, surrounded by blood and death and loving every bit of it. But I still hear a heartbeat in the room.

I look up to see the captain enter, clapping his hands. "Well done." He pulls out a handgun and aims it at me. "You almost got away." Without another word he fires a bullet into my forehead.

Dropping to the ground, I see Tara rush in. For a moment, I only think of her being killed. But before I can dwell on the surprising amount of sadness that would bring me, she picks up a gun. Pulling the trigger, she kills the captain with a clean shot to the head.

I sit up, holding my head as she hurries to my side. "Are you okay?" she asks.

Aside from the pain in my head, I am. "Yeah," I tell her. "I'll be fine."

Exhaling forcefully, she smiles.

A sly smile spreads on my face, "Did you just kill somebody for me?"

A serious look washes over her. "No," she snaps. "He was blocking my escape. Don't flatter yourself like that."

But I know what happened here, and my lopsided grin shows itself. "Get up," she says, pulling me to my feet. "We have to get out of here."

She is right, of course. There will be many other Nazis in this building. Although I do like killing them, I'm tired of being shot.

Motioning for the others, she goes to the double doors. They all run past me, except Roddy.

He stops in front of me. "That was pretty amazing."

I shake his blond hair lightly. "Thanks."

Taking my hand, he pulls me toward the door. There has never been a child who knew what I was and still approached me so easily. Never has a human treated me as an equal. I have to admit, I really like it and, for once, I am glad that I spared him.

Finn walks back and holds the sticks of TNT toward me. "What now?" he asks.

Taking them from his hand, I toss three of the sticks on the floor. I steal a lighter from one of the soldiers and light the short fuse. Dropping the last stick on the ground, I say, "We leave."

We rush outside. I feel the cold night air on my skin. Picking up Roddy, I take him away from the building.

Seconds pass and the TNT explodes, blowing out the windows and doors and knocking us to the ground. There is a second explosion, probably from the box we left behind, which causes the building to collapse in on itself. Then there is another, much larger, explosion, which I assume is from the stockpile of TNT somewhere inside, which throws chunks of blocks into the air.

Leaning over Roddy, I try to keep his head covered as the debris falls down around us. When it's just dirt and mortar dust hanging in the air, I stand up.

With Roddy beside me, I go to Tara, ignoring the coughing of the two girls and the tumbling of blocks as the building settles.

Taking her hand, I help her up. Looking at Roddy, she rubs his dirty cheek with her thumb and smiles gently. Then she looks back at me. "Thank you, Nicolas," she says softly. "Thank you for everything."

I nod at her. I suppose she does not realize that I know how grateful she is. I guess she does not understand that I owed her.

She wraps her arms around my neck. Surprised by her embrace, I stand still for a moment before I put my arms around her, too.

It seems odd to have a werewolf this close without having my teeth in them. But I let my eyes change back to green and my fangs recede.

I let myself look human and vulnerable again.

When she pulls away, I look the way I want her to remember me: kind. "Come on. Let's go home," she says, looking at Roddy, but I know she is talking to everyone but me.

She starts to turn when I speak up. "Tara?" As she turns around, I continue, "I don't have any werewolf friends. But I would like to."

Taking a deep breath, she steps toward me. "I do have a vampire friend, and I am hoping he comes to my house tomorrow night." She smiles. "I want to know that you made it back safe." She laughs to herself. "But don't expect to be invited in."

I chuckle lightly. "Of course not." Relieved that I will see her again, I smile and say, "I'll be there."

She does not give me her address nor do I want it. I like the challenge.

I watch them until they disappear into the woods before I start. Home would be so nice right now, but there is something I must do first.

*　　*　　*

Perched on the top of a building, I wait. Having fought my way out of that Nazi research facility and run most of the night, I have only a few remaining hours before daylight. A little nervous that I won't have the opportunity to finish this, I watch the sidewalks below.

I should not have stopped at the safe house for shower and clean clothes. But I did, and I may have missed my chance because of it.

At least it was a clear night and I was able to use the stars to guide me, which helped me make up some time.

I wonder if Tara and her pack had as much success at returning to their homes as I have. I suppose I will find out tomorrow night. It should not be too difficult to track her. I will start at the battlefield, knowing that Roddy could not have walked there from too far away.

Deciding my route for tomorrow night, I catch the scent of someone. Someone I have been waiting for.

I dig my fingernails into the edge of the roof as my fangs extend and my eyes change to black. My hate grows inside me, and I nearly snarl at the woman below me.

Jumping down into the alley, I wait for her to pass by. Unnoticed, I slip out behind her and watch her light brown hair bounce with each step.

I look around but do not see anybody. At least, not anybody who would take notice of us, so I walk faster.

As she gets close to the next alley, I flip a coin in the air so that it lands in front of her. Stopping, she bends down and picks it up. She holds it in the dim glow from a streetlight, studying it curiously.

Behind her, I lean close to her ear and say coldly, "It's for the ferryman." Dropping the coin, she turns to face me and inhales sharply.

Covering her mouth with my hand, I drag her into the alley. Ignoring her whimpering, I press her back against the brick wall of a building.

"I have waited for this, Nurse Klein. And I do not like to wait," I inform her. "I even had enough time to pay your mother a visit."

Tears roll down her face and my hand as I continue, "Those must have been your children she was watching." I lean close to her. "Cute. But so naïve."

I slide my hand down to her jaw. I want to be able to hear her beg. "Please. Don't hurt them," she says, sobbing.

I could tell her that I did not go inside. Could say that I do not plan on going back. But I don't. This needs to be as painful as I can make it.

"You should worry more about yourself right now. It's you who will not survive the night."

Whimpering, she cries harder. Perhaps I should not play with my food. But really, she does deserve it.

I rake my fangs across her neck, inhaling the scent of her sweet blood. Keeping myself from biting is harder than I expected, and my grip on her face tightens. Scared, she lets out a quiet squeal as her body begins to tremble.

Weeping, she says, "I'm sorry. I didn't mean to tell them."

But I can hear the lie in her voice, which is just as well, because I do not intend to back down now.

"I think you did. But you will soon wish you hadn't," I tell her calmly. Feeling her jagged breaths on my skin and hearing her heart race only makes me want to rush this along. The air is thick with her fear, and my revenge is pushing me to bite. At least I know that I will be more patient when it comes to killing her. Even though I'm anxious to bite, I'll be able to prolong her pain until the very end of the night.

"Please. I'll do anything," she offers through her tears.

"Anything?" I ask sharply. "Perhaps you have forgotten what you've already done. Maybe you do not know what torture you put me through. Possibly you cannot imagine the pain you've caused me."

I jerk her head to the side abruptly. "It felt something like this." And I sink my teeth into her soft neck.